"We interru

Natalie stared at the television as a group of reporters surrounded a man on crutches—a man whose blond hair and strong features were disturbingly familiar. A State Department official shook the injured man's hand, then looked toward the camera.

"I am pleased to announce the defection of Mikhail Illyovich Korolev. I'm sure you're anxious to ask him questions, so I'll turn this conference over to him."

Adjusting his crutches, Mikhail stepped up to the podium. "I have no prepared statement, but I would like to thank the United States government for granting me asylum."

"He speaks English!" Natalie murmured.

She was almost more shocked by the revelation than by the fact that she had unknowingly participated in his defection!

Dear Reader,

Do you want something more in your romance books?

Then welcome to the world of HARLEQUIN INTRIGUE!

You have chosen a story that interweaves the dynamics of a contemporary sophisticated romance with the surprising twists and turns of a puzzler. Mystery and suspense are the elements that provide "something more." We like to call it a *challenge*. And the romance you will find in a HARLEQUIN INTRIGUE is what has made Harlequin a household name—both nationally and internationally—for almost forty years.

We promise to bring you two exciting INTRIGUE novels every month and to uphold our standards of the highest quality. Our wish is that you will have many hours of pleasurable reading. We look forward to your comments with great interest.

Reva Kindser and Marmie Charndoff,
Editors

DEATH SPIRAL
PATRICIA ROSEMOOR

Harlequin Books

TORONTO • NEW YORK • LONDON
AMSTERDAM • PARIS • SYDNEY • HAMBURG
STOCKHOLM • ATHENS • TOKYO • MILAN

To Reva Kindser, for continuing to believe in my writing and because you're as fascinated with stories about Russians as I am.

Special thanks to Carol Myers of the Delaware Development Office, Richard Stuckey of the Skating Club of Wilmington and Erika Amundsen of the Professional Skaters Guild of America for their invaluable help.

Harlequin Intrigue edition published September 1987

ISBN 0-373-22074-X

Printed in Canada

Death spiral: a dangerous, compulsory movement in pairs skating during which the man goes into a pivot and, holding the woman's hand, spins her around him in a dizzying circle while she leans backward, her position vulnerable, her body parallel to and her head narrowly missing the ice.

Prologue

As night fell over Moscow, a man stepped out of the shadows and approached the Sandunovsky baths. Pulling up his frayed collar in spite of the mild late-May weather, he hunched inside his jacket and drove his fists into the pockets. Always cautious, he looked over his shoulder before he entered the building.

And it was caution that kept his pale eyes wandering as he strode through the ornate structure that dated back to czarist times. He had no appreciation for the much-darned flowered carpets, the lace-shaded lamps or the plaster Cupids that seemed to watch his progress.

He merely wanted to make sure no *human* was watching him.

Small groups of Muscovites flowed around him, some going to, others having come from the pleasures of the *banya*. Ignoring their chatter, he went into a dressing room and exchanged his street clothes for a sheet, which he wrapped around his body like a toga.

A moment later, he entered the steam room and nearly lost his breath. Inhaling a lungful of pure humidity, he could see only three other men through the thick white haze. They were flailing themselves with leafy bundles of aromatic birch twigs. This activity was part of a Russian's way of life—cleansing dirt from the pores while banishing the day's ills from the soul. In spite of Communist teachings, he thought with irony, Russians were very aware of their souls.

But that had nothing to do with his reason for coming to the *banya*.

He approached the man with the receding hairline who was picking wet leaves from his large body. The loose-jowled face turned up to his. "So you made it, comrade."

"And with good news."

"I presume it will wait." The tone of the man's voice intimated, *When we're alone.*

"Waiting is something I'm good at."

He'd been waiting most of his life for things—the food he ate, the vodka he drank, the clothes he put on his back. Why should now be any different? He had learned to be patient out of necessity; otherwise he could not survive the frustrations he faced every day.

Sweat was dripping off him before the other man led the way out of the steam room. A plunge into an icy pool was followed by a visit to a scrubbing room. They lay on long marble slabs while attendants scoured them with pine shavings, then doused them with buckets of cold water.

Ready for another session with the inferno, he was surprised at the command: "Now, comrade, it is time. Come."

They entered a paneled dressing room. Plates of dried salt fish and glasses of ice-cold vodka awaited them. He stood while the bulky man made himself comfortable on the couch and took a long drink of the alcohol.

When the glass was lowered, the man studied him, the too-small eyes sharp in the loose-jowled face. "Now we are alone. You are free to speak."

He took a deep breath before saying, "Money to a disgruntled employee goes a long way. The plans are in place to obtain Thwart."

Chapter One

Natalie Lundgren had a peculiarly foreboding feeling when she glanced up from her guidebook and stared out the windshield of her rented Ford Fiesta. The driver, Faith Osborne, slowed the car and swung it off the main road at an observation area. The darkening sky above the French Alps signaled impending rain. Angry-looking storm clouds shrouded the peaks of Mont Blanc, Europe's highest mountain, and the nearby glacier gleamed dully through a settling haze. The car came to a stop mere yards from a several-hundred-foot drop-off, one that made Natalie gasp for breath. She was glad that she'd let her friend do the driving.

"It's nasty out there," Faith said.

"I'm going to take a closer look anyway. After all, you insisted on bringing me here."

"Want me to come with you?"

Natalie shook her head. She never let irrational emotions rule her. She got out of the car, wrapped her arms around herself as protection against the chilly June air and strode toward the flimsy-looking guardrail, the only barrier separating Faith and her from certain death.

As she glanced down, her stomach knotted and her throat closed up. Wiping her sweaty palms on her jeans, Natalie told herself not to be ridiculous. There was no reason to be afraid. She was here for the view, not for a climb. Even so, mesmerized by the very thing she feared most, she pinned her gaze on the steep decline tumbling away into nothingness.

Then the wind picked up, ruffling the brown curls around her shoulders and sending icy shivers through the loose weave of her red cotton-knit sweater. It moaned through the peaks and valleys, its eerie sound portending danger. Natalie retreated with a sigh that was a mixture of disappointment and relief, and slid back into the passenger seat, happy to view her surroundings through closed windows.

"So much for our adventurous picnic," she said, trying not to sound dispirited. Wasn't a longing for adventure one of the reasons she'd agreed to come?

"We're going to have our picnic anyway," Faith insisted, her soft voice determined. "This is supposed to be a holiday for you, and I promised you a picnic with one of the most magnificent views in the world. Besides, we can't let all the delicious goodies we bought go to waste just because I didn't check the weather. We can eat in the car."

"Then what are we waiting for?" Natalie turned to grab the picnic basket from the back seat. "Don't worry about the weather. I know you had other things on your mind." She handed Faith two glasses, a bottle of regional red wine and a corkscrew. "I'm no good at this, so you get to do the honors."

"No problem." Faith lowered her golden brown eyes to the bottle. "Anyone who's lived in France for more than a year had better be an expert."

Natalie organized the food. They'd raided a specialty shop before driving out from Aix-les-Bains, the fashionable Alpine spa where they were staying for the weekend. From the basket she produced a fresh loaf of French bread, a wedge of Brie cheese, two pieces of spinach quiche and raspberry tarts. Setting the individually wrapped items on the dashboard, she wedged the basket between their seats as an impromptu table.

"You know, you're more fun than Bernard ever was," Faith remarked, giving the corkscrew a vicious twist. Her head was bent to her task, and the fall of silky blond hair hid her face. "He never would have responded to a friend's plea for solace unless there was something in it for him."

Natalie frowned. "The more you tell me about him, the more I wonder at your accepting his proposal in the first place."

"I was fooled. He was dashing and charming in his own way, but I was sure he was dependable—good marriage material. Do you realize I'll be thirty next month?"

"Turning thirty's no reason to get married!"

"Hah! You can talk, since you're younger than I."

"Right. I'm only twenty-eight. A mere babe in the woods."

In spite of the two-year age difference between them, they'd gone through school together after Natalie had skipped second grade. She'd refused a later double promotion so she wouldn't leave Faith behind. They'd joined the same activities in high school and had been roommates in college. Though they'd taken different paths since graduation, they'd stayed in touch with letters and telephone conversations, but their communication had become less frequent in the past couple of years. Still, there'd been no way Natalie could have ignored her friend's plea for a shoulder to cry on. When a tearful Faith had called the day Bernard jilted her, Natalie had agreed to fly to Lyon where Faith worked at the American consulate.

And it was a good thing she had come. Ever since yesterday morning, when Natalie had arrived, Faith had been a nervous wreck, first crying, then retreating into a depression Natalie couldn't understand—perhaps because she'd never met Bernard, but more likely because she'd never been in love herself. Or maybe Faith really *was* worried about being single at thirty. Natalie found she couldn't read her as easily as she had in the past.

"What happened to the way you used to view life?" Natalie was thoughtful as she unwrapped the Brie and set it on the basket. "You were the romantic one. If I remember correctly, the Lone Ranger was going to sweep you off your feet and you were going to ride into the sunset yelling, 'Hi-ho, Silver!' Who was that masked woman, anyway?"

For once, Faith didn't smile at her teasing. Her hand shook slightly as she poured their wine. "I guess she was an innocent who finally grew up, Nat."

Natalie's heart went out to her. Even when they'd been children, Faith had had a wounded-bird quality that made people want to help her; she'd always been petite and a little too thin. Natalie herself had been pointed out as the model of self-sufficiency even before she'd reached her maximum growth at age thirteen. Who could look at a five-foot-ten-inch, large-boned young woman and think of her as needing assistance with anything?

She took the glass Faith handed her and raised it. "To recaptured youth, then."

Faith stared out toward Mont Blanc. "Sometimes you can't go back, even if you'd like to," she said softly before taking a sip of her wine.

Poised to give her old friend a pep talk, Natalie was startled by a sudden banging on the car window next to her. Her wine sloshed over the rim of the glass as she turned and stared at a middle-aged man who was shouting at them, his expression anxious, his motions erratic. His clothing was torn and filthy, his face and hands were scraped and streaked with dirt, and his light blue eyes were filled with pain and fear. She set down her glass on the basket and started to open the door.

"Nat?" Faith whispered, her voice shaky. "What if he's dangerous?"

"I don't think so. He's been hurt."

"Bitte." The man pleaded with them through the half-open door. *"Sie müssen mich helfen. Bitte, Fräulein, bitte."*

Drawing on her rusty school German, Natalie said, "He wants us to help." But with what? Getting out of the car, she asked the stocky man, *"Was ist los?"*

He gestured frantically in the general direction of the narrow pathway leading to the glacier and rattled off an answer Natalie could only guess at from the few words she recognized. She couldn't misinterpret the urgency in his voice, however, or the desperation in his gestures. She poked her head back into the car.

"Something about another man out there on the mountain. A climbing accident. He's frantic for our help. Come on."

Faith took the keys from the ignition and handed them to Natalie, who pocketed them with her international driver's license. Then, seeming to get out of the car reluctantly, Faith stared at the man, now standing a few yards away. She whispered, "Are you sure you want to do this? He's acting awfully funny."

Natalie turned to look at him. His broad forehead was creased in a frown, and he was shaking with impatience. He mumbled something in German and shifted his eyes from side to side as though he expected to see an unpleasant surprise.

"I think he's in shock." Nodding broadly to the man, Natalie approached him and said, "All right. We'll go. Ah, *wir gehen*—"

"American?" He seemed to come out of a trance. "You are American?" he asked, his accent thick.

"Yes!" Natalie said excitedly. "Can you tell us what happened—in English?"

But either he didn't understand her or her question fell on deaf ears. He was already moving toward the path that would take them to his friend. Suddenly the enormity of their rescue mission sank in on Natalie.

The wind howled across the mountainside, reminding her that it had warned her of danger. She'd been so wrapped up in the man's desperation, she hadn't actually realized what she'd agreed to. She was going to have to walk on that narrow pathway, with the mountain wall on one side and the sheer drop on the other. And she'd been afraid of heights for as long as she could remember.

Sweat beaded her skin. Had she gone crazy? Facing her fear was one thing, but putting herself in unnecessary danger was quite another.

"Bitte, Fräulein," the accented voice called. The German was looking at her expectantly. "This way, *ja*?"

Faith took her by the arm, urging her forward. "Come on. Just don't look down."

"Easier said than done," Natalie muttered.

But she did do it, because she couldn't desert someone in such terrible trouble, even though he was a stranger. She concentrated on looking straight ahead at the German's back so she wouldn't be overcome by the familiar vertigo that threatened her.

Traversing the mountain wasn't as bad as she'd expected. The path itself was about five feet wide. Natalie hugged the cliff side of the mountain while remaining between the man in front and Faith in the rear. The experience gave her a feeling of unreality—as if she were watching someone else rather than participating. And yet she was well aware that what was happening was real, because she was breathing heavily, partly from the altitude and partly from stress.

"How much farther?" she gasped after they'd walked for more than ten minutes.

"Only a little way more," the man assured her, turning to face her. "Please, we must hurry."

Natalie's heart pounded as he began to walk backward, his feet getting closer to the drop-off with each step. Reaching out, she grabbed him by the arm and pulled him inward. "You were too close to the edge. Careful!"

He bobbed his head before he continued on, but she wasn't sure he really understood that he'd been in danger. It seemed as if he were still in shock.

Remaining motionless for a few minutes, Natalie willed her pulse to steady itself. She took a cleansing breath of the thin mountain air.

Beside her now, Faith asked, "You okay, Nat?"

"I'm fine. I just wish we'd get to wherever it is he's taking us."

Natalie caught up to the man quickly, but Faith practically had to jog to stay close behind her. "You don't think it'll be too bad, do you?" Faith lowered her voice as if she didn't want the German to hear. "I mean, do you think this guy's friend is dead?"

"No, of course not."

Actually, it was a possibility—one she hadn't considered before. But as they kept trudging along the narrowing path, which snaked in and out while steadily slanting upward, she had plenty of time to think about it. She merely chose not to.

Instead, as Faith dropped back behind her, Natalie studied the texture of the terrain, which had changed during the last half-mile. To her left, the mountain wall had metamorphosed into a series of hills. A few trees were scattered across the landscape, mixed with boulders, some of which seemed precariously balanced. Smaller rocks and pebbles lay strewn about the path in increasing quantities, making Natalie wish she'd worn jogging shoes instead of leather-soled loafers.

The sooner they were on their way back to the car and the highway, the better, she thought. Rain could make the path even more dangerous. The wind blew in gusts and positioned the storm clouds directly overhead, like a damp gray blanket. Eyeing the sky with trepidation, Natalie called to the man, who was rushing forward in a sudden burst of speed. "Excuse me, but how—"

"Only a short distance more," he interrupted, obviously anticipating her question. He pointed to a hairpin curve ahead, where a distinctive rock formation jutted up and over the path, creating a rocky canopy of sorts. "Just there."

She hoped so. The feeling of unreality prevailed, protecting her from her phobia, yet the impending storm was a real threat that she'd be stupid to ignore. They were in the middle of the mountains with no shelter in sight. No roads or other human life was visible. Then they rounded the curve, and in a large open space she saw a pair of long legs clad in brown corduroy stretched out across the path amid loose rocks and pebbles.

The man's upper body, covered only by a lightweight gold turtleneck sweater, was turned away from them, draped over the small boulders perched haphazardly at the base of the slope. A rock careered down the hillside and out into oblivion, but the man didn't move. The German ran the few yards to his friend and knelt beside him. He spoke in rapid German but got no immediate response.

Were they too late? Natalie wondered as she and Faith stopped a yard away from the still figure. Had they traversed the dangerous mountainside in vain? A moan of pain told her they hadn't.

"Help me," the German said, waving to her. "We must turn him carefully."

Natalie got down on her knees next to the unconscious man. Sitting back on her heels, she helped brace his body while the German did most of the work of shifting him into her arms. When his dark blond head rolled toward her, coming to rest in the valley between her sweater-covered breasts, she saw that he was much younger than the other man, perhaps in his early thirties. Something about his vulnerability struck a responsive chord in her. She cradled him tenderly.

"Oh, Lord, look at his face!" Faith cried.

It was an arresting face, with high cheekbones, a commanding, straight nose and sculpted lips, but the entire right side was scraped and streaked with blood. Natalie noticed that the jagged cut on his broad forehead had clotted.

"He's stopped bleeding, but I don't like his pallor." His skin had a gray tinge, as though it had absorbed the coloring from the sky. She slipped her fingers under his sweater and felt for an artery. "His pulse is weak but steady."

"Thank God!" Faith whispered.

Natalie glanced at her friend and realized Faith's complexion wasn't very healthy, either. She looked a little queasy, as if she were about to be sick. Then the German crouched next to his companion, lifting first one blond-lashed eyelid, then the other. He mumbled something to himself that Natalie couldn't understand.

"Concussion?" she asked.

"I'm afraid so." The man shook his head. "I think we must carry him."

"We can't!" Faith cried. "I'm going to go back to the road."

Natalie looked up in shock. "You want us to leave him?"

"Not you. Me. We can't carry an unconscious man his size. I'll flag down a car with men who can help. Or maybe I can contact a mountain patrol."

"That does make sense," Natalie admitted. "Go ahead, then. And hurry, for God's sake."

But Faith was already on her way, disappearing into the fog that had begun curling greedy fingers around the mountain.

The German got to his feet and stared down at the injured man. "I only hope it will not be too late."

There was a slight stirring against Natalie's breasts, and a hoarse whisper. "Peter?"

"I think he's coming around." The man's pallor had faded somewhat, and Natalie slipped her fingers under his sweater again. "Pulse seems to have picked up a little."

"Peter?" The voice was louder this time. The eyelashes that fanned out above his high cheekbones flickered. His lids opened slowly, revealing pale gray eyes. He squinted, trying to focus on Natalie's face. *"Sie sind nicht Peter,"* he muttered.

"No, I'm not Peter," she agreed.

"Hier," the German said.

The injured man's eyes were drawn to Peter, who launched into a rapid conversation in his native language that Natalie found nearly impossible to follow. He said something about not being where they should be. The younger man answered, his voice weak and filled with pain. Something about his leg. Obviously it had been hurt in the accident. Then Peter gestured toward her and said she was American and had come to help.

The blond man stared at Natalie. Words were not necessary. Understanding gleamed from his eyes as he nodded his thanks.

"We'll try to help him up," Peter said. Natalie realized he appeared to be clearheaded and thinking straight; his command of English was better than she'd first thought. He stooped over and hooked a hand under the man's armpit. "Like so."

"What if he's got internal injuries?" Natalie asked.

"I have checked. Only his right leg seems to be injured."

While they supported him, Natalie made sure to stay away from his injured leg, as Peter had told her to do. It took them several tries, but somehow the man was able to draw on his inner strength and help them get him up on his feet. Nevertheless, his mouth was a thin line of pain, and his eyes glazed over.

"Now we help him walk."

At the first step, the man groaned. His complexion became even paler than before. Natalie knew he was in agony, and yet he desperately forced himself to walk. Sweat broke out on his forehead, but he kept going around the curve and farther. Their progress was slow, hindered as well by the fog that lathed them with its moist embrace. They managed to get a third of the way back before the man's injured leg folded under him and he crashed heavily into her.

"I've got him!" she assured Peter, for once thankful that she wasn't a lightweight like Faith. Even so, she had to muster all her strength to keep him from falling. She braced herself, quickly spreading her feet for balance. The man wasn't a lightweight himself. She guessed he was six-one or six-two, and he had an athletic physique with broad shoulders and a lean yet well-muscled torso. Wherever she touched him, he was as solid as a man could be.

Peter removed the live weight from her and helped his friend to sit on a boulder. He said something in rapid German, keeping his voice low as though he didn't want her to hear. When the other man replied in the same manner and nodded slowly in agreement, she began to get anxious. What in the world was going on?

Peter straightened up and turned to her, his dirt-streaked face wearing a determined expression. "You will give me the keys to your automobile, please."

"What?"

"You will wait here while I go back to the auto and bring it to you." Before she could tell him he was crazy, he said,

"It is the only way. He cannot walk off this mountainside. Would you be responsible for this man's death?"

Shaking her head, she said, "I won't be responsible for your death, either. There's not enough room to get a car out on this ledge. Besides which, the fog—"

"Will not stop me! Your auto is small. I will succeed." There was a strange harshness to his tone when he added, "I must, for *all* our sakes. There is more at stake here than I can explain, but you must trust me."

His words froze her to the spot. She stared first at Peter, then at the man they'd come to rescue. As if she were seeing them in a dream, they appeared as shadow figures, enveloped in mist. She had no idea who they were or what they were about, yet this stranger was asking for her trust.

And for her car keys.

A gust of wind blew her hair in her eyes, blinding her for a moment.

Hadn't she thrown herself blindly into this rescue? She'd acted on instinct, not stopping to ask questions. It was a little late to ask questions now, though it was pretty obvious that these men were not ordinary mountain climbers or sightseeing tourists. She could run from them both, but that would mean leaving the injured man to die there, for surely that was a possibility if help didn't arrive. Her conscience wouldn't allow it.

Although she hadn't a reason in the world to trust Peter, Natalie did trust her own instincts. She reached into her sweater pocket, pulled out the key ring and held out her hand to the German, praying to God that she wasn't making the biggest mistake of her life.

"This you will not regret," Peter said gravely, taking the keys from her.

"I hope you're right."

He disappeared into the fog, which had settled around them like a white blanket. She shook her head. He could walk right off the mountainside and they'd never know it. And if he did get back to the road, he wouldn't be able to drive the car onto the ledge, not with the weather conditions as they were. Finally, it was starting to rain.

Stepping closer to the injured man, she saw that his shoulders were slumped and his head was drooping. The steady drizzle wouldn't do him any good. Natalie didn't hesitate before stripping off her sweater and crouching next to him. Rather than making the man struggle to put it on, she covered his back and shoulders with it. When she began to tie the sleeves together around his chest so the sweater would swathe him snugly, he stared into her face as though searching for something.

Oddly enough, in spite of the cool rain that quickly soaked her white cotton shirt, Natalie felt a stab of heat flush through her. It was fear, she told herself, knowing she wasn't sure of its source. She avoided the man's eyes until he raised a hand to push the wet hair out of her face. His fingers seared her skin where he touched it, but no more so than his steady gaze, which seemed to look straight through her to her very soul.

She rose and backed away, blinking in confusion, telling herself that the atmosphere was starting to get to her. She was imagining that an attraction that couldn't possibly exist had sparked between them.

Swallowing hard, Natalie forced herself to focus on the situation at hand. She began to wonder whether or not she should stay and wait, as Peter had instructed. One good, long look at the man convinced her that she had to try to get him off the mountain path herself. Slumped over again, he seemed to have turned into himself. Resigned. Waiting for his fate. Rainwater dripped from his dark blond hair onto his face, streaking the ruggedly attractive features with dirt and dried blood. He began to shiver in spite of her sweater.

He was already suffering from a leg injury, concussion and shock. She decided he didn't need to have exposure added to the list. Grabbing his right arm, she said, "Come. *Kommen Sie*."

He shook his head stubbornly, but she continued to tug at him while ordering him, in both English and German, to get up. Finally he stopped trying to fight her and forced himself up. He wrapped his right arm around her shoulders and adjusted his stance to take the pressure off his bad leg. His natural body heat seeped through their wet clothing; she assumed hers was doing the same for him. At least they could try to keep each other warm.

The fog was so thick now that she couldn't see her fingertips when she stretched out her hand in front of her. They could walk right off the edge of the earth....

There was a hollow feeling in the pit of her stomach as she set out, making him take one slow step at a time, but she ignored it. Instead, she concentrated on guiding him and taking the brunt of his weight. She felt her way along the slope, using her foot or her hand and hugging the mountainside. A couple of times her leather soles slipped on wet pebbles in the path, but she regained her balance before she could cause any more harm to his leg.

As they went on, the rain let up a little, but his grip on her shoulder grew tighter. Natalie felt his pain vibrating through her own body, yet she had to be ruthless. She couldn't give in and let him sit for a while. He might not be able to get up again.

"If you can feel pain, at least you know you're alive," Natalie told him, as though he understood English.

She repeated those words silently as they hobbled along for what seemed like an eternity. And his pain became hers through some odd kind of bonding she couldn't comprehend, because all her schooling and work had honed Natalie to be logical rather than emotional.

The idea of indulging in her emotions was as foreign as the phobia she'd developed as a child.

"I hate heights," she told him suddenly, wanting to hear the sound of her own voice for comfort. "I was what Americans call a tomboy. This other kid I knew—an older boy—dared me to climb into a tree to save a stray kitten. She was mewing pitifully because she couldn't get down."

He seemed to be listening to her ramble, yet there was no sign of recognition in his expression. Maybe the sound of her voice comforted him also. At least it gave him something other than his leg to concentrate on. The very fact that he couldn't understand what she was saying allowed her to speak freely.

"As I went up into the branches, so did the kitten. All the way to the top. You can imagine how far down that seemed to a seven-year-old."

Of course he didn't answer, although he studied her face intently. His grip on her shoulder had lessened, and some of the tension had left his body. Or maybe that was just her own wishful thinking.

"That rat of a boy left me stuck up there for hours, as terrified as the kitten," she went on. "I couldn't get down. It was dark before my father found me and brought a ladder. When we got to the ground, I threw myself into his arms and sobbed." Natalie hesitated a second before adding, "Father told me I was being irrational."

She'd almost forgotten those words—perhaps because they made her father sound cold and uncaring, when he hadn't been like that at all. At least she'd never thought of him that way.

"It happened more than twenty years ago, but I still can't look down a stairwell without holding onto the railing. Standing on a ladder to paint walls is a trauma in itself. And I occasionally get dizzy standing on a chair to change a light bulb."

The man's gray eyes were on her rueful smile. He had soulful eyes. Warm. Comforting. Caring. The kind of eyes a woman might wish belonged to her man.

The startling thought made Natalie uneasy. She wouldn't tell him what this rescue had done to her nervous system: that being brave enough to get out of the car and look at the landscape had been challenge enough for her. Somehow she sensed he might know this—maybe the bonding had gone both ways—because Gray Eyes seemed sympathetic.

Suddenly wondering if he understood some English after all, Natalie felt a little foolish. Even though she had a sense of humor about her shortcomings, she'd never told those personal things to a complete stranger. She looked ahead, realizing that the rain had stopped altogether. And the fog was lifting. Her hope that they would make it back was renewed.

Glad to have something other than the silly one-way conversation to think about, she focused on the faint smudges of glowing red that appeared to be coming toward them.

"Taillights! My God, he did it!"

She stopped and waited for the car to do the same. Peter backed up to within a couple of yards from where they stood, then halted. The driver's door was inches from the edge of the mountain. Scrambling out across the passenger seat, Peter carefully made his way around the vehicle to them. As Natalie wondered where Faith was, the two men exchanged a few sentences in German, after which Peter looked at her in awe.

Together, they helped his friend get into the car, Peter first backing himself in toward the driver's seat. Natalie gently lifted the injured leg. Gray Eyes moaned, making her let go as soon as his foot touched the car's interior.

"You will ride with us?" Peter asked, nodding toward the rear seat.

Although she'd had enough of the mountainside and wanted off as quickly as possible, Natalie shook her head. "Thanks, but I prefer to walk."

Gray Eyes caught her elbow. His grip was incredibly strong for an injured man, even one as well built as he. She looked at him questioningly. The intensity of his gaze made her mouth go dry and stopped her from moving away. Natalie's pulse picked up as he touched the side of her face, drew it closer with his free hand, then did something totally unexpected.

He kissed her.

It wasn't a passionate kiss, but one of thanks, full of warmth, comfort, caring—all those things his eyes had promised.

And then he released her and let his head fall back in exhaustion.

Uncertain and a little embarrassed, Natalie glanced at Peter. He was staring out the driver's window. She didn't say a word, merely pulled away and closed the passenger door. When she'd backed off, he allowed the car to creep forward slowly. She followed, several yards behind.

Fortunately it was a short haul. She managed to keep up with the car until they came in sight of the observation area and the vehicles waiting there. That was when Peter grew bolder and stepped on the gas, leaving Natalie a good distance behind.

She could see the flashing lights of a mountain-patrol ambulance ahead. Faith was talking to the medics, pointing to the oncoming car. Several spectators milled around, undoubtedly waiting to see what was going on. They crowded the small Ford after it had stopped and Peter got out. When the medics tried to get to the passenger side, however, Peter waved them away.

Natalie frowned, wondering if he really hadn't gotten over the shock of the accident. She hurried forward as he ig-

nored the medics and said something to one of the spectators. She was close enough to see him take a roll of bills
from his pocket and peel off several. The other man took the
offering, then helped Peter get Gray Eyes out of her car and
into his own red Fiat. Faith seemed to be the only one trying
to stop them.

"Peter, wait!" Natalie yelled, still a hundred feet or so
away. She heard the car start but was determined to reach it
before it drove off. Gray Eyes needed medical assistance!
She had questions that needed answers! The Fiat defied her
concerns and crept out toward the road. "Wait!" she
screamed again.

And then it zoomed away and disappeared, vaporized by
the mists that still clung to the mountain. Natalie stared after it in frustration. Her chest heaved as she tried to get her
breath. The medics and the other people climbed into their
vehicles calmly, as if now that the performance was over, it
was time to leave. A performance . . . unreal . . . yet it had
actually happened.

She'd helped save a man's life and didn't even know his
name. He'd kissed her, but she'd never see him again.

A gust of wind mocked her, making her hug herself for
warmth. Natalie looked down at the damp cotton shirt she
wore and realized a part of her had gone with the mysterious gray-eyed stranger. He still had her sweater wrapped
around his neck.

Whoever *he* might be.

Chapter Two

Natalie continued to wonder about the identity of the blond stranger, who had not only her sweater but her international driver's license as well. Faith convinced her she could drive with her U.S. license, so at least the loss didn't spoil the rest of the weekend at Aix-les-Baines. Still, Faith seemed thoughtful and restless by turns. And the hot springs, racecourse and casino of the mountain resort barely distracted Natalie from memories of the gray-eyed man.

She was still thinking about him after they had returned to Faith's small apartment in Lyon. She'd probably never forget him, or so Natalie thought as she chopped ingredients for a salad to accompany the veal she was cooking for dinner their first night back. Unable to stop herself, she conjured up his image as she'd seen it right before he'd kissed her: his brow creased, his gaze intent, his expression determined. For some strange reason, that gentle kiss of friendship stood above any other kiss in her past, both in her mind and in her heart.

She didn't know her mystery man's identity and probably never would. Peter had seen to that when he'd refused help from the mountain patrol Faith had managed to contact. Instead, he'd made sure they were gone before anyone could ask them questions, despite his friend's injuries. Thinking about Peter's suspect motives, Natalie heard the apartment door opening. She glanced at the clock. Faith must have left the consulate early.

"I'm home," Faith called. "It smells wonderful, but why are you cooking?"

Natalie stuck her head out of the tiny kitchen area. "I thought we could eat in tonight instead of having a five-course dinner in a restaurant. You could use a few extra pounds, but I've got to start cutting back or I won't fit into my plane seat on the way home."

"You know you're exaggerating ridiculously. And don't talk about leaving." Faith set her briefcase on the floor and stripped off her suit jacket. "You just got here."

"It's been almost a week. Only two days before I go home."

Rather than responding, Faith wandered over to the television set and turned it on to the English-language news station, just as she'd done at every available opportunity during the past few days. Natalie guessed that Faith's obsessive interest in current happenings stemmed from her work as a foreign-service officer.

Shutting out the noise of the television, she went back to her task at the cutting board. "Dinner won't be ready for a while. I was going to surprise you by having the food completely prepared and the table set with linens and the flowers I bought at the market."

"You're a dear. I can set the table while you cook. Just give me a chance to change."

"Sounds fair to me."

The newscaster droned on in the background. Natalie found a bowl for the salad and dumped in the ingredients she'd just chopped.

"I want to hear all about your day as a tourist on your own," Faith yelled from her bedroom. "I'm going to miss you when you have to go back, Nat! It's been too long since we've had the opportunity to be close."

It was true, Natalie thought as she turned to the frying pan on the two-burner stove. She flipped the meat and added a few more dashes of spice as well as a generous squeeze of fresh lemon.

After graduation, Faith had gone to work for the government. She'd been assigned to posts that took her to exotic places far away from their native Delaware, while Natalie had remained behind to teach and to continue with her schooling. Until now, she'd seen nothing of the rest of the world. She'd always wanted to travel through Europe—to travel anywhere!—but adventure had been put aside in lieu of her career.

Great things had been expected of the only child of two brilliant scientists, and Natalie had made sure she lived up to expectations. After receiving her Ph.D. the year before, she'd been promoted to assistant professor of mathematics at the University of Delaware. She'd achieved her professional objectives in record time. That winter, her father had been able to die content, knowing his daughter was a success.

Unfortunately, a Ph.D. and a promotion hadn't been enough for her. She'd been dissatisfied for quite some time, but it had only been recently that she'd realized what was bothering her: life was passing her by.

Analyzing why she'd let that happen, Natalie had first blamed her dedication to her father's wishes, but in the end she'd decided it had been her own fault. She'd always thought of herself as unexciting and not particularly attractive. Unconsciously she'd tried to make up for those shortcomings by developing her brain to its limits.

Although others had admired her lustrous brown hair, large blue eyes, and good skin and facial bone structure inherited from her Slavic and Scandinavian forefathers, she'd always been self-conscious about her size. Feeling the need for camouflage, she'd adopted an unassuming style for herself in her wardrobe—and in her life.

But when Faith had called a little more than a week ago, begging her to come to Lyon, Natalie had wanted to help herself as well. She was long overdue for a change. Perhaps she'd never redo her outer self, but she could broaden her interests and experiences. She could seek out the adventure she'd always secretly wanted.

Adventure. She'd certainly had more than she'd bargained for in one afternoon, she mused, remembering the mountainside. Made restless by the images that came to her unbidden, she left the meat cooking over a low flame and wandered into the living room. She was surprised to find Faith standing very still in front of the television.

"And now let's return to the U.S. embassy in Paris for an unscheduled news conference," the Oriental woman reporter on the screen was saying.

"Hey," Natalie protested. "I thought you were going…" Her voice trailed off as the picture on the tube changed to a wide shot of reporters surrounding a man on crutches. A man whose blond hair and strong features were disturbingly familiar. A gray-haired State Department spokesman welcomed him to the podium, which was faced with a seal of the United States of America. After shaking the injured man's hand, he turned to the microphone and the cameras.

"As you know, a few minutes ago the ambassador announced the defection of Russian skating coach Mikhail Illyovich Korolev. I'm sure you're anxious to ask him questions, so I'll turn this conference over to him." He stepped back and to the side, saying, "Mikhail."

Adjusting his crutches, the Russian took the last step toward the podium. The camera zoomed in to a medium shot of him alone. Weak-kneed, Natalie felt for the couch and sat down.

"I have no prepared statement," Mikhail began, his English perfect, his Russian accent pronounced. "But I would like to thank the United States government for granting me asylum. I will answer your questions to the best of my ability."

"He speaks English," Natalie murmured. She was almost more shocked by that than by the fact that he was a Russian, one whom she'd unwittingly helped to defect! She'd assumed he was German, like Peter. All those personal things she'd told him—he'd understood every word!

"Where and how did you defect?" asked one reporter.

"I came to France with my skaters," Mikhail said. "They were to compete in the Chamonix Invitational. A friend guided me along a mountain path that led away from the town."

"Is that where you were injured?" another reporter asked.

"Yes. By a rock slide."

He didn't mention that two women had assisted him after he'd been injured. But that might be for the best, Natalie thought. Perhaps he didn't want to involve them in case there were repercussions from the Soviet government.

"Who was this friend who helped you seek asylum from the United States?"

Mikhail hesitated and looked off to the side as though seeking permission to answer. He nodded, then faced the reporters and the cameras once more.

"Someone who understood the difficulties," he replied. "Another skating coach, who now works with members of the United States team. Peter Baum."

"The East German defector?"

A murmur went up through the crowd at the announcement, so that the next woman to ask a question had to shout to be heard. "Why did you defect?"

Mikhail looked straight into the camera as it zoomed in on him for a close-up. His gray eyes seemed to fill the screen. Natalie studied them, but they were devoid of expression.

"For the same reason that my friend Peter defected twelve years ago," he finally said. "Artistic freedom."

Satisfied with the pat answer, the reporters yelled at once, each wanting to be the next to have his or her question heard. After a few minutes of this, the camera shot changed to that of a reporter holding a mike and surrounded by three young people.

"I have with me members of the American skating team—brother and sister Jan and Ken Butler, as well as Wendy Prentiss," the reporter said to the camera. He turned to the pretty blonde next to him. "Jan, let me start with you. What do you think about Korolev's defection?"

"I think it's super. Korolev is a great skater and a great coach. He could be a shot in the arm for our amateur skaters."

"Wendy, what about you?"

"I was in one of his skating seminars as part of an exchange program a couple of years ago." Although her mind was already wandering back to the Russian, Natalie vaguely heard Wendy continue. "Being able to work with him again is . . . exciting. He has an intensity about him that's inspirational."

"This is a lot of bunk." Ken Butler's remark startled Natalie into giving the program her full attention. "He's a Ruskie."

"Would you clarify that statement?" the reporter asked.

"What's to clarify? He's the enemy. I wouldn't trust him to sharpen my skate blades."

Ken Butler's words made Natalie uneasy, especially when the cameras cut back to Mikhail, who was still being questioned by the press. She stared at the magnified emotionless eyes she'd been able to read so well on the mountainside.

Why weren't they reflecting the happiness he should be feeling? Where was the joy that should come naturally with being free of a repressive government? Was it possible that Mikhail Illyovich Korolev was lying about the reason he'd defected?

EVEN WITH PRACTICE, DECEPTION didn't come easily to Mikhail Korolev. He felt that each lie he told was a cancer eating away at his soul. But knowing that didn't change a thing. He'd left Moscow with a mission, and he meant to fulfill it, no matter the cost to himself.

If he failed, all would be for naught. He had to remember that.

As things stood, his beloved Russia was like a dead mother to him: a sometimes beautiful memory to be cherished. Nothing more. He accepted this, as he'd accepted so many objectionable things in his life that he could do nothing about. Agreeing to leave had been his choice, after all.

But if he could choose right now, he'd be anywhere else in the world but in this cramped, airless room fouled with cigar smoke. Anywhere away from Elliott Drucker of the Central Intelligence Agency.

Although he was of average height and medium build, Drucker had an undeniable aura of strength. It was evident in the way he held himself when he paced—ramrod straight with an arrogant tilt to his dark-haired head—and in the way he looked through a man when he questioned him. Drucker's brown eyes constantly tried to penetrate Mikhail's protective barrier. His face wasn't cruel, exactly, but with its crooked nose and thin-lipped mouth, it looked as tough as the rest of him.

At least this time Mikhail was sitting in a chair at a table and not lying helpless in bed. He no longer had a concussion, and he wasn't in shock. Despite the severity of his ruptured tendon, he was able to walk with an elastic bandage and crutches.

He was more determined than ever not to let the agent get to him, but he was so tired. And English was difficult for him when he was tired. He had to speak carefully and not make a mistake. Mikhail knew Drucker was the kind of man who'd give no quarter if he learned even a fragment of the truth. A mistake could be fatal.

As if on cue, the CIA man demanded, "When are you going to tell me the real reason behind this defection, Korolev?"

"You ask the same questions always."

"And you keep shoveling the same crap at me. Do I look stupid?"

Mikhail merely raised an eyebrow as Drucker puffed on his obnoxious cigar and waited. Two could play at the same game. Russians were masters of gamesmanship.

Drucker was the first to lose his patience. "All right! You want me to rephrase the question?"

"No. You know my reason. The whole world knows, after the broadcast."

The press conference had come as something of a surprise. Having superseded the man from the State Department who'd arranged for Mikhail's medical care when he'd shown up at the embassy, Drucker had been hammering away at him for three solid days. The debriefing had been so intense and unsympathetic that Mikhail was surprised when his defection was announced.

Drucker stopped pacing directly in front of him. The agent reached into his pocket, withdrew an object, then threw it on the table. "And does the whole world know about this?" "This" was an international driver's license. "Who is she? What does she mean to you?"

The card identified the woman as Natalie Lundgren of Wilmington, Delaware. Mikhail stared at the typically unflattering official photograph. Remembering her differently, he picked up the license and touched the plastic-coated, lifeless representation of Natalie. It was nothing like her. The real woman was full of life; she had forced his own on him when he'd been ready to quit. Even with her hair wet and straggly, she'd seemed the epitome of womanhood to him. Strong, determined and unyielding, yet soft and vulnerable. Willing to put aside her own fears to help someone else.

Unlike most of his Russian comrades.

In some ways, so very like his ex-wife, Galina Temka. The biggest difference between the two women was in orientation—a matter of politics. Natalie Lundgren had seen beyond politics to save his life. Of course, she hadn't known he was a Russian, but Mikhail felt instinctively that she would not have cared.

Drucker put out his cigar in an ashtray. Then he leaned forward, his hands grasping the back of a chair, the expression in his eyes that of a predator ready to pounce. On whom? Mikhail wondered. Himself? Or Natalie?

"Come on, Korolev. The truth. Who is she?"

Taking a steadying breath so he wouldn't show his fear for the woman to whom he owed his life, Mikhail casually tapped the driver's license. "Where did you get this?"

"Why do you care?"

"Why do you show me this?"

Drucker leaned closer, practically sticking his face into Mikhail's. "Are you denying you know her?"

"No, damn it!" Mikhail finally exploded, throwing the card down on the table so hard, it flew across the polished surface and onto the floor. "I do not want to give her trouble. She does not deserve trouble."

He put his head in his hands. What had he done? He should have pretended he'd never seen her before. For all he knew, Drucker could have her arrested for questioning. He had no idea how these things were handled by the U.S. authorities. He'd been in the States for training and competitions several times during the past dozen years, but that was as far as his knowledge of authorities went.

"Who is she?"

Mikhail shook his head. "I did not know her name until you showed me her license. She is just a woman, a kind stranger who helped me after the accident."

"Interesting that she'd help a Russian defect and not tell anyone about it."

"She knows nothing. Not even that I am Russian."

"Just where did she think you were from, with that thick accent of yours?" Drucker asked, his expression disbelieving. "The Bronx?"

Not understanding the reference, Mikhail shrugged. "I never spoke. Peter thought it would be too dangerous for us. And for her."

"Don't you think it's time you gave me the whole story rather than the edited garbage you've been feeding me?"

There wasn't much else he could do now that Drucker knew about Natalie, so Mikhail told him what had happened as he remembered it. The concussion had made him confused about many things, but he did the best he could, leaving out nothing but the personal details and the one thing that counted most—the item that Drucker would give anything to get from him.

When he'd said all he intended to, Mikhail sat silently until the CIA man asked, "Why didn't you tell me this before?"

"She has done nothing wrong. She has a kind heart. Do not give her trouble."

Instead of responding to his plea, Drucker asked, "Who was the woman with Natalie Lundgren?"

"I saw her once. Briefly. I cannot even remember what she looks like."

Would the incessant questions never end? He'd thought he was through with the interrogation when his defection had been announced, but Drucker would never let him go, Mikhail decided. He would keep him in the room all night if he had to, until Mikhail's English became so jumbled that he would make a mistake. He should never have refused the offer of a Russian interpreter, but it was too late for regrets.

"My head hurts," Mikhail said, not really lying. "I would rest now."

Drucker walked around the back of Mikhail's chair to the other side of the table. Bending over, he picked up the driver's license and held it out. "This was in the pocket of that red sweater they took off you when you came in."

"Then it is mine. I can keep it."

Perhaps if he got the license, Natalie would be safe. Mikhail held out his hand, but Drucker slid the card into his own shirt pocket.

"I think I'll keep it for now. Question time's over. You'd better get some sleep. You're heading for Washington in the morning."

ONCE IN WASHINGTON, MIKHAIL was put up at a hotel in which he'd remain until he could find work or until his State Department contact found it for him. Before leaving for a coaching seminar in China, Peter had made inquiries of the major ice-skating training facilities on Mikhail's behalf. All three were interested, but, depressed and lonely, Mikhail had not yet followed up on the leads.

He was starving, not for food—he'd been provided with money for that—but for company. He was a man who needed people. He'd always been surrounded by others ever since he could remember. Born in Moscow, he'd been raised in a communal apartment, which was common in the days before prefabricated apartment buildings had converted the

beautiful city into a poorly constructed patchwork quilt.
Each of the three bedrooms had belonged to a different
family, although the kitchen, toilet and living areas had been
shared. One had to learn to like people in order to survive
in those conditions.

Mikhail was an only child, which wasn't unusual in Moscow, then or now. That was why he'd become so attached to
the only other child in the apartment.

Two years older than Mikhail, Aleksei Rodzianko had
treated him like a little brother. He had seen to it that Mikhail's skating talent had been recognized. Mikhail had been
taken out of his regular school and sent to a physical culture institute, where he had received both an education and
the best athletic training. Mikhail had idolized the bold, attention-seeking Aleksei, who had always wanted to be a hero
and had pulled crazy, dangerous stunts. He had stood up for
Mikhail and gotten him out of several scrapes over the years.
Now it was Mikhail's turn to save Aleksei before it was too
late.

If only things hadn't gone wrong, he could have settled
everything in Paris. He and Aleksei might have been reunited, perhaps even today. Instead there'd been the accident. Before he'd passed out, at least he'd had enough wits
about him to hide the carefully wrapped package he'd
smuggled out of Moscow.

A lot of good his care did Aleksei now.

Mikhail didn't have enough money to return to the place
where he'd secured the package, and even if he had it, he
didn't want to involve Peter Baum anymore. The German
would have to lead him to that mountain path because he
had only a selective memory about the escape. Alone, he'd
never find the spot. As a matter of fact, he remembered little of the time between the accident and waking up on a
couch in the Paris embassy.

But he did remember Natalie. Natalya, he thought, liking the Russian name better. No, he'd want to call her his Natasha. But she wasn't his and never would be. He'd never see her again.

To distract himself, Mikhail left the hotel and, with the aid of a cane, walked to the library to do the research he now knew was necessary. He would do it for Aleksei, and damn his own ethics! There was no other way.

Once there, Mikhail quickly found the article in the March issue of *Newsweek*. He read the headline: "Thwart Uncovered in spite of Maximum Security." The article that followed was a long one, detailing the years of research that had already gone into developing Thwart—the code name for the radar-invisible aircraft being built for the U.S. government by Aircon—without actually giving away any secrets.

Photographs of the three scientists leading the project accompanied the article. Mikhail was drawn to one in particular, a woman with graying brown hair and round blue eyes surrounded by fine lines. There was something disturbingly familiar about her. Perhaps it was her facial bone structure—typically Slavic. The caption under her photo read: Catherine Lundgren of Wilmington, Delaware.

Reading her name jolted his gut like a shot of pepper vodka. Mikhail studied the face and imagined it without the age lines and with a fuller, more sensual mouth. As much as he wanted to deny it, the picture did not lie.

He was staring at a likeness of Natalie.

"HOME ONE DAY, AND YOU'VE already got this place topsy-turvy," Catherine Lundgren complained to her daughter good-naturedly.

Natalie looked up from the bed of pansies she'd just finished planting. "I don't intend to waste a minute of this summer, C.L. It's the first time I've had the freedom to do anything I wanted since I started high school. I was always too busy taking classes. But this year I'm determined to try all kinds of new things."

"That's all very well, but what are we paying the gardener for?"

"To cut the lawn, prune the trees and trim the bushes." Natalie rose to her full height, which made her two inches taller than her mother, who wore sensible inch-and-a-half heels to go with her business suit. "He can do all the grunt work, but this summer the flowers are mine!"

Catherine eyed her daughter's grime-covered exterior. "Well, you've certainly gotten into your project wholeheartedly, haven't you, dear?"

Natalie knew her bare legs were streaked with dirt, and her hands were covered with it. She liked the feel of the earth at her fingertips and had chosen not to wear gardening gloves. "Isn't that a Lundgren trait, Mother?"

"I guess so."

Using the back of her hand, Natalie swiped at her forehead to get at the stray curl that had come loose from her ponytail to tickle her. "You certainly look cool and professional today. What are you up to?"

"Another news conference. What a bother!" Catherine started toward the front of the house, Natalie right behind her. "It keeps me from my work."

Her mother's giving up the time to talk to reporters was quite a sacrifice. "Do I correctly assume you'll be staying at your lab tonight?"

"If I don't, I won't get anything done." Catherine opened the screen door and led the way into the living room. "I'm sorry. I know I promised you we'd have dinner together."

"Forget it. We'll have dinner tomorrow. Just remember to eat tonight."

"I'll get a bite somewhere. There's always peanut butter and bread in the lab refrigerator."

Natalie rolled her eyes. "You'd better listen carefully to those questions the reporters aim at you. I can hear them now. 'Dr. Lundgren, how do you survive when you hole yourself in your lab for days at a time?' Then you'll say, 'Why, on peanut butter.' Real impressive, C.L.," Natalie said playfully.

"What have I done to deserve such a disrespectful daughter?"

"You love it. Admit it."

"I love *you*, Natalie." Catherine moved in to peck her on the cheek but couldn't do so without getting dirty. Natalie obliged her by leaning over. "But I hate wearing these ridiculous clothes." She picked up her overnight bag and briefcase from where she'd left them in the middle of the living room. "Now I hope I haven't forgotten anything. I always get flustered before these grand displays. If only your father were here. He used to be so good at taking care of such unpleasantries."

"He used to be good at a lot of things."

"I'd better hurry or I'll be late. You have fun with your plants."

"I will."

Natalie locked the front door behind her mother, then wandered through the house to the back door and the garden, where she gathered up her tools. Actually, she was done for the day, ready to clean up and bring out the grill. But cooking for and eating by herself weren't much fun. She wondered if her mother had peanut butter in one of the kitchen cabinets.

Eating alone had become a bad habit. Catherine worked late most nights, often sleeping on a cot at the lab. Natalie was thoughtful as she placed the bucket of tools in the shed. Since her father died, her mother seemed to be trying to do the work of two people to make up for his absence. Living with Catherine was very much like living alone, but there were times when they drew close, giving each other what they could. Natalie wished there were more times like that.

She entered the house, stopping in the mud room next to the kitchen, and slipped out of her shoes. She was about to strip off the filthy shorts and tube top when the doorbell rang. She thought her mother must have forgotten something in her frenzy. Undoubtedly her keys, or else she would have let herself in. Grinning, Natalie planned to tease her about being an absentminded scientist. Her hand was already on the knob and pulling the front door open when the bell sounded a second time.

"All right, what did you forget...?"

The man standing on the other side of the screen door said, "But you are confused. It is you who forgot something." He held up her red sweater. "Hello, Natalya. I've come to thank you for saving my life."

Her gaze lifted and locked with his. Then her pulse lurched as she recognized anticipation mixed with something else—something far more complex and confusing—in the gray eyes of Mikhail Illyovich Korolev.

Chapter Three

"Won't you let me in so I can thank you properly?"

The softly issued question jarred Natalie into action. Blinking, she opened the screen door for him. Mikhail never took his eyes off her as he entered the hallway. She noticed he was using a cane. Dozens of questions whirled through her brain, but only one found its way to her lips.

"H-how did you find me?"

"Your international driver's license." His simple answer made her feel foolish. She should have remembered. "You left your license in the pocket," he continued, offering her the sweater. "The authorities—they have returned it?"

Taking the garment from him, she shook her head. "No, not yet."

For a moment, he seemed to tense and she couldn't read his expression at all. But then he relaxed and let his eyes drift over her appraisingly. Natalie was immediately self-conscious of her disheveled appearance. Mikhail's hair was neatly combed, and his light gray trousers and gray-and-white striped shirt were obviously new. When his glance swept the length of her dirt-streaked legs, she felt like hiding behind something. Instead, she crushed the sweater between her suddenly damp palms.

"I was working in the garden," she said as though she had to explain.

His eyes seemed to return to her face reluctantly. "Then I have interrupted your work. Perhaps I should come back at another time."

"No, not at all. I'm finished. I was just about to get cleaned up. If you'd like to wait, it'll take me just a couple of minutes. I have questions," she said, letting her voice drop. Undoubtedly, he'd had enough questions in the past several days to last him a lifetime.

But Mikhail's smile belied her thoughts. "Good. Then I would like to take you to dinner. It's not enough thanks for my life, but—"

"I'd love to have dinner with you, but why not right here? I was going to barbecue tonight. My mother couldn't make it, though, and since there's only the two of us, that meant I'd be cooking for myself, which wouldn't be much fun." From his slightly dazed expression, she gathered her explanation was too rapid for him to follow. Natalie slowed down. "Would you like to eat here? Please say yes. We can relax. Talk."

"Talk," he echoed. "Yes."

She smiled and awkwardly backed away into the living room. He followed, limping slightly. "You can wait in here. Or outside on the deck." She gestured toward the patio doors in the dining room. "There's a nice breeze out there."

"Good."

"Would you like something to drink?"

He nodded. "Later, with you." His lips twitched as if he were amused. "And I can let myself out."

She escaped to the attic she'd refurbished several years before, when she'd decided to remain in the Lundgren home instead of finding an apartment. Her father had been ill even then, and her brilliant mother hadn't known how to cope. As an only child, Natalie had felt responsible for her scientist parents, who looked out for their "fellow man" more than they did for themselves.

She'd never regretted staying. She was alone most of the time, but she loved living under the eaves, her own oasis with its lofty view. Pale blue walls with white trim reflected the light let in by the skylight as well as by the French doors, which opened onto a small deck overlooking the garden. Her bed, plumped up with a bolster and pillows, was tucked in under one slanted side; her built-in desk hugged the opposite wall.

Natalie was out of breath by the time she reached her third-floor room, but she wasn't sure if it was because of the climb or the prospect of spending time alone with the Russian. No, that would be silly, she decided, throwing the sweater down onto the bed. There was nothing romantic about the situation. Mikhail was grateful to her and wanted to thank her for her help. Period.

Yet as she peeled off her clothes on her way into the dormer bathroom, she remembered the last time he'd thanked her. His kiss had been a gesture of friendship, but her memory of it seemed different now. Had there been an underlying eroticism in the way he'd touched her?

She really was being silly and far too romantic. Natalie reminded herself that she was not the type of woman to inspire those kinds of notions in a man. Even Warren Young, the graduate-student lover she'd once thought she'd sensibly marry, hadn't seen her that way. He'd respected her mind and thought she carried herself well. But when it came down to committing himself, he'd become engaged to a woman who was smaller, prettier and less competitive intellectually.

So much for romance.

Still, as she stepped into the shower she couldn't help but speculate what it might be like to kiss Mikhail as a lover.

MIKHAIL DIDN'T MOVE UNTIL Natalie's long legs had disappeared up the staircase. It would be too much to hope that she might wear shorts when she returned. She'd been un-comfortable because he'd seen her that way, but he liked her womanly fullness. He'd never appreciated the Western countries' penchant for bone-thin women. He frowned at the thought. It wouldn't do to speculate further in that direction.

Leaning lightly on his cane, he looked around him. The large living room and the dining room and kitchen beyond were neat. The furniture was obviously expensive, al-though plain. There was no individuality about the place, nothing special that made it stand out from the American homes he'd been in when he'd visited the U.S. in the past. The lack of personal touches or of family pictures gave the impression that the occupants of this house didn't actually live here.

After standing indecisively for several minutes, he wan-dered, not to the dining room with its deck beyond, but in the opposite direction, to a closed door. It wasn't locked.

Mikhail entered a room whose walls were lined with books. A worn leather couch and two chairs faced a fire-place that had been used recently. The scent of cherrywood lingered in the room. Technical and scientific magazines covered a low table in the middle of the seating area. On the other side of the room, a hutch sheltered a computer ter-minal hooked up to a modem and a printer. Next to it, the huge oak desk backed by a window was piled with folders and papers. A coffee cup sat on top of a stack. A framed photograph of a couple with a small girl was half hidden by the mess. Someone lived in here.

He walked to the low table, lifted one of the magazines and read the address label: Dr. Catherine Lundgren. He'd been correct, then. So why didn't that give him the sense of satisfaction it should? He stood there, looking at the girl in the photograph, the scene on the mountain replaying itself in his mind.

Setting the magazine down exactly as he'd found it, Mikhail left the study, pulling the door shut quietly behind him. It was only when he turned around that he grew aware of the woman standing on the stairs, watching him.

He thought quickly. "I'm afraid I'm lost," he told Natalie, flushing with the embarrassment of his lie. "I was looking for the toilet."

"Oh, the bathroom!" She came to life, her stiff posture softening at his fabricated explanation, then descended the remaining few steps. Her gullibility made Mikhail feel guilty. "It's right over there. I'll be outside, setting up the charcoal."

She pointed to a closed door on her side of the hall as she headed for the kitchen, her full hips swaying a little, beckoning to him in spite of his good sense. He was sure she allowed herself this touch of femininity only unconsciously. Dressed in loose tan pants with a wide elastic waist and a cotton-knit shirt with short sleeves and a collar, she'd hidden the best of herself. Even the length of her beautiful brown hair was camouflaged in a loose French braid at the back of her head.

Mikhail went into the bathroom and forced himself to wait a few moments—he didn't want her to be suspicious. Then he flushed the tank and washed his hands before exiting. When he came into the kitchen, Natalie was outside on the deck, setting down the bag of charcoal.

"Do you need help?" he asked, joining her.

"Not really. Sit down." She nodded toward one of the cushioned chairs surrounding a redwood table, then picked up a can of charcoal starter fluid. "We can relax and talk over a drink until the coals are ready. Anything in particular you'd like?"

Iced vodka, Mikhail thought, setting his cane on the ground under the chair. He could use the jolt the shot would give him. But, knowing he needed to keep his head clear, he said, "No alcohol. I'm on medication."

"Oh, that's right. Your leg." Natalie frowned at it as though she could see the injury through the material of his trousers. Shifting her attention back to the job at hand, she doused the contents of the grill with the starter fluid. "Are you in much pain?"

"No. Not now. Sometimes it still..." He paused, searching for a word. "Twinges, I think you say. A ruptured tendon isn't serious, but I use the cane when I walk outside. The doctor says I can be back on the ice in less than a week."

"I hope you don't rush it."

Natalie lit a match and dropped it on the mound of charcoal. The flame flared high, tinting her clear skin with warm tones, animating her face. Mikhail couldn't look away. She caught him staring and froze for a second, as if fixed by his gaze. The fire died down, yet he noted that the delicate tinge of rose remained on her cheekbones. Either the flames had made her very warm, or she was very self-conscious around him.

"I'll get us some iced tea." She started for the house but hesitated when she got to the doorway. "Unless you'd prefer soda or juice."

"I like tea."

Mikhail thought she would say something more, but she went on inside. He let out a sigh of relief once she was out of sight. He needed a moment in private to compose himself. This was going to be even more difficult than he'd imagined. Not only did he owe this woman his life, but there was something appealingly vulnerable about Natalie that belied the strength he knew her to possess. The knowledge both stirred and discomfited him; he hated the idea of crushing her particular kind of innocence.

And yet, he reminded himself, it was too soon to decide how to proceed with his mission. For the moment, he was merely continuing with his research. That thought made him feel better, but just barely.

When Natalie returned, she was carrying a tray with a pitcher and two glasses. She placed everything on the red-wood table and poured the tea, sneaking a peek at him through lowered lashes. Although she seemed to be trying to make up her mind about something, she didn't say a word until after she had sat down opposite him and taken a sip from her glass. Then curiosity won out over hesitancy.

"Why didn't you speak to me in English on the mountain?"

"Peter said not to," Mikhail told her truthfully. Natalie nodded as if she'd known that all along. "He said to use German if necessary, but that it would be safer for everyone if I could avoid speaking at all."

"That was some escape."

"I don't remember much of it myself." This was true. If he did remember more, he wouldn't have to be here, wouldn't have to consider hurting her. Realizing she was looking at him questioningly, Mikhail added, "The head injury made me forget most of what went on."

Her eyes flickered to his forehead. "Looks like you'll have a slight scar. It'll add to your romantic image." Then, as if embarrassed by her statement, Natalie quickly asked, "The man Peter paid to drive you away from there—where did he take you?"

"All the way to Paris. I'm very grateful to him. And to you. You're a brave woman, Natalya Lundgren."

"Brave?" She shook her head. "'Afraid' is more like it."

"I know." Mikhail smiled as he remembered her humorous admissions about being afraid of heights. "That makes you even more brave than someone who had no fears at all."

After rapidly swallowing the remainder of the iced tea in her glass, Natalie poured herself some more. Mikhail was sure she did this to avoid looking at him.

"Now that you're in the United States," she said, changing the subject, "how do you feel about life here?"

"It's lonely, but that will pass."

Her vivid blue eyes revealed her compassion. "You miss Russia, don't you? I can hear it in your voice."

"Yes, some things. And as time passes, there are many more that I will miss about my native country." Mikhail clenched his jaw grimly as fleeting images of things he'd never again experience flitted through his mind—flower-bedecked horses pulling a troika in the winter; he and Aleksei playing chess at one of the tables in Gorky Park in the summer. "But there are many advantages to being here, too."

"Artistic freedom," she said, her expression intent.

"Yes." Frowning down into his glass, Mikhail absently swirled the tea and watched the ice cubes bob. "Also, living conditions are so much better here. A house this size for two people would be unheard of in Russia. A couple is lucky to have even a three-room apartment in Moscow." Like the apartment he and Galina had lived in until his defection, Mikhail thought. "When I was still married, we got one because of Galina's importance as a computer hardware designer and because of my own previous international recognition as an Olympic ice-skating champion. I became a coach just before our marriage," he clarified.

"So you're divorced?"

Mikhail nodded, mentally comparing their situations. Natalie could leave her mother's home at any time and find an apartment. In Moscow, where shortages abounded and changes occurred slowly, the dissolution of a marriage didn't mean one could find new living quarters. He'd been divorced since last winter, but he'd never moved out of the apartment because he'd had no place to go. He'd been on a waiting list for housing. At least he'd been away with his skaters most of the time....

To think that only a month ago he'd been so anxious for the authorities to find him another place to live—and now he'd never have to worry about it!

"But what about the outskirts of Moscow? We call them suburbs. Don't people own any kind of homes away from the city?"

"Yes, some have dachas—country cottages not too far from Moscow. But only special people—artists, politburo members, high-echelon party members—are so lucky." Like Aleksei, who'd been granted one because of his status as a writer, before he'd become "unofficial." Now his friend had a prison cell to call home. That disturbing thought reminded Mikhail of his purpose. "It is your turn. I want to know more about you. What were you like as a child? What kind of work do you do?" He paused only a second before adding, "And your mother... What kind of a relationship do you have?"

Their discussion of life behind the Iron Curtain had put Natalie on edge, reminding her of the suspicions she'd had about Mikhail's defection. And yet his obvious interest in her pleased Natalie, making her push those doubts aside for the moment.

She told him a few amusing stories of her childhood, skirting the feelings of awkwardness she'd developed as she'd grown taller than every girl in her grammar-school class. There wasn't much she could say about her work except that it was satisfying.

"That's a family trait—choosing mentally challenging careers. I merely took a slightly different path from that of my parents. Science was all right, but I found mathematics more stimulating." Natalie rose and walked over to the grill. "Looks like the coals are ready."

"So your mother is a scientist," Mikhail said, sounding surprised. "Does she work on exciting projects?"

"At the moment she is. As a matter of fact, my parents started working on Thwart together."

"Thwart?"

"Oh, I guess you don't know what that is. The concept isn't exactly a big secret anymore—only the method. It's a plane Aircon is developing for the military. Radar-undetectable." She moved toward the dining-room entry. "I put everything on the counter earlier. I'll be right back with the chicken and corn."

Natalie moved swiftly into the kitchen. She'd prepared the food earlier, before her mother had announced her plans for the evening. And when she'd come in for the tea, she'd set out the corn, wrapped in aluminum foil, and the chicken she'd parboiled so it would cook quickly. Even so, she waited for a moment before picking up the two bowls and a jar of barbecue sauce . . . almost as if she were stalling.

Lord, she was behaving strangely for someone usually in command of herself! By turns, she'd been awkward and overeager to please ever since Mikhail had arrived. How absurd. He was another human being, complete with needs and faults, probably not unlike her own.

That brought Natalie back to her doubts about him. She told herself not to get too caught up with the man, just in case. But in case of what? Instinct told her Mikhail wasn't a bad person, even if she had questioned his reasons for defecting. She would think positively about him until he gave her grounds to think otherwise. With that settled, she picked up the bowls and rejoined her unexpected dinner companion.

"I love cooking outside," Natalie said, laying the ears of corn directly on the coals. "It makes everything you cook special, somehow. It gives food a unique flavor." She adjusted the cover on the grill, then arranged the chicken over it. "I hope you like your barbecue sauce hot."

"I don't know what I like, since I've never had any of your American barbecue. But unless yours is hotter than Mongolian sauces, I will love it."

"Hmm." She remembered an experimental Chinese dinner she and Warren had tried a long time ago. She'd sworn her stomach would never recover. "If you're used to things like Mongolian beef, this might seem pretty tame by comparison."

"If you like it, I'm sure I will also."

Natalie knew Mikhail was merely being polite, but she couldn't help smiling at his response. As a matter of fact, she'd be smiling if he didn't say anything at all. It gave her pleasure just to look at him.

"Tell me more about your mother," he demanded, interrupting her musings. "You said she and your father started working on this Thwart together?"

"Yes, but my father died last winter." Natalie sat opposite him again, leaning her elbows on the table, playing with her glass. "Since then, my mother has thrown herself into her work with a vengeance, as though she could make up for his loss professionally—and perhaps personally, too. I know she misses him and she's lonely, but I hate to see her so single-minded. I stopped counting the number of times she's slept at the lab, which she's going to do tonight. And when she does come home, she invariably brings her work with her and stays in the study for hours."

"Many people react the same way after the death of a husband or wife of many years."

"So I've been told. The shame is that she's lost without my father, even though she's much younger than he was. She's only in her early fifties now—much too young to give up living."

"Your mother sounds like a very dedicated woman and a fascinating one," Mikhail said. "I would like to meet her sometime."

"I might be able to arrange that. She'd be especially interested in meeting a world-champion skater and coach. She's always been a big skating fan—she even insisted on my taking lessons when I was a kid. One of her best friends is on the Olympic committee."

"I will look forward to meeting her, then."

From his tone, Mikhail made Natalie think he was looking forward to much more than meeting her mother. The idea sent a jolt through her and made her doubt the veracity of her own perceptions. She might see Mikhail as a desirable man, but she was sure he saw her as a friend—one who'd helped him when he'd been hurt.

Trying to neutralize his effect on her, she determined to keep him talking. "We think of American cities like New York and Chicago as being melting pots of different nationalities. I imagine Moscow is the same."

Mikhail nodded. "If you stand in the middle of Red Square for a while, you will see faces of Russians, of Turks and Latvians, of Armenians and Mongolians—to name only a few."

"Red Square," Natalie repeated, thinking of the beautiful colors of St. Basil's onion-shaped domes, which seemed to dominate the pictures she'd seen of the square—more so than the Kremlin itself. "Now *there's* a place that has a history."

"It has been the focus of our national life since the Middle Ages, when people used to crowd onto the cobblestones to hear the czar's edicts read aloud. Today it is still the place for ceremonial events that are national *and* personal. On their wedding day, newlyweds bring flowers to Lenin's tomb," he added.

Without thinking, Natalie asked, "Really? Did you and your ex-wife do that on your wedding day?"

"Yes, of course." Mikhail looked away immediately, centering his attention on the grill. "I think the chicken may be burning. Would you like me to turn it for you?"

"No, I'll get it," Natalie said, although she knew the chicken wasn't even close to burning.

Mikhail had obviously wanted to change the subject, away from his ex-wife. She hadn't meant to offend him, but perhaps he was newly divorced and thinking about his ex-wife still hurt. Wanting to be more careful, she asked about his career as an athlete—a safe topic. He seemed to relax.

It wasn't until they were eating that she brought the conversation back to more personal matters. "With your training schedule added to all the traveling you did, it must have been difficult keeping up with your friends back in Moscow."

"One learns to make new friends in new situations," Mikhail told her with a tense smile.

"I'm sure Faith—the woman I was with in France—has made many new friends since she started working for the Foreign Service, but that doesn't mean she doesn't miss me. Or I her," Natalie added. "Didn't you have someone really close whom you hated to leave? A childhood friend, perhaps?"

"Real friends never forget each other," he said evasively, as though it pained him to remember.

Suddenly she realized she didn't know anything about his present life. "I never thought to ask where you're living or what you're planning to do here. Will you look for a coaching position?"

"I have already found one."

Natalie forced herself to continue smiling and said, "Then you'll be moving on soon."

"I will be moving tomorrow."

So she wouldn't see him again, and his saying he was looking forward to meeting her mother had been nothing more than a pleasantry. She tried to push down the disappointment that sprang up inside her, but it was a losing battle.

"Well, I'm glad you found the time to look me up before leaving."

"But I am arriving, not leaving," Mikhail told her. "Tomorrow morning I move from my hotel in Washington to a small furnished apartment here in Wilmington. I found it this morning, right after I toured The Skating Club of Wilmington, where I will be coaching."

"You're going to live and work right here in Wilmington?" The very idea made her pulse quicken, and Natalie found that she couldn't stop smiling.

The time she spent with him seemed to fly by. But when he finally got up to leave, Natalie didn't know much more about him than she had when he'd arrived. Still, she felt oddly close to Mikhail.

At the front door, he hesitated. His expression was serious—she'd say apprehensive if she didn't know better. "You will see me sometime soon?"

"I'd like that." How could he doubt it? Surely he could hear her heart thudding against her ribs.

"I will call you after I'm settled."

"My number is listed in the telephone directory."

"Yes, I know."

He was standing so close, inspecting her face so intently, that she thought he might kiss her again. And when he cupped her cheek gently, Natalie was sure of it. She felt a thrill of anticipation. Mikhail allowed his head to do no more than inch closer. Natalie was captivated by his wide mouth and wanted to feel it against her own. Would this be a kiss of friendship or one of passion?

Neither, she soon realized as he smoothed some stray hairs from her face, then let his hand drop and switched the cane to it. "Good night, Natalya."

Mikhail opened the screen door and walked outside, but turned back as though he really didn't want to leave. Or so she wistfully thought. He put his free hand out and flattened his palm against the mesh that separated them. Natalie did the same thing, seeking the closeness of that special bonding she'd felt on the mountainside. Wondering if he was remembering, too, she tried to read the message in his eyes, which seemed dark and mysterious in the dim porch light. Almost as though they held secrets . . .

"Good night, Mikhail," she whispered.

Unable to move, she watched him blend quickly into the night. When she finally pulled away and locked up, her movements slow, her thoughts muddled, she made a startling discovery.

Mikhail stirred wants and hopes and feelings in her that she'd thought were gone from her life forever. That he'd be living and working in Wilmington filled her with an unfamiliar longing. Mikhail Illyovich Korolev was a very fascinating man who had the power to make her dream again.

THE THOUGHT WAS ONE that Natalie couldn't seem to banish, not even in the cold light of morning. It was an idea she'd like to share, but she didn't know if she could confide in her mother about something so personal. She'd feel more comfortable sharing the information with one of her friends.

As she drove home from the post office after mailing a letter to Faith about Mikhail's unexpected appearance, Natalie reflected on the emotional distance she'd often felt with her parents. Perhaps they'd been too involved in their work and in each other; perhaps they'd never been capable of giving her more than they had. And they *had* provided her with all the necessities of life, Natalie had to admit as she parked her white Chevy Cavalier and left it—including love in their own fashion. It was only human nature that made her wish they could have given her more of themselves.

She was so caught up in her thoughts that she didn't see the dark-haired man until she was almost upon him. Although he was leaning casually in her doorway, his body seemed taut. His piercing brown eyes sent a chill through her. And when he removed the cigar from his mouth, his thin lips affected her the same way.

"Natalie Lundgren?"

She faltered, not knowing if she should speak to him at all. Her instincts told her he meant trouble. Unfortunately, he didn't look like a man who was easily discouraged, and he was blocking her doorway.

"Yes," she finally said, keeping her distance. "I'm Natalie Lundgren."

"Why don't we go inside so we can talk privately?" When she didn't readily agree, he pulled out his identification and held it out to her. "Elliott Drucker of the Central Intelligence Agency."

She stepped just close enough to check it. It looked legitimate. Because of her parents' sensitive work, she'd had previous experience with government agents. Somehow she didn't think she was going to like this particular man any more than those who'd been responsible for her family's security clearances or who'd been assigned to check on information leaks.

"What is it you want?"

"I have something that belongs to you." He slipped his hand inside his jacket and pulled out another card. "Your international driver's license."

Mikhail had asked if the authorities had returned it. Natalie was sure it wasn't standard procedure to have someone do so in person. Knowing she wasn't going to enjoy the next few minutes, she took the license from him.

"What do you want with me?" she asked. A foolish question. His appearance had something to do with Mikhail. Although she couldn't say why, exactly, her pulse quickened. "I've done nothing."

"You call helping a Soviet citizen defect 'nothing'?"

"I helped an injured man get to safety," she corrected him. "I didn't know there was a law against that."

"I didn't say there was."

But he'd implied it, and Natalie didn't like the insinuation. Nor did she like the way he was staring at her. Obviously she wasn't going to get rid of him until she'd told him what he wanted to know. *Or a reasonable facsimile thereof,* Natalie silently added. She glared at him until he moved out of her way so she could unlock the front door. The smoke from his cigar made her queasy—or maybe it was just Drucker himself.

She didn't bother to invite him in; he didn't bother to wait before following her inside. She chucked her purse onto the couch and spun around, irritated by the man's audacity. He sat down on the arm of an easy chair, puffing on his foul-smelling cigar as if he were in his own home. Natalie picked up an ashtray from the coffee table and shoved it toward him belligerently. She wasn't about to talk until he'd put out the cigar. He got the message. Surprise showed on his face at her silent demand, but then he recovered and squashed the cigar's lighted tip against the cut glass.

"All right, Mr. Drucker. Why are you here?"

He threw up his hands and gave her an innocent expression. "Just a few friendly questions."

She wasn't buying. "This should be interesting," Natalie said, ridding herself of the ashtray and sitting on the couch. She forced herself to seem more relaxed than she actually felt. Even though she had nothing to hide, Drucker made her nervous. "I've never been friends with a CIA man before."

"Contrary to public opinion, we can be pretty nice guys." His thin-lipped smile didn't reassure her of the fact. "How do you know Mikhail Korolev?"

"I helped him on the mountain when he was injured while trying to defect, as I'm sure you know."

"Who are his other contacts?"

"I have no idea. I was a tourist who just happened to be nearby when his friend was looking for assistance."

"Alone?"

"No, I was with a friend."

"Who?"

Natalie hated to implicate Faith in case there was trouble. She wished she knew more about the law and whether Drucker could arrest her for being uncooperative. Undoubtedly he'd find out before his investigation was through. "Her name is Faith Osborne."

"Another tourist?"

"No. She works in France. I was visiting her."

"What does Korolev mean to you?" Drucker asked, the switch in direction startling her into momentary silence. "Do I need to repeat the question?"

"No. Mikhail is just a man who needed—"

"Mikhail?"

"That's his name."

"You're on a first-name basis, yet you weren't one of his contacts?"

"Wait a minute!" Natalie exclaimed, her heartbeat accelerating. The agent was making her feel as if she had something to hide or was guilty of some crime. "You're treating me like I'm on trial here."

The thin-lipped smile appeared once more. "I'm merely trying to find out exactly what happened."

"You're merely badgering me, hoping I'll say something incriminating. But who are you trying to incriminate?" she demanded.

"Korolev."

"Are you crazy? The man defected. He turned his back on his own country, his family and his friends to seek asylum here."

"And all in the name of artistic freedom."

Natalie shifted uneasily. When she'd seen the newscast announcing Mikhail's defection, he'd looked so devoid of joy or relief that she herself had wondered if his declared reason had been the truth.

"That's what the man claims, anyway," Drucker added. "But what if that was just a cover for his real reason? What if he's a plant?"

"A spy? That's ridiculous!"

"Then you know him well enough to deny it?"

"No, but—"

"But you know him well enough to invite him to dinner."

Natalie rose, fury added to her increasing fear. "You're the one who's been spying—on me!"

"Not on you. On him." Drucker left his perch on the chair and walked toward her. He stopped when they were inches apart and eye-to-eye. "I have reason to suspect Korolev is a very cunning man, one who can endanger this country. And if he succeeds, that makes you an accessory."

"You're not making sense. I don't have to listen to this."

"No, you don't—at least not here and now. But in a court of law . . ." He left the sentence unfinished.

Natalie felt her skin crawl at his unspoken threat, half issued mere inches from her face. He was trying to use her fear against her, but she refused to be intimidated into acquiescence. She wouldn't back down mentally or physically.

"I assume you have proof that Mikhail is up to no good."

Natalie was surprised when Drucker moved away before saying, "A gut feeling, but not proof."

"Then exactly what do you think he wants?"

"I'm not sure." He began to circle her. But Natalie, not willing to give him her back, centered herself, turning in place like the hub of a spiral. "That's where you come in. Mikhail Korolev could use closer watching by someone he has no reason to suspect: you."

"Your suspicions are crazy."

"Then prove me wrong."

"I won't do your dirty work."

"Think about it."

"Nothing you say—"

"I won't take no for an answer," Drucker said coldly, his eyes emotionless as he came full circle, completing the spiral.

Natalie couldn't say a word. Her breath caught in her throat, threatening to choke her. She was angry, but even more, she was afraid. Fear made the room spin around her, although she was now standing still.

Drucker backed out of the living room. "I'll be in touch, Natalie." His voice was soft now, coaxing, transforming him from challenger to confidant. "Think about what I've told you. I'll give you another chance to save yourself and do your country a service."

Then he was gone.

Natalie took a deep, shuddering breath but couldn't regain her equilibrium. She found the couch with her hand and sank into it, lowering her head between her knees. She felt the same way she did when faced with heights she couldn't conquer.

How dare that man spy on her!

How dare he make her suspicious of Mikhail merely because he was a Russian defector!

But she'd had a few suspicions of her own, fueled by that young skater's statement about not trusting a Ruskie to sharpen his skate blades. Had that been mere anti-Soviet paranoia, or *did* Mikhail have a different reason for defecting than the one he'd declared? Her heart wouldn't allow her to believe that Mikhail Korolev was capable of undermining any country or government.

So what in the world could he be hiding?

Chapter Four

A few nights later Natalie stood in front of the Quonset-hut-shaped building that housed The Skating Club of Wilmington and told herself that Mikhail's reasons for defecting were his own business. She'd convinced herself the Russian wasn't presenting any risk to national security, as Drucker had intimated. Then why did she hesitate before entering?

Mikhail had telephoned earlier, inviting Natalie and her mother to watch him coach and to get on the ice. An innocent-enough request. Excited at the prospect of meeting someone with Mikhail's reputation in the ice-skating world, even if she herself had never been on skates, Catherine had had to beg off because of her work. But Natalie hadn't been able to resist being in Mikhail's company once more. There was an attraction between them she couldn't deny. Perhaps that was what made her hesitate now.

She shifted the weight of her well-used skates from her left shoulder to her right, then set one foot in front of the other. Hesitating over a little attraction was nonsense. She was going inside.

The number of people still wandering in and out of the building didn't surprise her, although it was close to 10:00 p.m. Most were leaving, but a few were just arriving. She knew they would be part of some special-interest group such as a precision team that took advantage of the club's off-hours. They wouldn't begin their practice until eleven or so.

Natalie entered the arena. A half-dozen skaters and coaches were working on the ice, but her eyes were immediately drawn to the tall figure in navy sweatpants and matching pullover. She slipped into a bench seat located at the yard-high barrier, where Mikhail was working with his student on a patch of ice.

"Turn into the circle like so before making a small loop," he was saying to the red-haired young woman who was intently watching him demonstrate the school figure with practiced ease. "Then change to the same edge of the other foot to complete the circle."

His execution was perfect. It was only because she knew his leg must still be bothering him that Natalie could tell he wasn't as loose as he might have been. She was amazed that he'd gotten back on the ice so soon, but that special kind of discipline was common to dedicated athletes.

Not that she'd ever had an ambition to be a serious athlete herself. Sports had always been a form of entertainment for her, including the lessons she'd taken right here at the skating club. It had been several years now since she'd been on the ice. Work on her doctorate had pushed her personal interests to the back burner, and she'd allowed her membership in the club to drop. The idea of getting back on the ice now—especially with Mikhail—was an exciting one.

As if he could hear her silent thought, he looked away from the redhead to where Natalie sat leaning forward, her arms resting on the retaining wall. Their gazes touched only for an instant before he turned back to his pupil, leaving Natalie almost breathless with anticipation. The next few minutes went by in a blur as she anxiously waited for him to finish the lesson.

Then he stood in front of her, within touching distance. "So you have come," he said, his voice rich with satisfaction. He bent forward and rested his elbows next to hers, making her pull back. "Alone?"

"Yes. Mother was sorry to pass up the opportunity to meet you, but she couldn't leave her work."

An odd expression flitted across his features—one that Natalie couldn't read. Before she had time to think about it, he asked, "Did you bring your skates?"

She lifted them from the floor. "Right here. I even remembered to sharpen them. But are you sure it's all right? I haven't been a member of the club for several years."

"I know that public skating hours are on the weekend, but I don't think anyone will object this once. If so, I will take the blame. I will say I was trying to convince you to rejoin."

An appealing idea. Natalie decided she would seriously consider it. About time she put some fun back in her life. And if that included seeing more of Mikhail, all the better. From the way he was looking at her, she guessed he knew exactly what she was thinking.

"If you're sure you're up to it, considering your injury," she mumbled, ducking her head to put on her flesh-colored skates. "I wouldn't want you to be hurt."

"Don't worry about me." He skated away from her, so she barely heard him add, "It is not likely that I will be the one to be hurt."

The odd note in his voice made Natalie look up from the skate she'd been lacing, but his back was to her. Touched at his concern about the possibility of her hurting herself on the ice, she called after him, "It may have been a few years since I was on skates, but I was always tough."

Then she bent over to concentrate on her task once more, glad that she hadn't worn one of her old short-skirted costumes. Instead, she'd chosen beige stretch pants and a beige and blue striped sweatshirt that hung loosely to the middle of her thighs. She'd worn them both for comfort and sensibility—wanting to be well-protected when her bottom hit the ice! Natalie had no illusions when it came to her rusty skills.

She finished lacing her skates just as Mikhail executed a camel spin. He made a perfect T—his weight accurately balanced over his left hip, and his right leg and left arm stretched out high, even with his body. Considering the ease with which he accomplished the spin, an uninformed observer wouldn't have the slightest clue that his right leg had been injured.

Natalie found the blue banana clip she'd stuffed into her sweatshirt pocket. She smoothed her long hair back from her face and secured it so it wouldn't get in her eyes while she skated. "Here I come," she called, willing her ankles to support her as she rose from her seat. They wobbled a little, but she made her way to the gate without mishap.

Mikhail beat her there and took her hand, leading her onto the ice and closing the gate behind her. "You can leave your skate guards here," he said.

She slipped off the strips of rubber that protected her newly sharpened blades and put them on the retaining wall. Taking a deep breath, she met his eyes and nodded. She was as ready as she'd ever be, or so she thought until he put his arm around her waist and gently pulled her to his side. Suddenly her pulse lurched, her blood skating through her veins more swiftly than her feet had ever done on the ice. The attraction Natalie had felt toward Mikhail was suddenly running rampant.

She forced herself to concentrate on putting one skate in front of the other, pushing off the left blade, then the right, allowing him to lead her in whatever direction he chose. Her eyes roamed the gleaming surface ahead, and her ears were attuned to the *shush* of their blades. She was doing her best to ignore anything more personal, but it wasn't easy.

"You are doing well for someone who has not skated in years," Mikhail assured her.

"I owe it all to sheer bravado," she replied as they continued in a large circle, covering one end of the arena. "And to your able assistance. If you let go of me, I can't predict what might happen."

"Then I will hold on until you tell me otherwise."

Which might be never, Natalie thought, leaning closer into him. Of course, their minds were on separate tracks, hers on one more intimate than his. And in a public place, too! But when she looked around, she saw that only one other coach and student remained on the ice. It would be another half hour before the next group arrived to practice. She and Mikhail were practically alone.

His body's warmth seeped through his clothing, then through hers, making Natalie want to get even closer. Her ankles wobbled and her adrenaline speeded up. She felt light-headed and could hardly see the ice directly in front of her. Afraid she'd embarrass herself by falling or doing something equally silly if she didn't change her situation quickly, she pulled away, relieved to feel the chill of the ice reaching up between them to cool her off.

"I've got to try this on my own," she told Mikhail. "It might as well be now."

"Just hold my hand, then."

Even as he said it, his hand sought and found her wrist; then his long fingers twined themselves through hers. The light touch seemed safe enough, and she allowed herself to enjoy it as they completed their tour of the arena. When they stopped by the gate where she'd entered, Natalie was slightly out of breath but more exhilarated than she had been in years. Whether being on skates had anything to do with the feeling or not, she wasn't sure.

"When you took lessons, were they by yourself or with a partner?" he asked.

"Mostly singles. I've done a little pairs skating for fun, but only side-by-side stuff. Lifts give me vertigo, and I have the distinct feeling the death spiral really would be deadly for me." Natalie shivered as she thought about the movement in which the woman arched the length of her body horizontally over the ice, letting her head almost touch it while she rotated around the man, who held her by one hand. "I've never had a partner in whom I could put so much trust."

"I would not let anything happen to you, Natalya," Mikhail told her. His features were set into an unfamiliar expression of concern, his gray eyes intent on her face. "I would protect you with my life."

It was a peculiar thing for him to say, and it immediately made Natalie wonder if for some reason he might *have* to protect her. He was a Russian defector, after all, and one who was suspect—as if she could forget that after Drucker's visit! And if the CIA man had tracked her down so quickly and easily, why not a member of the KGB? Soviet agents could be after Mikhail right at this moment, and after her as well for her part in his escape.

She glanced around warily. The other coach and his student had disappeared. Every shadow in the far reaches of the arena seemed to hold an ominous warning. Before her imagination could embellish on that dark line of thought, however, Mikhail distracted her.

"Natalya, could we not try some of the safer spirals together?"

Her awareness of him as a man superseded that of him as defector. They were alone on the ice now, at least for a short while. Her body thrummed with the knowledge, attraction warring with deep-seated caution. "All right, let's do it," she agreed.

They began with side-by-side spirals, Natalie in front, Mikhail in back, their bodies so close they might as well have been touching. Natalie fought the urge to turn into his arms and to face him, to look into his eyes and discover whether or not his natural instincts were clouding his thoughts as hers were. She reminded herself that he was coaching her, mixing business with friendship, nothing more.

Nevertheless, her heart pounded in a slow, deep rhythm when his hands impersonally moved her body parts into the correct positions—chin high, right arm and leg lifted and parallel to each other. She could imagine what it might feel like if passion were guiding those hands. The sound of their blades on the ice competed with her own labored breath as she tried to hold the pose for more than a few seconds. Then her muscles protested, her knee gave way and she stumbled into Mikhail's broad chest. A giggle of embarrassment caught in her throat, and they went zooming backward with the force of her displaced weight.

The strangled sound echoed through the empty arena. Mikhail wrapped his arms around her for support. One of his hands accidentally brushed the underside of her breast, sending a shock wave through her. As they slowed on the ice, she found herself turning, facing him, recognizing her own reactions reflected in his face. Such an arresting face, a face a woman would never forget, she thought, mesmerized as he drew closer.

"Natasha," he whispered huskily, his lids lowering, his dark blond lashes closing her off from the truths she would read if only she could.

It was his mouth that told her what she wanted to know— that he felt more than friendship for her. This kiss was no tender pledge of comfort, but a statement of desire. His lips plundered and separated hers while he pulled her close and shoved his weight forward, moving them lightly over the ice together.

As she had done earlier, Natalie allowed him to lead her, blades skimming on the frozen surface, tongues tangling boldly in exploration. Fire and ice. A steamy combination. Mikhail turned and wedged his thigh between hers, then sent them into a spin that was at once thrilling and frightening.

The shock of their intimate contact startled Natalie into opening her eyes and moving her head back. The surroundings whirled around them in a blur, making her remember where they were. She levered her hands against his chest. Breathing heavily, he held her fast while slowing their movement. Their eyes met for a brief second before his slid away, as if he were feeling guilty about something.

Natalie told herself she was being ridiculous, merely allowing Elliott Drucker's insinuations to get to her. She needed to stay levelheaded until she knew the truth about Mikhail, but there was no reason to go around imagining things. Mikhail was probably just as embarrassed by the unexpected embrace as she was.

She was sure of it when she saw where his eyes had settled—on several skaters who'd entered the arena.

"Bravo!" one of the men yelled, clapping loudly. "What do you do for an encore, Korolev?"

"We have not yet worked that into our routine," Mikhail said with humorous bravado. He released Natalie but held her hand. "Don't expect us to demonstrate when we figure it out."

"You're no fun!"

Natalie laughed nervously as Mikhail led her straight to the retaining wall, where they retrieved their guards and slipped them on their blades. She didn't know what to say or where to look. It wasn't every day she had an audience when a man kissed her. As a matter of fact, it wasn't every day that a man kissed her at all!

"Natalya, what would you like to do now?" Mikhail asked as though nothing were wrong.

"Actually," she said truthfully, "I'd like to go home."

IT WAS ONLY LATER, when they were well on their way to her place, that Natalie realized Mikhail might have misunderstood her request. If he thought she wanted to be alone with him to continue what they'd started on the ice, he didn't say so. Yet he sat next to her quietly, his arm on the back of her car seat, his fingers lightly massaging her shoulder. The unconscious possessive gesture made her nervous.

"It's late," she said suddenly. "Maybe I should drop you off at your apartment."

"I am not what you Americans call the early bird."

"Yes, but you don't have a car to drive home, and I'm pretty tired now, so I thought it might—"

"No problem. I can autostop."

"Autostop?" She flashed a questioning look at him. He aimed his thumb in explanation. "Oh, you mean hitchhike. That's okay in Europe, but here it's not a good—"

"Then I will walk."

Natalie acquiesced. Mikhail was certainly determined to be alone with her. She was flattered. And upset.

For no matter how much she tried to relax, to think of him only as a date, she couldn't. He wasn't just any man, and the value judgment had nothing to do with the fact that he happened to be great looking and incredibly sexy. He was Mikhail Illyovich Korolev.

Olympic champion.

Russian.

Defector.

It always came back to that.

By the time they'd left the Chevy for the house, Natalie was in a fine state of nerves, wondering what Mikhail wanted of her, wondering why she'd let him persuade her to do as he wished. Maybe it was because, in spite of her sensible objections, she was destined to be close to the Russian. At will, she could relive the escape from the mountainside. No other incident from her past stood out so clearly in her mind, and she doubted anything that happened in the future could ever take its place.

"Do you need help?"

Startled out of her thoughts, Natalie saw an amused Mikhail leaning against the doorjamb and staring pointedly at her hand on the key. How long ago had she inserted it? A flush crept up her neck as she unlocked and opened the door, then led him into the darkened hallway. From the living room came the soft glow of a single lamp, which she didn't remember turning on before she left.

"Natasha," Mikhail said softly, his hand on her shoulder banishing thoughts of everything but him. "Look at me."

With only the distant lamplight reaching them, his face was a contrast of shadow and light, exactly the way she saw him. Part of him was open and inviting, yet another part was foreign and elusive.

Her eyes swept down past the healing scar on his forehead. "I'm looking," she said breathlessly, waiting for whatever it was he'd do next. Maybe it was time she listened to her instincts and forgot suspicions and warnings.

"I, too, am looking. What do you think I see?"

A woman whom Mikhail seemed to find attractive, she silently answered as she probed the depths of his eyes. But, based on past experience, she had trouble with that evaluation. What if he had an ulterior motive for being with her—to throw Drucker off, for example? Or what if he was merely expressing his gratitude for her having saved his life? She didn't want to believe either.

"Why don't you tell me?" she finally suggested.

"I see someone very special. Brave, kind, compassionate. A woman of strength and softness. Beautiful, inside as well as out."

Beautiful? Her?

When Mikhail touched her cheek, gently gliding his fingers toward her neck until she shivered with the growing power of her own attraction, Natalie thought she might believe anything he told her.

And then the momentary spell was broken.

"Natalie? I thought I heard you come in." Catherine Lundgren stopped in the doorway leading to the living room, her eyes wide. "Oh, sorry." She backed away, obviously embarrassed at having interrupted them.

"It's all right, Mother," Natalie said, feeling relieved. "I wanted you two to meet anyway." She slipped away from Mikhail and went into the living room, where she turned on another lamp. He followed, limping slightly, his right leg undoubtedly strained by the workout. "Mother, this is Mikhail Korolev. Mikhail, this is my mother, Catherine Lundgren."

He took the older woman's hand. "I am honored."

"That makes two of us." Catherine smiled broadly, and Natalie thought the expression removed a decade of years from her still-pretty face. "I'm a big fan of anything having to do with figure skating. I saw many of your performances on television, and once I watched you skate in person at Lake Placid. You were wonderful." Quickly she added, "As I'm sure you still are."

Mikhail laughed. "Or will be when my leg is back in shape."

"Yes, your leg. Natalie told me all about that horrifying incident."

"I will be forever grateful to your daughter."

Not wanting them to discuss her, Natalie changed the subject as they made themselves comfortable on the couch. "By the way, what are you doing home, C.L.? I thought you had to work."

"I didn't feel like being alone at the lab tonight, after all, so I brought it home with me. I was in the study going over some papers when I, uh, heard you."

Heard what? An unwelcome flush of heat made Natalie move toward the kitchen. "I'll be back in a minute. I thought I'd make us some tea."

"That's a nice idea," Catherine said before turning her attention back to Mikhail. "Now that you're here, what kind of plans do you have for your career?"

"To continue coaching," he replied. "But your career sounds much more interesting—"

Natalie was at the kitchen sink with the teakettle. The water pouring out of the faucet cut off Mikhail's words, but she knew he could get Catherine to talk about her work all night. Her work! The thought that the Russian might be interested in Thwart startled Natalie into shutting off the water immediately.

"I am serious, Catherine," Mikhail was now saying. "You look so youthful and enough like Natalie to be her sister."

Natalie grinned at the well-used line he was handing her mother. She put the kettle on the stove and reached for the tea. Mikhail had merely been polite when he'd asked about Catherine's work. She'd better be careful, or Drucker would have her jumping at shadows as well as to conclusions.

"Another cliché destroyed, right?" Catherine said, sounding delighted. "Now you know the truth. All scientists aren't crusty old fuddy-duddys."

"I never thought that. It is just that Natalie told me how much time you put into your work, so I had a somewhat different picture of you in my mind." Mikhail laughed. "Someone hunched over a drafting table, perhaps."

"I'm actually hunched over a computer terminal, although I don't have anything to do with the structural design of our aircraft."

The kettle whistled as though sharply reprimanding Natalie for not paying attention to her task. She set about measuring the tea and pouring the water while continuing to listen to the conversation in the living room.

"What about your parents?" Catherine asked. "Are they still working or are they retired?"

"They work, of course, since everyone must have a job in the Soviet Union." His voice had changed. Natalie heard a note of caution. "My father drives a taxi and my mother is a clerk at GUM, the largest department store in Moscow, owned by the state."

"You must miss them," Catherine said sympathetically. "And your friends, also. Did anyone know you were going to defect? How do you think they felt when they heard about it?"

"There will be those who regret it and those who will not," was all Mikhail would say, evasive once again.

Natalie entered the room then, carrying a loaded tray. Catherine rose, as if to help. "Sit down, Mother. I can handle this."

After placing the tray on the coffee table, Natalie took the chair closest to Mikhail, surprised by his sudden turn of awkwardness. He was having trouble looking at her. She was touched and pleased that he could feel self-conscious around her. And he'd been so nice to her mother, even if he'd sounded strained answering her questions.

It seemed only natural that he'd be cautious with strangers who questioned him about the defection and his people in Russia. He probably didn't feel safe or comfortable yet. He might even have the exact same doubts about her that she had about him. Her leftover nerves suddenly dissolved, and Natalie relaxed for the first time that evening. From the way he'd behaved with her before, she suspected Mikhail was indeed attracted to her. Getting used to each other—trust—would take time.

What in the world had she been worried about?

NATALIE INSISTED ON DRIVING him home, after all. Barely an hour later, Mikhail was in his own place, comparing his one-room apartment to the Lundgren home. It seemed dismal by comparison. After pouring himself a tall glass of vodka, he shut off the table lamp and sat staring into the dark, although it wasn't the shabby furnishings that he objected to. It was the lack of human warmth and companionship.

He downed half of the vodka, savoring the way the raw heat made his throat and stomach flame. Catherine's mentioning his parents and friends had depressed him. That, and seeing Natalie's artless smile of trust, which he didn't deserve. For the moment, the fiery pain in his gut gave him something else to think about. Something safe. He shut his eyes against the darkened room as though that would shut out Natalie's image. It wasn't enough. She was there with him, a constant reminder of the reason he'd left Russia.

But could he accomplish what he'd come for? What he'd given up everything for?

This time the vodka lathed his insides more gently, helping him to force his mind to happier times, to recapture all that was good about his native land. And there *had* been good things, good people. If some memories were bad, at least they were familiar. He'd known how to deal with them. A man didn't grow up in the Soviet Union without learning the intricate angles of survival—not if he wanted a decent life without too much government interference.

In Russia, Mikhail had known where he stood and what was expected of him. He'd lived half his thirty-three years in shadows, learning to coexist with the KGB, as most Soviet citizens learned to do. He'd accepted the threats and intrusions into his life and work while he'd grown to hate the system. After all, he'd been one of the minority of people who'd had something with which to compare it. His trips to the West had opened his eyes and had made him discontent.

And yet, under the Soviet system, his days had had structure and purpose. Here he was on his own, trying to find his way through a maze of new experiences. It was called freedom. But to a man who had had little opportunity to make important decisions in his life, freedom was a frightening concept. If he went wrong, there'd be no one to blame but himself.

The last of the vodka soothed him, made him feel more self-confident. He couldn't go wrong—not with Aleksei's freedom, and probably more, at stake. That was his purpose. He had to remember that; to remember Aleksei, his brother in spirit if not in blood.

Mikhail rose and walked to the window, intending to open it for air. The vodka had warmed him well. But his hand got no farther than the sash. A full moon cast silvery light into the room. Onto the dresser. Mikhail frowned at what he saw there. Part of a newspaper, one he hadn't bought. His hand moved toward it, his eyes scanning the Cyrillic characters before it struck him that someone else had put the paper there. Someone who hadn't belonged in this apartment.

He held up the day-old issue of *Pravda*, Moscow's leading newspaper, to the moonlight. Aleksei Rodzianko stared back at him from the front page. The article accompanying the muddy photo detailed the beginning of his trial as a dissident, an unofficial writer banned by the union but who dared to continue writing what he chose in defiance of Soviet policy. The reporter speculated that Aleksei would be found guilty and sentenced to Siberia.

Aleksei's paper face crumpled in Mikhail's fist as easily as the flesh-and-blood man would crumple under the Soviet system of justice.

Found guilty? What a joke! No other verdict was possible. No one in the Soviet Union went to trial unless he was already convicted in a closed pretrial session. The public hearing was meant to humiliate the guilty one. To cow him. To sentence him. Aleksei's lawyer could plead only for mercy, asking that his client not be sent to Siberia.

Mikhail knew his friend's chances were slim; he feared there'd be no mercy for Aleksei Rodzianko. He leaned his forehead against the window and closed his eyes, as if that would help obliterate the truth he could clearly see in his mind.

From the distant past came an image so bold and frightening that it made him shudder: KGB agents waiting for him in his room; he and Aleksei entering laughing, unaware, feeling manly after having made fools of themselves over a couple of girls at a party; books, magazines and papers tossed all over the floor.

Contraband. Black-market ideas. Things he'd brought back with him from his various trips to the West.

He'd seen the results of his own foolishness clearly at that moment. His career as a skater was over. No matter that he was the Soviet figure-skating champion, world champion, favored in the upcoming Olympics. He was about to be arrested.

Then Aleksei stepped forward. Brave, defiant Aleksei, *official*, highly praised writer, boldly stated that he'd gotten the stuff underground, that he'd wanted to read Western writings out of artistic curiosity. He didn't give Mikhail the opportunity to protest or to admit the truth. And so it was Aleksei who had been taken away. The next day he was released with no more than a verbal slap on the wrist. Although Aleksei had always loved attention and wanted to be thought of as a hero, the magnanimity of his intervention wasn't lessened in Mikhail's eyes. This episode had been the start of Aleksei's troubles with the KGB. From that moment on, he'd been watched closely, every phase of his life studied, dissected and analyzed under a microscope.

Mikhail crossed the room to where he'd left the vodka bottle. This time he didn't bother pouring the alcohol into a glass. This time the long swallow didn't help. It couldn't rectify the perfect example of the unjustness of the corrupt Soviet political system.

And he couldn't delay his painful decision any longer.

Ah, he'd thought himself so clever when he'd smuggled out of Russia what he'd meant to trade for Aleksei's freedom. He'd never once considered he might have an accident that would change his plans. He'd never imagined he'd have to leave his bargaining tool on a mountainside in France, in a hellish place he wouldn't be able to find by himself.

There was always Thwart. He knew that. He'd been preparing himself for it. Even so, he'd convinced himself he was only doing research, that he'd never have to use the knowledge he had gained. He'd been fooling himself.

Unbidden, an image of Natalie's face came into his mind. He turned on the lamp as if the light would make her vulnerable eyes and her trusting smile disappear. It didn't work, and he knew that he couldn't free Aleksei at her expense. He couldn't betray her so cruelly. He'd never meant to. There was no reason to start feeling guilty again, as he had more than once that evening.

He would come up with another plan.

Desperate now, Mikhail convinced himself he could bluff the Soviet government into believing he still had the article he'd smuggled out of Russia. They'd be frantic to get it back. He could delay Aleksei's trial merely by threatening to turn it over to the Americans.

Then what?

Peter Baum. Mikhail hadn't wanted to involve him any deeper, but now he had no choice. Peter would understand;

Mikhail was sure of it. His old friend had defected himself, hadn't he?

Mikhail would have to let Peter in on his secret so the German could help him. He wouldn't leave any of the details out, not this time. They could return to France, retrace the escape route and find the plastic-covered package he'd left on the mountain ledge. In the meantime, he'd contact the Soviet ambassador in Washington with his demands and pave the road for Aleksei's release.

His plan would work. It had to, for everyone's sake.

Chapter Five

"C.L., are you going to use your computer this afternoon?" Natalie asked, poking her head into the study.

It was Saturday, but that didn't stop her mother from working. Catherine looked up from her terminal and peered over the reading glasses she'd been forced to start wearing a few years before.

"No. I thought I'd check in at the lab. As a matter of fact, I'm just about finished running this program. Did you want to test that new spread-sheet software you bought the other day?"

"Actually, I wanted to write a letter to Faith." Natalie had never been known for penmanship, but she was great at word processing. "I thought I'd give her an update on things around here."

"Didn't you mail a letter to Faith a few days ago? I could have sworn you were going to the post office, because you asked if I needed any stamps." Catherine's attention was drawn back to the monitor screen. When Natalie didn't answer, she glanced at her daughter, and a knowing smile tilted her lips. "Oh, I see. You want to tell Faith all about Mikhail."

Natalie shifted uncomfortably and wedged a shoulder against the doorjamb. "She knows about Mikhail. She helped rescue him, remember? I figured she'd be interested."

"But not as interested as you are."

"I guess not." After their passionate embrace the other night, Natalie was more interested than ever. And frustrated, too, because it seemed as if nothing would come of it. "So I can use the computer, right?"

"How interested?"

Natalie blinked in surprise. "I like him. He's a friend."

"And that's all you want him to be?"

What had gotten into her mother, anyway? Natalie eyed Catherine suspiciously. It wasn't like her to pay so much attention to Natalie's private life. "Something bothering you, C.L.?"

"No, not at all." Catherine slipped off her glasses and stared directly at Natalie. "I was merely curious. Can't a mother be curious?"

"Sure. I guess so."

"I found Mikhail charming. And he thinks so much of you."

"He's grateful."

"More than that. He's attracted."

Natalie tried to joke about it. "All of a sudden you're an expert, huh, C.L.?"

"I've always noticed when men were attracted to my daughter, even if I never said anything."

"Gee, I wish you had told me when you noticed those things," Natalie said in mock aggravation. "Maybe I could have done something about it."

"It's not too late to do something now. When are you going to see him?"

Natalie shrugged, remembering how quiet Mikhail had been when she'd driven him home two nights before. He hadn't said anything about a next time. He hadn't even kissed her again—a major disappointment as far as she was concerned. And how could they build trust between them if they never saw each other?

Her silent musings didn't stop her mother. "Why don't you invite him to do something with you tonight?"

"I don't think so."

"Why not?"

"Well, he's Russian!" Natalie protested. "Who knows how they do these things in his country? If I call him, he might be offended."

"He's not in his country, is he? He'll have to get used to the way we do things in the United States, including the fact that women invite men out. Besides," Catherine added persuasively, "maybe in Russia the men and women take turns. He called you first. Now he may very well be waiting for you to call him."

"I doubt that."

"Do you really? Or are you afraid he'll turn you down? Only one way to find out." Catherine put her glasses back on and faced the terminal, muttering, "If I'd been that timid, I never would have gone out with your father, we never would have gotten married, and you never would have been born." Stunned into silence by the unexpected and startling revelation, Natalie merely stared at her mother until Catherine turned around in exasperation. "Well? Are you going to call him or are you going to let some other woman snap him up? A gorgeous, talented hunk like him won't be alone for long."

"I'll think about it," Natalie croaked, backing away from the study and this new facet of her mother.

Not that she resented Catherine's unusual interest. Actually, she was pleased. But thinking about taking her advice and picking up the telephone were two different things. Perhaps Mikhail didn't want to see her after the other night. He'd approached her in friendship, but things had quickly gotten out of hand—something he might regret. He could be afraid she'd misinterpreted that kiss. Maybe that was why he'd been so introspective in the car.

Natalie spent the next few hours alternately avoiding the telephone, glaring at it and willing it to ring so she wouldn't have to make the decision herself.

"HEY, KOROLEV!" Karen Johnson, one of the other coaches, called from the doorway of the arena. "You've got a phone call."

Her casual words froze Mikhail at the retaining wall, where he was working with his last student of the afternoon. His heart immediately began to pump blood through his system in a great rush.

"Thank you. One moment!" he shouted in return. He glanced at his student, a talented fourteen-year-old boy. "I have been expecting an important call, but I should not be long." Not when he would have witnesses to his conversation. The office wasn't exactly private. He was already moving toward the doorway. "Continue practicing that double Salchow and concentrate on keeping your free leg away from your skating knee."

Adrenaline pushed Mikhail through the door. Finally. He thought he'd never hear. He'd called the Soviet embassy in Washington at nine o'clock yesterday morning, more than thirty hours ago. He hadn't been allowed to speak to anyone important, of course, only a clerk. After identifying himself, he'd suggested that he had a trade the ambassador might be interested in pursuing. He'd given the woman the club phone number, expecting to hear from the embassy sometime yesterday.

When he entered the office, Karen looked up from her conversation with another employee long enough to point to a receiver lying on one of the desks. Mikhail smiled at her and turned his back, willing his voice to remain steady.

Not wanting to speak in Russian in front of an audience unless it was absolutely necessary, he merely said, "Korolev."

"Mikhail, it's Natalie."

His throat tightening, he sank to the edge of the desk, leaning against it for support as his energy flowed out of him. Frustration that it wasn't someone from the embassy made him clench his jaw rather than answer. The Soviets had to know he wouldn't have called if he hadn't been serious. How long were they going to make him sweat this out?

"Mikhail?" Natalie sounded hesitant, unsure of herself. "If you're busy—"

"I was out of breath from running," he lied, wanting to hear a smile in her voice. "You caught me in the middle of a lesson."

"Sorry. I didn't know your schedule, so I took a chance on catching you between sessions. I can call back."

Mikhail forced himself to sound casual, natural. "Why *did* you call?"

Now it was she who was silent, making him wonder if something was wrong. Had someone approached her—threatened her for helping him? But before he could ask, Natalie's words spilled out in a rush.

"Would you like to do something together tonight?"

Nothing wrong, then. He breathed a sigh of relief. He shouldn't see her again, not until this horror was over and Aleksei was released. Then he could come to her with a clear conscience.

"Yes," he heard himself say, "I would like to see you."

It was a mistake. He knew it. He shouldn't tempt himself with her mother's knowledge of Thwart. But every fiber of his being yearned for her softness, her warmth, her caring.

"Anything in particular you'd like to do?" she asked.

Anything that would get his mind off the tension growing inside him. "A movie. Something amusing." That should help him relax.

"I'll pick you up. How does seven sound?"

It was after five now. He had the lesson to finish and needed time to get home and clean up. "Seven will be fine."

The idea of seeing her in less than two hours picked up his spirits. He needed a distraction from this awful waiting. If he didn't hear anything by morning, he'd call the embassy again and insist on speaking to the ambassador himself. He refused to think beyond that.

The rest of the lesson went quickly and well. Then Karen offered him a lift home. He accepted, thinking he'd have to do something about getting a valid driver's license—not that he'd have the money to buy an auto for a while.

How could he think about doing something so trivial when he had Aleksei to worry about?

Karen dropped him off in front of his building, an old house that had been converted into several apartments. He thanked her, then hurried around the back and up toward the second-floor apartment that was now his home. He checked his watch: a quarter past six—less than an hour until Natalie was to arrive.

The thought distracted him, and it wasn't until he had his keys in his hand that he realized something was wrong. The door was slightly ajar. He stopped short, mouth dry, heart hammering in his chest. Drucker? Or whoever had left the copy of *Pravda* for him?

He pushed at the wooden panel so that it swung open slowly. The creak of the old hinges scraped up his spine. It was dark inside—the shade had been pulled—but his eyes didn't miss the human bulk in the easy chair facing the door.

"I've been waiting for you, comrade," the burly man said silkily in Russian, placing a bottle on the table next to him.

"Yuri Simansky." Mikhail controlled his breathing. It wouldn't do to let the bastard know he was afraid. "Is this a social visit?"

"Yes, of course. I wanted to welcome you to your new home." His pig eyes wandered from one wall to the other, then settled on Mikhail. "I would have thought you would have chosen something larger, though."

The relaxed speech and innocent expression didn't fool Mikhail. Neither did the man's soft looks—the unhealthy pallor, the increasing paunch and the receding fine blond hair. Mikhail had known the KGB agent far too long. Simansky was ambitious. Ruthless. Feared. And Mikhail had made him look bad by escaping his men in Chamonix—something Simansky wasn't about to forget.

Needing to feel in charge of the situation, Mikhail turned on the room light, making the other man squint. "I would offer you vodka, but I see you have already found it."

Simansky lifted his drink in a silent toast and downed the clear liquid. Then he set the glass down next to the bottle and shook his head. "Inferior quality."

"Go back to Russia. You can get what you want there."

Simansky's jowls lifted as his face took on an evil expression akin to a warped smile. His meaty hands spread wide. "But I have what I want right here, comrade."

Sweat began to trickle down Mikhail's sides and the middle of his back. He should have known Simansky would come for him. It wasn't the agent's style to let offenses go unpunished. What sentence would he prescribe? Instant death?

Mikhail had to think quickly! Suddenly it came to him. "Actually, you don't have what you want right here, because it is not in this room."

The flicker of interest in the close-set eyes told Mikhail that he'd guessed correctly. Simansky wasn't here solely on his own. He knew about the call to the embassy. No wonder it had taken so long for a return contact. They'd flown the agent in from Moscow. Mikhail was equally sure Simansky had already searched his room, although nothing seemed out of place.

"What do you have that you think I want?" the agent finally asked.

"A computer board."

"Boring."

"One that encrypts and decrypts secret messages."

"Our computer experts can break any code the Americans can come up with!" Simansky boasted. He reached for the vodka in spite of its inferior quality.

"Not American. Soviet." Simansky's hand remained fixed on the bottle. "The board your worldwide network of spies has found so helpful." The other man slumped back into the chair, his face mottling with color. Satisfied by the reaction, Mikhail sat down on the couch, his pose as casual as he could make it. The board was the heart of an incredibly complex and expensive computerized system the Soviets had recently put into use. "Is that more interesting to you, comrade?"

"Explain."

"You know what I'm talking about. And you know I had the opportunity—because Galina developed it."

"I refuse to believe your wife helped you in this."

"Ex-wife. I took it from her laboratory." Mikhail was gaining confidence. The sweat under his armpits was drying. "For once the Russian system that doesn't usually work for the individual did work for me. Since I was still living with Galina while waiting for housing, I had access to her keys."

Simansky's loose jowls swayed as he shook his head in denial. "If you took one of the boards, she would have noticed. She is an exemplary Communist. She would have reported you, no matter how mistaken she might once have been about your future with her and the party."

Mikhail nodded, knowing the last evaluation was correct. Galina was a zealous Communist, all right. "She wouldn't necessarily have noticed it was missing, not if it was one of several prototypes."

The agent threw his head back and laughed. "A prototype! You think this is something worth trading?"

"It's close enough to the real thing." Simansky couldn't bluff him. He knew the Soviets would want it back. "American computer experts could use it to break the Soviet encryptions."

"Why should I believe you have this board? I don't suppose you want to show it to me?"

"I told you, I don't have it here, as I'm sure you well know."

"Then how can I believe you? Security at the Moscow airport is tight, even for frequent world travelers such as you. Amuse me. If you can't produce it, tell me how you got it out of the country."

"I don't think so, comrade. Why don't you amuse yourself by trying to figure that out?"

Mikhail thought about the way he'd smuggled the pocket-size computer board out of Russia. He'd sewn it into one of the costumes he was to have worn for a skating exhibition. The garment had been embroidered with metallic threads. He'd assumed that if his luggage was X-rayed by airport security, the fine lines of soldered metal on the thin plastic board would appear to be part of the metallic threads of the costume. It seemed he had been correct.

But now was not the time to congratulate himself. Simansky was simmering. Now was the time to make demands.

"I want Aleksei Rodzianko freed and brought to the West."

The mottling on the agent's face quickly became a single shade of bright pink. Mikhail's stomach lurched as the KGB man lunged agilely to his feet and stood over him.

"You think you are so smart, don't you, Korolev? You think you can make fools of the Soviets. I have no interest in your offer. Rodzianko is a dissident. He will be made an example."

"You're the fool, Simansky." Mikhail rose, butting the bulkier man out of the way with his shoulder. "I was smart enough to get away from your men in Chamonix. While you had the roads watched, I walked out on foot behind you." He whipped around and stared the KGB agent in the face, determined not to look away, not to show the renewed fear that was eating at his gut. "I know you can't afford to make two costly mistakes. You need that computer board returned."

"And you want your dissident friend delivered safe and sound. I wonder which of us is the more anxious at this moment." Mikhail felt the sweat trickle between his shoulder blades. He wanted to interrupt but thought better of it. He let Simansky continue. "Think about this, Comrade Korolev. If you are not alive, you can't give the computer board to the Americans."

The room was as silent as if they'd both stopped breathing. The threat shook Mikhail, almost making him break eye contact. The only thing he could do was bluff his way out.

"Are you sure I haven't already given it to an American? Someone who will get it to the right people if something happens to me?"

Simansky swore loudly, using every vile expletive in the Russian language. "Traitor!" he went on. "You would do this to your own country? To your mother who nurtured you? Who molded you into what should have been an example for our youth?"

"Mother Russia is no saint. She has much to answer for. Or her government does."

The pig eyes narrowed. "No deal, Korolev. The computer board is not enough compensation for the embarrassment of releasing an outspoken dissident like Rodzianko. You will have to give me something far more valuable."

"I have nothing else to offer."

"Then get it." Simansky paused dramatically. "I want Thwart."

Mikhail felt as if his heart had stopped for a moment. Then he shook his head in denial, but the self-satisfied KGB agent was already on his way to the door. When he turned around, Simansky pulled his jowls into that imitation smile.

"Don't tell me you can't give me what I want, comrade. You're a clever man, as you've taken great pains to explain. You smuggled a computer board out of Russia. You got away from my men and defected in France. This little thing I ask you to do should be…how do the Americans say it?" He switched to English. "A piece of cake."

With that he walked out of the apartment, leaving the door open and Mikhail feeling defeated. He should have known Simansky would never be satisfied with what he had to offer, that the man would go for the jugular.

He wandered to the window. A dark blue sedan waiting at the curb on the other side of the street caught his eye. A few seconds later a door opened and Simansky got in. Mikhail hadn't noticed the car before. He should have been prepared. He'd have to be more careful in the future.

If he had a future.

MIKHAIL WAS BEHAVING so peculiarly that Natalie was starting to worry about him. He hadn't been ready when she'd arrived to pick him up. He'd apologized profusely, then retreated into silence. Even the hilarious movie they'd gone to had gotten only a few laughs from him. She'd wanted to believe that he hadn't understood the jokes, but instinct told her something else was responsible.

Afterward, he suggested that she take him home, since he wasn't in the mood for a restaurant or a bar. Not wanting to part so soon, Natalie convinced him to go for a quiet walk in the center of Wilmington. The evening air was pleasantly cool as they strolled down Market Street, a mall area closed to traffic. Eventually they stopped in a dimly lit parklike area off French Street and settled themselves on a bench, Mikhail remaining as quiet as he'd been all evening.

Natalie couldn't stand to see him so unhappy.

"What is it?" she finally asked. "Tell me what's wrong, Mikhail. Maybe I can help."

His eyes shadowed, he turned his face away from her. "No, I cannot allow it, Natalya. No!" he repeated emphatically. "There is nothing I want from you."

In spite of his harsh tone, Natalie wouldn't let it go. "I have a strange feeling that your mood has something to do with your defection. I know you don't like talking about it, but maybe it would help if you did."

"You cannot know, cannot understand."

She'd hit the right nerve. She could hear it in his voice, feel it in the tightening arm next to hers.

"Try me. Tell me about your life in Russia—how you saw things, what dissatisfied you."

"Every country has its drawbacks."

"But not everyone who's dissatisfied defects." Thinking about what life might be like if that happened, she grinned. "That certainly would be a mess, with people switching countries all over the place. Governments would go under from the sheer volume of paperwork." When his laughter didn't join hers at the whimsical idea, she sobered and placed a gentle hand on his arm. She didn't say anything more until he looked at her. "I want to understand why you had to leave."

A muscle twitched in his cheek, and even in the semi-darkness she could see an angry flash in his eyes. When he finally answered, Natalie decided it wasn't aimed at her.

"First, you must understand the Soviet Union is under lock and key in the most literal sense. Newspapers, television, literature and art, even speech, are all regulated by the government."

"But they couldn't regulate your thoughts. You had that, at least."

"Perhaps it would have been better..." His voice trailed off, but soon he continued. "I knew Western countries operated differently because I was lucky enough to visit many of them. I traveled extensively, first as a skater, then as a coach. I have been in the United States several times. I even spent the better part of one summer at a training camp. That is why my English is not so bad."

"Actually, it's excellent." And with that wonderful strange accent of his, she could listen to him all night without tiring. "But I didn't know that kind of a deal was possible."

"Many things are possible. Exchanges. Americans come to Russia also. I have worked with a few of your current world-class skaters. David Barron has a good chance to take the next Olympics."

Natalie figured that if she let him, he'd lead her away from the subject. She steered him back in the direction that she thought would do both of them the most good. "So seeing the West made you discontent."

As if he knew exactly what she was about, he asked, "You don't want to talk about your skaters?" His tone was lighter, more relaxed. "I can tell you some amusing stories."

"I want to discuss the things that are important to you personally, Mikhail. Truly."

He nodded soberly and slipped an arm around her shoulders. She snuggled into him in hope that he'd find as much comfort in her warmth as she did in his.

"The more I learned about the West, the more the idea of living here appealed to me."

He rested his cheek against her head so that his breath gently ruffled the hair around her face. Natalie sighed in contentment.

"Did you ever think about escaping before you actually attempted it?" she asked softly.

"Many times, but the word *defector* always conjured an image of a man without a country. You must understand that I love my country as much as I hate her political system." His voice grew deeper. She could feel the charged emotion that surged though him and could better understand the depth of his loss. "Abandoning Russia meant cutting away part of my soul."

"The indecision must have been very difficult for you."

"Especially during the past several years," he agreed, hugging her closer. "I could not condone the corrupt system that allowed its leaders to set ideology while doing what they pleased themselves—something brought home to me after my marriage to Galina. She was a nationally known computer-hardware designer. More important, she was a loyal, well-placed member of the Communist Party."

"So you got special treatment?"

His nod felt like a caress. "We got a new apartment and an auto with minimal wait. Luxury items and cheap groceries not available to others were ours for the asking. Little things became more important when you saw how many people did without. And Galina wanted me to become a Communist. She insisted I work toward admittance. I refused in spite of her pleas."

Natalie had read that only a small percentage of the people in the Soviet Union were Communists. It was an elite group, not one that a Russian or any other Soviet could join at will. Members were handpicked by other Communists.

"Our love turned to bitterness; our marriage, to divorce. It was frustrating for me."

Natalie slid her hand along Mikhail's sweater-covered chest in a sympathetic attempt to be closer to him. She wondered if it was her touch or the memories that made him shudder slightly.

"I could not get away from her. Because of the continuing housing shortage in Moscow, I had to stay until my application for new quarters was granted. I slept on the couch at night and listened to Galina's political lectures during the day. She became more hostile about my refusal to listen attentively after the marriage ended."

"So that was the impetus you needed to defect. How sad."

Mikhail didn't answer. He couldn't tell her how mistaken she was without giving away his secret.

Actually, he'd resigned himself to living in Russia without Galina. He'd stayed away from the apartment as often and for as long a time as he could. Then he'd finally been assigned a new apartment. That had brought him to another crisis in his life: should he move and continue to live like half the man he thought he could be? Or should he think seriously about defecting and become a whole person for the first time in his life?

Ultimately, however, Aleksei's imprisonment had been the immediate catalyst for his defection. He had made the decision fully aware that he had to be on the outside with something valuable to trade for Aleksei's freedom. He'd left knowing what the Soviets wanted most—the secrets that would render Thwart useless—but he hadn't planned on helping them. Not that he'd expected there would be a way for him to do so, anyway.

How ironic that he'd literally fallen into the opportunity, the accident having given him the contact he needed, almost as if it were his destiny to get the plans for Thwart. But Mikhail had already rejected that notion, believing that it was up to him to determine his own future.

And giving the Soviets these American military secrets would bring about an imbalance of power between the two rival nations—an ethical impossibility as far as he was concerned. On one level, it would mean betraying the country that was sheltering him. On a deeper, gut-feeling level, it would mean betraying his beloved Russia; because if anyone were to suffer for his perfidy, it would certainly be his own people.

Stealing the computer board had been his way of ensuring the continuing balance of power as well as of easing his own conscience. The U.S.S.R. would merely recover its own property in exchange for Aleksei Rodzianko's freedom. But Mikhail's alternative bargaining tool now seemed to be worthless, and he was faced with having to make a terrible decision—one that was tearing him to pieces.

"Mikhail," Natalie murmured with what sounded like amusement, "you're crushing my ribs."

He immediately loosened his hold on her and touched her face with his free hand. "I wouldn't hurt you if ever I could help it, Natasha. You must believe that."

Her eyes clouded with confusion. Of course, she had no way of knowing what he was thinking. He was sure her mind had been wandering in more romantic circles as they sat enveloped in each other's warmth. He stroked her cheek and felt, rather than heard, her breathing quicken.

What a cruel fate: to be torn between a lifelong friendship and growing feelings for a woman who'd risked her own life to rescue him. He knew that since Natalie's mother worked at home, he could find the opportunity to get his hands on at least part of the plans for Thwart. He tried to rationalize that if he did steal them, Natalie wouldn't be hurt, not physically. But if he didn't get them, the result could very well mean Aleksei's death.

"Come," he said, suddenly rising and pulling her up with him. "It is time to go home. We both need sleep."

Disappointment added to the confusion in her expression, and he could tell she'd expected him to kiss her. He wanted to do more than that, but he had to think of her best interests.

And Aleksei's.

How long could one put off making an impossible decision?

Chapter Six

On Monday morning, Natalie strolled across the tree-lined walkway of the University of Delaware campus, reflex alone allowing her to dodge the students zooming by on bicycles. She'd picked up several weeks' mail from her office as well as the books she'd need to plan a new class for the fall semester. Her business finished, she was on her way back to the parking lot, immersed in thought about the other evening. Just when Mikhail had started opening up to her, he'd retreated into himself again. And she'd spent two restless nights wondering what he had meant by saying he wouldn't hurt her if he could help it.

Distracted, she didn't see the crack in the walkway until her loafer caught in it, throwing her off balance. The pile of books shifted in her arms. One volume slid from her grip, and then they all went flying. She stooped to retrieve them.

A furtive movement out of the corner of her eye made Natalie whip her head in that direction. She searched the crowd of students milling around her like a herd of lost sheep, but the feeling that there had been someone more dangerous lurking among them remained.

A warning tingle crept along her spine as she gathered up her books, but Natalie did her best to blame her imagination. She didn't succeed. She'd been jumpy all morning, struck with the weirdest sensation of being followed. Unfortunately she'd failed to catch the culprit in the act. Thinking about who might want to keep tabs on her, only one name came to mind: Elliott Drucker.

Was the CIA agent walking in her footsteps?

"Natalie, watch out!"

The shout of caution came in time for her to straighten up and jump out of the way of a careening bike. "Sorry!" its pretty blond rider cried as Natalie's heart reacted in the expected way. "I haven't quite gotten the hang of all the speeds yet."

"Natalie, are you all right?"

She recognized the voice as belonging to Jerry Lubin, another member of the mathematics department. "Thanks for the warning. I'm fine."

He shook his dark-curled head in disgust. "I swear these kids should be required to have a license to ride bikes on this campus."

"Bring it up at the next meeting when the administration asks us for meaningful suggestions." Natalie grinned, knowing exactly how much good that would do. She started walking toward the parking lot again, Jerry keeping pace with her. "How's summer school going?"

"Not bad. I teach in the morning and get to play in the afternoon." The skin around his hazel eyes crinkled. "Want to join me?"

"I think I'll pass."

He was a likable guy—and a nice-looking one—but he inspired nothing more than feelings of friendship in Natalie. Although she often shared lunch with him, she'd never accepted any of his repeated offers for dates.

"So you already have plans?"

"Not exactly." Again, Mikhail hadn't said anything about a next time. "But I'm hoping to hear from him."

"Him, who? The Russian?" Jerry asked artlessly. "What's his name—Korolev?"

Natalie stopped short within sight of the parking lot, unable to keep the surprise from her face. "How did you know about Mikhail?"

"Maybe we Russians are psychic about each other. Something to do with our souls..."

"You're two generations removed from the Old Country, if I remember correctly." Natalie was aware that Jerry felt a special affinity for the land of his ancestors. He'd visited Russia several times, and he'd even spent a few days this spring in Moscow.

"Word gets around, Natalie. Wilmington isn't that large."

"Seventy thousand people isn't exactly a small town."

Jerry sighed. "You win. Your mother told a few people at Aircon, one of whom happens to be my father's brother-in-law's cousin once removed. How's that for a complex explanation?" he said with a grin.

"I should have guessed."

"So what's Korolev like? When can I meet him? I've got a million questions to ask."

"I don't think that would be wise. Not just the questions," Natalie explained as they entered the parking lot and she spotted her white Chevy Cavalier two rows ahead. "I think it's too soon for a get-together. I doubt Mikhail's ready to meet anyone who'd want to delve into his past."

"Why not? Is he depressed or something?"

"Wouldn't you be if you'd just left the only home you'd known for more than thirty years?"

"Hmm. Russia is far more fascinating than Delaware."

"For a visit, maybe. But to live there?"

Jerry shrugged, but didn't answer directly. "Korolev's depression seems pretty natural under the circumstances. He needs time to adjust. He's probably feeling guilty about betraying his country and his family."

Betrayal? Natalie couldn't think of it that way, but Mikhail might. It was a sensible explanation for his changing
moods. She stopped at her car door and took the keys from
her jeans pocket.

"I hope you're right," she said. "Still, don't count on
that invitation to meet him too soon, okay?"

"From what I hear, you know him best. Who am I to argue? But if you change your mind—about spending time
with me, that is—I'm listed in the faculty phone directory."

"I'll keep that in mind," Natalie promised noncommit-
tally. She got into her car and drove out of the lot by rote,
her mind far from her actions. The situation with Mikhail
was getting to her in a very basic way. She wasn't only drawn
to the man physically; it went deeper than that. Her feelings were being caught up in their odd relationship. Becoming so attached to a stranger from a hostile country was an
idea that took some getting used to.

Mikhail had the power to make her uneasy with his
slightest mood shift. There were times when she listened for
hidden meanings in everything he said. Was she being un-
fair to him? Natalie was beginning to think so. Damn
Drucker, anyway! She'd probably be over her initial suspicions if it weren't for the CIA agent's accusations. She had
to remember that Mikhail was going through—probably the
biggest, worst crisis that anyone could experience—and be
more understanding.

That settled, Natalie relaxed and paid more attention to
her driving. But she was on a side street a block and a half
from home before it registered on her that a dark blue sedan had made the same turn off the main road as she had.
The warning tingle crept through her again. She tried to
shake it off. Still, remembering how determined Drucker
had seemed, she took her foot off the accelerator to see what

the sedan would do. It kept an even distance from her, its driver obviously slowing down.

With her eyes glued to the rearview mirror, she deliberately made a wrong turn. The dark blue sedan turned also. Panicking, she pulled over in front of a strange house, expecting the other car to do the same. Instead, it accelerated, speeding past too quickly for her to get a good look at its occupants through the tinted windows. She could tell there were two men in front and one in the back. Somehow she was sure Drucker worked alone.

Suddenly relieved, Natalie leaned back against her car seat, wondering why her imagination had waited twenty-eight years to rear its frightening head.

NATALIE SPENT THE EARLY PART of the afternoon at her desk going through the books she'd brought home, taking notes and trying to decide which to use as her text for the new class. The fall semester wasn't far away; concentration wasn't easy. She kept rereading the note her mother had left her.

Natalie—
Mikhail called. Anxious to see you. Can you meet him at the club later tonight? Said he might not get the chance to call again. Leave him a message with someone in the office. You lucky girl, I'll kill you if you don't go!

Love,
C.L.

P.S. Won't be home tonight. We've made a breakthrough in my coating formula for Thwart! Keep all fingers crossed!

Natalie smiled at the little-girl pleasure her mother took in her work. Catherine sounded as excited as she herself felt at the thought of seeing Mikhail. She'd left a message of affirmation at the club more than an hour ago. So why couldn't she put thoughts of the Russian aside so she could concentrate on organizing her notes?

For once, she couldn't say her work was engrossing. As a matter of fact, she longed to do nothing more stimulating than sleep, to be rested when she saw Mikhail later. Two disturbed nights in a row added to the rush of panic she'd had earlier were doing her in. She'd just about decided to indulge in the luxury of a nap when the telephone rang.

Mikhail! He'd found time to call her back, after all. She picked up the receiver eagerly. "Hello," she said.

A far-off crackle was followed by "Nat, is that you?"

"Faith?" Disappointment that it wasn't Mikhail warred with happiness at hearing from her old friend. "What are you doing calling me from halfway around the world? You are in Lyon, aren't you?"

"Yes, for the moment I am. I've got to be in Washington on business for a couple of days, so I thought I'd drive up to Wilmington sometime on Wednesday. Can we get together?"

"If I didn't have time to see you, I'd make it."

There was a slight pause before Faith said, "Your Russian isn't keeping you too busy?"

"He's not my Russian. But I kind of like the way that sounds. Shall I ask him along?" Natalie teased.

"No!" Faith's sharp retort was startling, not at all what Natalie had expected. "Nat, I never thought you'd get involved with the guy."

Natalie frowned. "Why? Because he's Russian? Don't tell me that just because you work for the State Department you're automatically prejudiced."

"I'm not prejudiced, I'm worried! I got your letter about Elliott Drucker's visit. He came to see me, too." Faith's shuddering breath was audible. "What an awful man."

"When did he show up?"

"Yesterday."

If Drucker had been in France the day before, he could not have been following her that morning. Natalie was relieved that she could put her imagination to rest on that score.

"Oh, Nat, Drucker grilled me like I was some kind of criminal."

"I guess that's his charming technique."

"He kept after me until I thought I would scream. He believes you and I know something we aren't telling. Nat, there's something wrong here. You know that, don't you?"

"What?" Natalie asked cautiously, hoping Faith wasn't going to criticize her for seeing Mikhail.

"Drucker never should have approached you like he did, not once he was back in the States, not alone. CIA agents are international operatives. Drucker should have turned his information over to the FBI and worked with one of their agents. The FBI is in charge of investigations dealing with internal security."

Faith's explanation made Natalie uneasy. She'd never thought of that. "Why would Drucker pursue it on his own, then?"

"I don't know, but I have the feeling something underhanded is going on. I've already put out feelers for information on the guy. Maybe for once my State Department contacts will be of use. In the meantime, swear to me you'll be careful. Please, Nat. I feel responsible for this whole mess. If it hadn't been for me, you never would have come to France. You never would have gotten involved."

And she never would have met Mikhail. "It's all right, Faith." Natalie mentally shrugged the unease away. "I promise I'll be careful."

MIKHAIL LEFT THE OFFICE, Natalie's message in hand. He shouldn't have called her and he knew it. It wasn't fair to her. But he was so alone. So desperate. He needed her.

Before he could analyze what that meant exactly, he glanced toward the outside doors. What he saw paralyzed him. He struggled to breathe naturally, to make his legs move toward Yuri Simansky, who leaned against the bank of bleachers, waiting.

As Mikhail drew closer, the KGB agent nodded his approval. He hefted his navy-suited bulk from the bleachers and opened the door. Of course. Simansky would want to talk outside, where there'd be no witnesses. Mikhail folded Natalie's note and shoved it into his pocket, cursing himself for luring her to the skating arena. He didn't think Simansky knew anything about her, and he wanted to make sure things stayed that way.

They'd walked half the length of the parking lot in the semidarkness of dusk before the agent finally stopped and turned to him. Mikhail didn't miss the dark blue sedan with KGB reinforcements mere yards away.

Simansky spoke in Russian. "Well, comrade? How are your plans for obtaining Thwart coming along?"

"They're not."

The close-set eyes narrowed. "That is a foolish statement."

"But it's the truth."

Mikhail had struggled with demons since Simansky had shown up on his doorstep. Aleksei's face had haunted him, but so had Natalie's. He hadn't been able to make a decision one way or the other.

"If you refuse to help us without incentive, Comrade Korolev, there is always the woman."

Mikhail felt his gut wrench. "Leave Galina out of this," he bluffed, guessing the agent wasn't referring to his ex-wife.

Simansky confirmed it. "I was talking about another woman. Tall. Good bone structure." His meaty fingers twirled around his shoulder as he added, "Brown curls, like so."

"Leave her out of this!" Mikhail wouldn't say her name. Maybe they didn't yet know who Natalie was.

"Such passion I see in your eyes, comrade. But how can I forget about this woman when she could be the key to your doing as I demand?" Simansky asked smoothly. "If you are as concerned about her as you seem to be, you will make sure that I am not forced to hurt her."

"Bastard!" Mikhail yelled, grabbing the agent's lapels and, in spite of Simansky's greater weight, dragging him around in a half circle. He heard the metallic sound of doors opening. "If you so much as touch her—"

"You'll what?"

His face mottling, Simansky tried to push him away, but Mikhail held on like a bulldog. They struggled until they went down on the pavement together, Mikhail on top. Suddenly he was grabbed from behind and jerked off the larger man. Rough hands on each arm sent him flying backward. A parked auto halted his progress. Pain shot through his recently healed leg as well as up the length of his back. He lay against the metal, watching the two flunkies help Simansky to his feet.

"You amuse me with these theatrics, comrade." The agent was barely breathing heavily as he dusted off his ill-fitting suit. "I will get what I want, one way or the other. The path to a single end is yours to choose." His pig eyes held Mikhail's tortured gaze steadily. "Don't take too long. My superiors in Moscow are annoyed that I have no progress to report. I will not be made to seem the fool a second time."

Mikhail clenched his jaw against shouting something stupid. He merely watched the three KGB men clamber into their car. It sped off immediately, and he pushed himself away from the parked vehicle. What was he to do now? They knew about Natalie—if not her name, at least the fact that she existed. A flash of white on the ground caught his eye. Her message. He picked it up and strode toward the Quonset-hut-shaped building, planning on calling her right away. He'd tell her not to come, that it wasn't safe....

Once inside the club, he hurried to the office, intent on using the telephone.

"Looking for this?" Tom Jackson asked. The older coach sat with his feet up on a desk, waving a recently published book on skating technique Mikhail had purchased. "I'd like to read it when you're finished with it."

"Yes, of course." Mikhail took the book from the man and stuffed the folded message inside its pages. "In a few days."

"Thanks." Jackson dropped his legs and stretched. "You're okay. I've got to get going. I promised the little woman I'd be home early tonight. You know how women are."

Mikhail did indeed know how they were. He thought of Natalie: brave, caring, innocent.

He picked up the telephone receiver and dialed her number. Jackson grabbed an athletic bag and sauntered out the door. Mikhail counted how many times the phone rang. Four. Seven. Thirteen. Damn it to hell, where was she? He couldn't stop her from coming if he couldn't find her!

"Hey, Mikhail." Jackson was poking his head back through the doorway. "Your student is waiting for you."

With a curt nod, Mikhail dropped the receiver and headed for the arena.

The lesson didn't go well. Mikhail was too distracted by thoughts of Simansky and his men getting their hands on Natalie. He tried to calm down by convincing himself they didn't know who she was or where she lived, and that since they'd left in such a hurry, they wouldn't be around to see her when she arrived. Finally his conscience made him suggest that the lesson be continued another time.

The student agreed.

Now what? Natalie wasn't due for nearly an hour. He'd go crazy waiting for her if he sat around and did nothing. Looking out over the shimmering expanse of ice broken only by a couple of figures working at the other end, Mikhail knew there was one thing he could do to distract himself.

He changed cassette tapes and set the portable equipment where he could get at it. A few minutes later, after doing some floor exercises to help warm up his muscles, he was on the ice.

Russian music softly filled the space around him. Mikhail closed his eyes and absorbed it for a moment, then began moving, slowly at first, stretching his tendons, ignoring the twinges of pain caused by the scuffle in the parking lot. He was both athlete and artist, and this was his medium. He could erase everything from his mind at will, but he didn't want to. He needed to think of the past.

Memories of Russia haunted him as he lengthened his strokes, changed direction on the ice, tested a spin. The blur of the arena walls became images of his boyhood, his proud parents, Aleksei—images he hadn't allowed himself to think about since Chamonix, when he'd betrayed and abandoned everything he'd ever known except the one man he still hoped to save.

As he skated, the music enveloped his thoughts and became part of his soul. His body responded, anticipating rather than waiting to be programmed. The low, throbbing tune, typically Slavic in its sorrowful intensity, spoke to him of tortured minds and unending guilt. It whispered his name, *his* guilt in leaving his country. He hadn't allowed himself to think of that until now. But here on the ice he could face anything.

The music picked up in tempo, sending a feverish energy coursing through him. He executed complex footwork, the patterns as classically Russian as those danced by the people of his homeland. He'd chosen to abandon that homeland rather than try to change it. He was a man with a conscience that had awakened too late in his life for him to make a difference—or so he'd convinced himself. But what if he'd been wrong? He was free, but it didn't look as if Aleksei would ever join him. And what of the others he'd left behind, no better off than before?

He skated for them, for the millions who would remain repressed under a government that could take away a man's living and his pride, strip him of his few possessions and threaten him with eternal banishment if he dared to speak out too loudly.

Mikhail fought back instinctively the only way he knew how, with blades of steel on ice, feeling more determined than ever that he had to get Aleksei out. Each stroke was a step in the right direction, each jump an attempt at flight.

He stopped suddenly, his heart beating like mad. Had he made his impossible decision without even knowing it? Would he really do anything to justify his defection? Instinct compelled him to turn around. He did so and looked straight into Natalie's trusting blue eyes.

NATALIE APPROACHED THE SKATING CLUB, eagerness putting a spring in her step. She was early, but she didn't think Mikhail would mind if she watched him coach again.

Strains of melancholy music floated to the outside from the arena, and even before she went in, she knew Mikhail would be skating to it. Still, as she stepped through the doorway, Natalie wasn't prepared for the power of his tan-clad body in motion.

She walked forward slowly, mesmerized. She had the oddest sensation that Mikhail wasn't aware of his audience, even though all other activity in the arena had stopped and every eye was focused on him. He seemed to have turned inward, to have become so absorbed in his thoughts that his impromptu performance was merely an outward expression of his emotions.

And then, his back to her, Mikhail stopped on a dime—his toe picks digging into the ice with a hair-raising screech—seemingly unmindful of the music that continued to fill the air with its woeful sound. He stayed frozen for a moment before turning. His haunted gray eyes rested on her face.

Her heart went out to him. She took the last few steps toward him. "Mikhail?" she mouthed. Silly. He wouldn't be able to hear her.

He tore his gaze away and headed for his portable cassette player. The music died in the middle of a high note. Silence. No movement in the arena. Then applause, a spattering of hands coming together enthusiastically.

If the half-dozen people there expected Mikhail to take a sweeping bow, they were undoubtedly disappointed. For, other than an acknowledging nod of his dark blond head, he didn't respond. Instead, he replaced the guards on his skate blades while Natalie approached him at the edge of the ice.

Her mouth went dry as she realized she didn't know what to say to the man. His features were set in an impenetrable mask. She could feel his awful despair, but she couldn't understand it or help him unless he was willing to talk about what he was experiencing. All she could do was be there for him.

"Natalya." His eyes were now filled with regret. "You shouldn't be here tonight."

"But your message . . ."

"A mistake." When she took a step backward, he added, "Mine."

"I'll leave."

"No!" His hand shot out, grabbing her wrist to stop her from moving farther away. Natalie flinched. He loosened his grip but didn't let go. His thumb caressed the inside of her wrist, as though it were wiping away the momentary pain he'd caused. She felt a languor seep through her, right down to her knees. She didn't know if she could move if her life depended on it.

"I'm feeling so foolish, Natalya. I am sorry."

Yes, she could hear the sorrow in his hoarse voice as clearly as she had heard it in the music. She remembered what Jerry had said about betrayal. Maybe Mikhail had played a piece that had reminded him of his family. Whether or not he was aware of it, he needed her to be with him tonight. She sat on the bench behind her and sensed his immediate relief. He dropped her wrist, sat next to her and bent over to undo his laces.

"It's okay," she said. "To be foolish, I mean. I often am."

"Then we are the same in some ways."

And so different in others, she thought. She'd had more than one taste of suspicion since she'd met Mikhail. What would it be like to live on guard always? Natalie had no idea, but she was sure he knew, just as she was sure it was possible to get past the stumbling blocks their cultures had purposely put in their way.

Developing a relationship would take time. She was prepared to be patient.

Mikhail Illyovich Korolev was a man worth waiting for.

Chapter Seven

Her silent musings startled Natalie. *Developing a relationship... a man worth waiting for*—those sounded like statements made by a woman who was ready for a commitment. She shifted uncomfortably in her seat.

"I will only be another minute," Mikhail said, packing his carryall. The sweat of exertion still beaded his forehead and soaked through the torso of his jumpsuit.

"Don't you want to shower and change?" she asked.

"It would take too long."

"I've got the time."

"No!"

He said the word too quickly, as though he were afraid. Was he worried that she might disappear if he left her alone? Whatever the reason, she was convinced it had to do with his emotions, which were obviously in turmoil.

Natalie decided to take a different tack. "Where would you like to go from here?"

"Anywhere with you."

It was the right answer. She smiled at the sincerity with which he gave it. "Not specific, but we'll think of something." Natalie rose as Mikhail zipped his bag closed. "Of course, if we choose any place other than a dark bar, you might be uncomfortable in what you're wearing."

He looked down at his sweat-stained work clothes and frowned. "You are correct. I should take the time to clean up," he muttered. "You will wait here, in the arena, not outside."

"I won't move," Natalie promised in response to what had sounded more like an order than a request. It wouldn't hurt to make allowances this once. She picked up the book that had been lying on the bench beneath his bag. "Is this yours?"

"Yes."

"*Skating-perfect*." The title indicated the book was about skating techniques. "Do you mind if I take a look at it while I wait? If I'm going to rejoin the club, I certainly could use a refresher course."

"You plan to rejoin?" Pleasure removed some of the tenseness from his tone. "Then you shall have all the help you need from me."

She sighed. "Does that mean I can't look at this book?"

It was his turn to smile, and with the softened expression came the tender touch of his fingertips grazing her cheek. "It means that you will not need it. But look all you want while you wait for me."

Mikhail retreated toward the door leading to the office, snack bar and locker rooms, and Natalie tried to make herself comfortable on the bench. The book opened automatically to a page in the middle marked by a folded note. Ignoring it, she flipped to the front and began to read.

YURI SIMANSKY WAITED ALONE in the sedan while his underlings, Gregor and Ivan, kept a closer watch on the club building. He picked up the cellular telephone—a touch of decadence that a man in his position appreciated—and punched out the sequence of numbers he'd memorized earlier.

After the prescribed number of rings—four—he hung up and hit the redial button. An amazing piece of technology, he thought with satisfaction. This time there were only three rings before the receiver on the other end was lifted. There was no greeting, only a hollow, crackling sound.

Simansky spoke first. "Our employers will be pleased."

"You got the message, then?"

"It was very precise."

"And you've made progress?"

"The spiral tightens," Simansky said.

"Are you sure?"

"There is always the woman. He is attached."

A pause told Simansky his contact was thinking seriously about that statement. He hoped this one wouldn't prove to be as soft as the last with whom he'd had to deal. The situation had become irritating enough. What man wouldn't feel humiliated when he had to take orders from a neophyte who was considered more valuable than he was, and after twenty years of loyal service!

"You'll have to instill more fear in her."

The answer gave Simansky some satisfaction. "Yes," he agreed. "Her fear will work on him to our advantage."

"How much do you think he'll tell her?" the voice on the other end asked worriedly.

New recruits! Full of fervor and stupidity! Simansky sighed deeply, wondering why he should have to explain every detail.

"It does not matter how much she knows, comrade. The woman," he said distinctly, wanting to make sure his point got across, "is expendable."

NATALIE CLOSED THE BOOK with a loud thump that echoed through the arena. She couldn't concentrate on the words in front of her. For the past ten minutes her mind had kept wandering to the commitment she seemed to be making to a man she hardly knew. Besides that, although she wore a rose cotton-knit pullover and jeans, the chill of the rink was getting to her. And the unnerving quiet. She was alone right now, yet she had the distinct feeling that she was being watched.

The book slid easily into her oversize purse. Natalie looked furtively over her shoulder. No one was there. A shiver crept up her spine anyway. From where she was sitting, she couldn't see the doors that led to the parking lot. Rising from the bench, purse clutched to her side, she listened intently while stealthily making her way toward the bleachers, which were folded back against the wall for storage. She'd have a great view of the doors as soon as she reached the last row. Disappointment speared her a few seconds later when doors were the only thing she did see.

Wait—one of them was cracked open a few inches, in the process of closing. Natalie thought quickly. She would have heard if someone had come out of the office area and walked toward the exit. She stepped closer, trying to see out the narrowing crack into the dark night on the other side. Her pulse fluttered with anticipation . . . then jumped with fright when strong fingers clutched her upper arm.

"I thought I asked you to stay inside."

Natalie's mind raced as quickly as her pulse. She hadn't heard Mikhail come through the office area, so she might not have heard someone else. How foolish she was! She willed her heartbeat to stabilize, a difficult demand with him holding on to her.

"Where were you going?"

"I wasn't leaving without you," she assured him.

Mikhail released her but didn't move away. For once, his nearness made her more jumpy, more anxious to put space between them.

"I thought perhaps you were impatient with me," he said.

The words were right, but his tone wasn't convincing. Natalie eyed Mikhail suspiciously but didn't have time to ask questions. He was already escorting her through the door. When she was outside, the feeling of something being wrong persisted—and so did the sensation that she was being watched.

Natalie looked around, trying to keep her own surveillance as natural as possible. She didn't spot anything unusual. No one lurked in the shadows. Only a dozen or so cars were left in the lot, including hers. She had her key out and in the door before she turned to scan the others more closely.

What she saw made her suck in her breath in a sharp gasp.

Mikhail stopped halfway to the passenger door. "Natalya?"

"That car over there, on the other side of the lot—I've seen it before, earlier tod—"

"Get in!" Mikhail was already taking the keys out of her hand and pushing her into the vehicle and across the driver's seat. "Move!"

"What are you doing?" she demanded, trying to untangle her legs.

"Driving."

Her eyes widened. "Do you know how?"

"I hope so," he said, starting the engine.

"'Hope'?" He was already turning on the lights and shifting into drive. "Mikhail, wait a minute!"

He was deaf to her protest. The Cavalier leaped forward. She looked across his shoulders, out the window toward the other side of the lot. The dark blue sedan's lights flashed on as Mikhail stepped on the accelerator, making her car zoom forward with a screech of tires.

"Your seat belt!" she cried, strapping herself in. "It's dangerous to drive without one."

"We will be in more danger if I don't lose them!" he told her, guiding the Chevy out of the parking lot and through the Rock Manor Golf Course.

"If we don't lose who?"

"KGB."

A lump settled in her stomach. "Are you sure?" she asked in a small voice, not expecting an answer. Mikhail was concentrating on the road.

Natalie drew into herself for a moment, barely noticing as they passed Carruthers Lane. A car chase between woods and cornfields was as unreal as a rescue mission on a deserted mountainside. She couldn't believe what was happening to her. She'd been visited by the CIA, and now she was being tracked by the KGB. She'd suspected the possibility of that happening, but she hadn't wanted to consider its implications.

Reality registered and she thought quickly. "Faulk Road," she said, looking over her shoulder. Headlights kept a steady pace behind. "Make a right on Faulk instead of getting on the highway. Maybe we can lose them down some suburban side street."

Natalie was almost sorry she'd suggested this, for Mikhail swerved onto the shoulder and accelerated around a moving car in the cross traffic. He'd ignored the fact that their light had just turned red. Swearing she could hear her own heartbeat, she looked back again. "They're caught. They won't be able to make a turn until the light changes again."

"Don't be too sure of that."

He was right. He hadn't driven far before the sedan moved out at the first break in traffic. Horns blared, cutting through the night quiet. Hoarse words squeezed up through Natalie's throat. "Faster, or they'll catch up to us!"

Instead of doing as she demanded, Mikhail got off the four-lane road at the first opportunity. He made a series of left and right turns and slid into a development of middle-class homes. He turned off the car lights and kept going, though admittedly more slowly.

"Mikhail, you can't drive without headlights."

"That never stopped a European," he said, referring to the fact that drivers in many European towns didn't use headlights. "Do not worry. The moon is full."

But she wasn't looking at the street ahead or the moon above. She was watching their rear. "I think we've lost...oh, no. There they are, stopping in the middle of the last intersection. I think the driver is trying to decide which direction to take. He decided—they know we're here."

"They are only guessing," Mikhail muttered under his breath. A sudden swerve of the Cavalier startled Natalie into thinking the car was about to hit something, but it coasted directly into an open garage attached to a house. Mikhail cut the engine. "Get your head down."

She obeyed immediately, leaning toward the middle of the car. He pressed her farther down into the seat, his body over hers. Within seconds, they heard the larger car's engine as it crept along the street behind them. Natalie held her breath until it went by and the sound faded away.

"Can I sit up now?" she asked. The seat belt was cutting into her, and Mikhail was getting heavier with each moment that passed.

"No. They could come back."

"How long do we have to stay like this?"

"All night, if necessary."

His fear was tangible, stronger than hers; he had more reason to be afraid than she did. She could feel the uneven, rapid beat of his heart where his chest pressed against her back.

"My whole body is going to sleep," she complained.

"You will survive," he muttered in return, shifting his weight but not releasing her. "No matter what I have to do."

That had an ominous ring to it. Before she could demand an explanation, a shrill voice cried, "Who's there?"

The garage suddenly filled with light, and an angry fist banged on the half-open window. Mikhail eased his weight off Natalie and she sat up to face an old woman dressed in a robe, her silver hair in curlers.

"What do you mean, using my garage for some illicit tryst?" she yelled, her expression outraged. "Perverts!"

Mikhail gave Natalie a significant look; she had to answer for them, because of his accent.

"We pulled into the wrong garage, sweetheart." Her giggle was forced for effect, but the heat creeping up her neck wasn't. She knew what their positions must have looked like! "Sorry," Natalie said. "Our pulling in here was an honest mistake."

"Mistake, my aunt Fanny!" The woman's curlers bobbed in fury. "Get out of here, right now, before I go call the police."

"We'll do that," Natalie agreed, nudging Mikhail.

He started the car and backed it slowly out of the garage.

"And next time you two get hot pants, use a motel, like decent folk!" the old woman shrilled after them.

Natalie's forced giggle turned into genuine mirth. Halfway down the block, Mikhail must have seen the amusing aspect to the situation, because his laughter joined hers. "She thought that you and I . . ."

"I know," Natalie said, gulping for air.

"If only she knew the truth."

The truth. The laughter stilled on her lips. Being chased by the KGB was nothing to laugh at. Mikhail picked up her quick shift in mood. She could tell he was checking his rearview mirror closely.

"Nothing," he said as she turned to look for herself.

He was correct. Nothing. Yet some of the fear burrowed its way back into her consciousness.

"Can you direct us home from here?" Mikhail asked.

"I think so."

But how safe was home?

"THE FIRST THING we have to do is call the police."

Natalie was feeling pretty shaky as she snapped on a lamp in the living room and went to the telephone. Mikhail turned the light off just as quickly and took the receiver from her hand before she'd finished dialing.

"Forget the police." He walked to the window and stared out. "They wouldn't be of any help in a situation like this."

"Like what, Mikhail?"

He hadn't said a word all the way back to the Lundgren home. After they'd arrived, he'd driven the car into the garage and closed the door, as if he thought the KGB's sedan might be cruising her neighborhood, which was across town from where they'd lost it. And still he didn't seem inclined to talk, although she could almost hear his mind working as he paced in the dark. Did he think he was protecting her by keeping her ignorant? She hated being treated like a child.

"Why would the KGB want to follow us? Tell me," she insisted.

His moving silhouette in front of the windows was ringed by moonlight, making his blond hair glow with a bluish cast, but she couldn't get a glimpse of his expression. "They meant to harass me."

"And me?"

There was more; she knew it. Natalie wanted to hold on to Mikhail for comfort, but he seemed so distant with the darkness of the room separating them. She grabbed the high back of the couch, smoothing the texture of the fabric with fingers that trembled.

"It is not you they want," he assured her.

"Then what were they doing following me home from the university this morning?"

The pacing in front of the window stopped. "The university?" He muttered heatedly in Russian. Cursing, no doubt. "Why the hell didn't you tell me?"

Why the hell was he angry with her? "That's what I was trying to do in the parking lot, but you didn't give me a chance to finish explaining."

"So they know where you live and where to find us."

"Not exactly." Natalie took courage from her own cleverness. "I thought I was being followed, so I deliberately made a wrong turn and stopped in front of a house a few blocks from here. They drove right by me."

"Do not be naive, Natalya." Mikhail's chastisement quickly wiped the tepid smile of victory from her lips. "If they found you in the first place, they know who you are, where you live, everything about you. I should have known...."

"Known what? Never mind." She picked up the phone again. "I'm calling the police."

He didn't try to stop her physically this time. "Do so, and you make more trouble for me, Natalya."

That stayed her hand. Natalie clenched her jaw and replaced the receiver. "All right. But tell me what we're going to do now."

"We will wait. And tomorrow, perhaps I will find a way to get them to stop this terrorism."

"Here? You want to wait here in the dark all night?" she asked softly.

He moved directly toward her. His hand was unerring when it found the side of her face. Her breath quickened in response to his touch. And so did her heart.

"Take me upstairs, Natalya."

Natalie instinctively responded to the fervor in his words. She cupped her hand around his, turned her face inward and kissed his palm. He whispered something under his breath in Russian. Not a curse. Definitely not a curse. The foreign sound blended with the sudden rushing in her ears.

"Take me to your room, my Natasha."

"Natasha. That's a beautiful name," she whispered, hardly daring to breathe.

"You are beautiful, Natasha. The name declares my affection for you."

The tips of his fingers stroked the back of her neck, mesmerizing Natalie into believing him. She closed her eyes, felt him move closer. His breath mingled with hers. She waited for his kiss, but his lips barely brushed the edge of her mouth.

"Come, my Natasha. Lead the way for me."

An overwhelming feeling of sensuality stole through her at his words. If she took him to her hideaway under the eaves, there was no turning back in their relationship. She knew exactly what he wanted and expected at the top of those stairs: the same thing she did. And why not? She'd thought of him as a man worth waiting for, and she could have him right where she wanted him, if only she had the courage to agree.

"All right." The words spilled out, soft but choked. "A moment. Wait for me."

She crossed the room to a wall unit with a dropleaf. The vodka wasn't hard to find among the few bottles inside the recess, since its paper seal was still intact. Natalie had bought it earlier, thinking she might offer him a drink. Now she was afraid she needed one herself.

Her heart was thudding when she turned around and stared into the darkness where he waited for her. If she hesitated, she might change her mind. She didn't want him to leave, didn't want to be alone. This day had been filled with so much negative emotion, she needed him to counteract that, to fill the night with memories she could cherish.

She approached the couch, picked up her purse and held out her hand to him, whispering, "I will lead the way."

Mikhail's hand was warm and dry and strong. He should have been the one leading. Natalie thought she might follow him anywhere, with no resistance at all. She didn't know why he'd left the decision to her, but the fact pleased her.

Upstairs, she set the purse and the bottle on her built-in desk and gestured toward the daybed. "Sit down while I get some cups."

They were paper cups actually, taken from the dispenser in the bathroom. She was aware of Mikhail's eyes following her every movement. Before opening the bottle, she drew the blinds, then lit a candle. Its golden flicker warmed the darkened room. When she turned back to Mikhail, she gave him one of the paper cups and poured vodka for them both.

"Are you planning to stand all night?" he asked, looking inviting pressed back into her pillows. His shirt was open to his waist, the fine sprinkling of golden hair that matted his chest capturing her gaze. She sat down gingerly on the edge of the bed, her heart in her throat. Surely that was why she found it impossible to speak.

Mikhail lifted his drink. *"Nazdorovie!"* With a flick of his wrist, he downed the vodka. Natalie eyed her own cup uncertainly. "Don't sip. Do it at once."

Squeezing her eyes shut, Natalie did as he'd instructed. The liquid flamed down her throat, and fumes attacked her nose and eyes.

"Is it always this potent?" she gasped, crushing the paper cup with one hand and clutching the bottle with the other.

"Sometimes more so, depending on the kind of vodka." His hand circled her wrist, pulling her closer between his spread thighs. He took the cup and bottle from her and put them on the floor. "Another and you'll be drunk. I want you clearheaded."

"The kind of vodka—you mean the brand?" she asked, trying to delay the moment of truth.

Mikhail wrapped his arms around her. "No. There are many variations of vodka, and we Russians have learned to appreciate all of them." His words ruffled the top of her hair. "It is a tradition, like our *zakuska*, or small bites of various foods that precede dinner."

"Appetizers," she murmured, snuggling closer, lulled by Mikhail's delicious accent as well as the warmth of his body.

"More elaborate, and so is the vodka—*zubrovka*, with buffalo grass added; *rubinovaia*, the brilliant orange of mountain ash berries; and *pertsovka*, vodka fortified with black pepper."

"I think you'd better quit while you're ahead. My stomach is getting queasy just thinking about it."

Laughter rumbled through his belly, causing a tingling response in her breasts that made her shift restlessly. But she only succeeded in becoming aware of another part of his body that told her of his own anticipation. The hardness pressing into her side and the hands stroking her back and her buttocks were becoming all she could think about.

No, not quite. There was still part of her that wanted some questions answered.

"Why, Mikhail?" she demanded softly.

He put a finger to her lips. "Misha. Let me hear you speak this name."

She kissed his finger—"Misha, then"—but remained undaunted. "Why is the KGB after you?"

When he didn't reply, she nuzzled his chest with her lips and lathed his nipples with her tongue until a different kind of tenseness overtook him. His breath was shallow, his voice hoarse as he said, "The KGB is after anyone who does not conform."

"Have they harassed you for a long time, then?"

He didn't give her a direct answer. "In the Soviet Union, KGB agents number in the hundreds of thousands—enough to harass everyone."

"So many people involved in such an ugly business," she murmured, trailing kisses down to the softness of his belly. How bold a single ounce of vodka made her!

Mikhail groaned and pulled Natalie forward while sliding his body farther under her. "Most are ordinary citizens like you and I." He insinuated his hands under her knit top and unhooked her bra. Strong, lightly callused, they touched her breasts in a way that made her gasp. "Anyone could be KGB—a co-worker, a friend, a member of your own family. That is how the organization works, from the inside out, until you no longer know whom to trust."

He freed the fastening on her jeans and slid a hand downward, cupping the heat between her thighs. As his fingers began to explore her, Natalie raised her head and forced open her half-closed eyes. His face was shadowed. Foreign. How did she know that she could trust him? Lord help her, she had to. She wanted to forge more than a physical union in this bed.

"You can trust me, Mikhail," she whispered with a shudder when his fingers penetrated even deeper.

"I know that, my Natasha." His intensity touched something buried in her. "I know that."

His kiss was as passion-filled as the intimate touch. Yet he seemed oddly in control, transmitting his need without making demands, as if his goal were her total pleasure rather than mutual satisfaction. She moaned deep in her throat, arousal snaking through her even as her mind remained split in two directions.

Natalie broke the kiss so that she could think. The room was still except for her own labored breathing. Candlelight flickered against the walls. She rubbed her forehead against Mikhail's lips as if to steal his silent thoughts. She stopped suddenly realizing she'd been unconsciously seducing information from him.

What would it be like not to know whom to trust? Natalie wondered, shuddering against him. Right now he was protective of her even in his passion. She felt an overwhelming need to prove her words somehow, to give him the gift of trust. Her trust.

Murmuring softly in Russian, Mikhail freed his hands and lowered her jeans and underpants to the floor, then did the same with his own clothing. Flesh scorched flesh. His mouth took hers, the moist attack erasing any further conversation. She squirmed on top of him, aching to feel his throbbing hardness inside her, yet she wanted to draw out this pleasure that was uniquely theirs, to turn it into something far more meaningful than physical gratification. The feelings flooding her were new, compelling, confusing. She'd thought she'd known what involvement with a man meant....

Below her, Mikhail's eyes closed to slits as she allowed her hand to explore, her fingers to torture. He grasped her buttocks, rocking her closer. She poised herself over him, but Mikhail stopped her from completing the movement.

"Natasha, you must understand... I do not want you to be in more danger because of me," he murmured. He reached up and stroked the side of her face gently. Lovingly. "I want you and need you, but it is not too late for you to change your mind. Perhaps you should tell me to leave now, to free you from any future involvement."

"That's impossible," Natalie whispered. It was too late. "I am involved."

And as he pushed up and took her in a hot, quick movement that sealed them at the hip, she knew it was true. She could no more deny it than she could try to put off their mutual assault of the senses.

She was involved.

His hands sought her breasts under the knit top she still wore, deliciously torturing them until she lost herself in the sensations consuming her.

Deeply involved.

Moving over him with deliberation, she absorbed his thrusts, taking him as fully as possible with a need and an abandon that were totally new to her.

Emotionally involved.

For, as their bodies shuddered against each other in a quick release of fear-inspired passion, she knew that no matter how much she might want to deny what had happened in two short weeks, she felt more for this man than for any other she had known.

Mikhail pulled her closer, wrapped his arms tightly around her back as though he'd never let her go, and whispered "My heart" so fiercely that she had to believe him.

How could she not when she'd fallen in love with a man who some would say was her enemy?

MIKHAIL LOOKED DOWN at the naked woman whose luscious and now-familiar body was curled around a pillow. He pulled the sheet up over her protectively. After relieving their first burst of desire, they'd undressed fully and made love again, properly this time—slowly, lingeringly, an experience to be remembered always.

He smoothed a brown curl from her forehead and kissed her brow. Deep emotions for Natalie flooded him. The quick stinging at the back of his throat—a reminder of the way he'd involved her in his dangerous mission—made him leave the room immediately.

Catherine would not be home tonight. Mikhail knew that before he descended the stairs. She'd told him so on the telephone earlier, when he'd left the message for Natalie. Of course, her staying at the lab that night didn't mean she hadn't left anything of value behind.

The door to the study was unlocked, as it had been the first time he'd seen it. He opened it but hesitated in the doorway, unable to make his feet take that first step toward the ultimate betrayal of the woman with whom he'd just made love.

What would Natalie think of him when she learned why he'd purposely forced his way into her life?

What other choice did he have?

He stared into the dark, poised on the threshold of unforgivable treachery, knowing what Simansky required of him to save not only Aleksei but his precious Natasha as well.

Chapter Eight

Natalie struggled out of sleep. She'd been having such a fulfilling erotic dream that she didn't want to leave it. But stripes of bright light slanting across her face were forcing her eyes open. The midmorning sun was shining through the skylight blinds, which weren't fully closed. Sprawled on her stomach at the edge of the bed, she squinted at the mess on the floor: a bottle of vodka, two crushed paper cups and her clothing.

Making love to Mikhail had been no dream!

She twisted around and sat straight up, hugging the sheet to her naked breasts. "Mikhail?" she called softly. No response. The bathroom door stood open, allowing her to see inside. Empty.

She blinked in confusion as her fog-shrouded mind recounted the details of the previous night. The mirror image across from the bed stared back at her curiously. It was quite disheveled, seemed deliciously satiated, and didn't have the slightest trace of anxiety in its expression. What had started in fear had ended in ecstasy....

But where was the man who had provided it?

Natalie didn't exactly bound out of bed. She eased her way, afraid the single drink had been enough to give her a hangover. It hadn't. Her head felt clear once she shook away the last remnants of sleep. She'd never been an instant riser, but this morning, her actions fueled by a need to see the man she loved, she grabbed her robe from the closet and struggled into it, then ran down the two flights of stairs.

The man she loved. Those words warmed her all the way to her bare toes.

"Mikhail, where are you?" she called loudly, but got no response. Her frown of disappointment grew deeper when she reached the first floor. There was no sign of the Russian. Perhaps he was taking advantage of the early-summer sun. She was on her way to the patio when the edge of an open drawer in the wall unit found her knee. She rubbed the sore spot and cursed at whoever had left the drawer open. She herself, probably. But as she scanned the area, Natalie realized that other drawers and doors had the appearance of having been shut without care—almost as though someone had been looking through them.

She whipped around quickly, as if expecting to see someone behind her. Her imagination again. Even so, she ran to the patio door. It was secure; Mikhail was nowhere in sight. She checked the other doors. Both were locked.

While trying to decide what to do next, Natalie heard the soft hum of machinery coming from the study. Cautiously, she approached it and swung the unlatched door open. The room was empty, but the computer terminal had been left on, with papers strewn around it. Relieved, Natalie leaned against the doorjamb.

Her mother had come home last night, after all. That explained why things had been out of place in the living room. Catherine must have been looking for something. Then another thought occurred to her—the reason she might not have heard her mother come home. Heat rose to her face.

She shut down the computer and checked the papers to see if they should be locked in the wall safe. No, of course not. Although Catherine was often caught up in her own world, she wasn't careless enough to leave important documents lying around.

Natalie left the study and went upstairs. The door to the master bedroom was closed, so her mother must still be sleeping. At least any embarrassing questions would wait until later. But, as usual, Natalie had questions of her own—for Mikhail—the most immediate of which was why he'd left without waking her.

He'd said that he'd find some way to get the KGB agents to stop their terrorism. If that was what he was doing, Natalie was more than worried. It was difficult to believe he'd gone to the skating club to coach, as he would on any normal day. Difficult, but not impossible, she amended. He was a Russian, used to taking these things in stride.

She'd check to see if he was at the club as soon as she got herself together. After putting on a pair of loose white pants and a brilliant sea-green T-shirt, she searched for her hairbrush. It was as elusive as Mikhail. Maybe it was in the purse she'd thrown on the dresser the night before.

The moment she unzipped the bag, the title *Skating-perfect* jumped out at her. She'd forgotten about the book she'd borrowed from Mikhail. She slipped it out and set it carelessly on the edge of the desk. It fell to the floor, spine first. The white piece of paper that had marked his place fluttered away and landed on her foot.

Natalie retrieved the paper, then stared in amazement at the dark scratchings on it. Someone had hand-printed a message in Russian. The Cyrillic characters were tiny and cramped, all running together, barely recognizable. She remembered seeing some notes Mikhail had penciled in the margins of the book, the style neat, the letters flowing. She flipped to the first few pages and compared the notations he'd made in Russian with the message on the piece of paper. The latter had definitely been printed by a different hand.

How odd. Mikhail hadn't mentioned being in contact with another Russian since he'd arrived in Wilmington. Then again, she was sure there were many things he hadn't told her. She'd confront him with the note when she saw him, and if he feigned ignorance, she'd tell him where she found it and demand to know who it was from and what message it contained. She'd threaten him with a repeat performance of last night's tortures unless he talked. Natalie laughed aloud, not really believing that threats, real or playful, would be necessary. Surely Mikhail could trust her as she trusted him, after what they'd shared.

The phone interrupted her musings. Her smile broadened. Perhaps that was her Misha now. With the mysterious piece of paper clutched in one hand, she almost dropped the receiver with the other in her eagerness to talk to him. "Hello?"

"Natalie, darling, you sound cheerful." Her mother's voice doused a little of her enthusiasm. "The date must have gone really well."

Suddenly it dawned on Natalie that her mother wasn't tucked snugly in bed. "C.L., where—"

"Still at the lab. Where else? We've made such progress in the coating formula that missing one night's sleep is a small price to pay."

"You didn't sleep at all? That means you haven't been home." And if her mother hadn't been in the study...

Natalie was distracted by thoughts of what a potential thief might have been after. Mikhail had been in the house while she'd been asleep, but she couldn't believe he'd searched the place. And for what? She wouldn't even consider what immediately came to mind.

Catherine's loud yawn announced her exhaustion. "No, I haven't been home. I distinctly remember leaving a note telling you that I wouldn't be."

"I only wondered if you might have changed your plans like you did the other night."

Mikhail hadn't even heard of Thwart before she'd told him about it, Natalie reminded herself. Or had he?

"Not this time," Catherine said with another yawn. "We worked straight through. I'm sure I'll make up for the loss of sleep tonight. I promise I'll be home by late afternoon. I'll tell you everything—if you plan to be around, that is."

"Yes, of course I will," Natalie said, injecting a forced enthusiasm into her voice as she stared at the note in her hand. The Cyrillic characters portended disillusionment for them both, but she didn't want to taint her mother's happiness just yet, not when Catherine had worked so hard to make this breakthrough. "Congratulations, Mother. I'm so happy for you, and I want to hear every detail."

And what was she going to do after she'd finished listening? Natalie wondered, suspicions building once more. Who knew what secrets the missive contained? Maybe she should turn the note over to some government official. Someone like Elliott Drucker. Natalie disliked the thought of sparring with the man again. And if she involved him, she was positive he would manage to implicate Mikhail in something underhanded. Perhaps she was being incredibly naive, but she couldn't believe her Russian lover would betray her.

"Oh, Natalie, I only wish your father were here to share this moment with me. I merely carried out the work we started together."

"I wish he were here, too," Natalie admitted. "Father would have been so proud."

And he would have been able to tell his only daughter the right thing to do with the note.

DAMN THE RIGHT THING! Damn the note! Damn Mikhail for doing this to her!

Natalie felt like snapping her pencil in two, but that wouldn't help translate the frustrating message any more than the Russian-English dictionary had been able to. She compared the two pieces of paper she'd set side by side on the table in the university library. Convinced that the way the tiny cramped letters ran together had prevented her from figuring out what they meant, she'd made a duplicate with the aid of the alphabet guide in the front of the dictionary. It had been a smart move. The copy was much easier to read.

So why couldn't she translate the damn thing?

At first she'd thought the lack of space breaks between characters was the reason. She'd spent three hours trying to determine where the breaks belonged, using every normal left-to-right combination possible. No luck. No matter where she tried to begin a word, the succeeding letter combinations hadn't come together properly. None of them made any sense.

She folded the original note and put it back into her purse, then stared at the duplicate as though it would give up its secrets. The task seemed impossible until the form of the message suddenly jumped out at her. She counted characters, and light began to dawn. They made a rectangular grid or matrix, with the same number of letters in each horizontal line. She had to face it. The message wasn't translatable because it was an encryption of some kind.

The note's mysterious contents had made her uneasy since she'd found it, more so after realizing someone had searched the house while she'd been sleeping. *Not Mikhail. Please, not Mikhail.* Her instincts couldn't be that wrong about him, could they?

The Russian couldn't have seduced her merely to get his hands on her mother's work on Thwart.

There, she'd allowed her mind to form the unacceptable thought, but she still believed that Mikhail was guilty of nothing more than wanting to be with her. Maybe one of the KGB agents had broken into the house and scoured the study. Of course, there had been no signs of a forced entry.

If only the message could give her some clue as to what was going on! That was why she'd been so determined to translate it herself. She'd wanted to prove Mikhail's innocence in her own mind as quickly as possible. Now she couldn't even do that, not without a lot more work. She would have to decipher the code first, and she knew that could prove to be impossible. Ciphers, codes and secret writings had been her form of entertainment when other girls had been playing with dolls or experimenting with makeup. The unusual interest had had something to do with her naturally analytical mind, which had been evident even as a child. But this was no ordinary game piece she held in her hand.

"A secret message, huh?"

Startled, Natalie jumped at the unexpected intrusion into her thoughts. "Jerry." Her co-worker was leaning over her shoulder, looking at the open Russian dictionary and the paper she'd instinctively turned over, face down. "I'm surprised to see you. I thought you took off right after your morning classes."

"Usually I do, but I had some personal research to take care of. I just happened to spot you when I was looking through the stacks over there." He nodded toward the paper under her hand. "So what is it? A love note from your current squeeze? He poured his heart out to you in Russian, and now you're trying to translate, right?"

"Yes," she lied.

"Well, don't look so thrilled."

Natalie forced a smile to her lips and met Jerry's eyes directly. "Translating an unfamiliar language is hard work." That was true, anyway. "Unlike you, I'm supposed to be on vacation, remember?"

"All right, hand it over and I'll save you the work."

"Uh, I can't," she said, stalling.

Jerry wouldn't be able to translate it either, and Natalie didn't want him asking too many questions. But before she could dissuade him, he reached over and slipped the paper out from under her hand. When he got a good look at it, his brow immediately furrowed.

"What in the world do you have here? These are Cyrillic characters, but I can't find a word I recognize. I think your friend's playing a joke on you. This isn't Russian."

"A joke." Natalie's voice was faint as she took back the duplicate note. Certainly not in the mood to laugh, she tried to cover her growing anxiety with another forced smile. "No wonder I was having such trouble."

"Trouble. The way you say that..." His expression intent, Jerry sat down next to her. "Natalie, is something wrong? I am your friend, you know."

"Thanks, but it's nothing I can't handle myself." She shoved the note into her purse and started to rise.

Jerry caught her arm. "I don't believe that. Talk to me."

"I can't, Jerry. I don't know what to tell you."

"The truth."

The truth. If only she knew what that was. "Listen, I've got to get home before my mother does. But thanks, anyway."

"The offer stands. If you need someone, call."

"I'll remember. Thanks."

As Natalie practically ran out of the library, she hoped she was only having a bad dream and that when she woke up she wouldn't need help from anyone.

LESS THAN AN HOUR LATER, the dream went from bad to nightmarish. The doorbell rang, and Natalie opened her front door expecting to see her exhausted and keyless mother standing on the porch. Instead she was treated to the sight of Elliott Drucker, looking every bit as intimidating as she'd remembered him. He didn't even flinch under her unwelcoming glare, but merely smirked at her through the screen door.

"Don't look so surprised, Natalie." He said her name as if he were making a social call. "I told you I'd be in touch. Can I come in?"

"What if I said no?"

"Then I'll stay right here. But you'll talk to me."

"Maybe I'll slam the door in your face."

His voice chilled her when he said with certainty, "You may be foolish, but you aren't stupid. You know that, one way or another, we have a few things to discuss. We can do it right here if you want." He glanced over his shoulder, and Natalie followed his gaze to the couple next door who were working on their lawn. "I don't care if the whole neighborhood knows what I have to say."

But Natalie did, and she knew he was counting on that. She opened the screen door and let him enter. She used closing the inner door as a stalling technique so she could get herself under control. After taking a deep breath, she followed him into the living room, her chin raised defiantly.

"What's on your mind, Drucker?" she demanded.

"The same thing as last time: Korolev. I want to give you another chance to save yourself and to do your country a service."

"I'm still not buying."

His dark eyes penetrated her defenses, making Natalie shift uncomfortably. To cover her awkwardness, she dropped down onto the couch. A mistake. She'd given Drucker the psychological advantage by letting him stand over her, thereby granting him control.

His expression contemptuous, he shook his head. "For a woman with a Ph.D., you're very naive."

"If you're going to attack me—"

"Save the indignation! I'm not impressed."

"I don't get the feeling you're impressed by much."

"You'd be surprised, Natalie." Drucker softened his voice as if he were her friend, but she wasn't deceived. "I'd be very impressed, for example, if you'd wake up and see the Russian for what he really is."

A surge of adrenaline almost made her jump off the couch. Natalie controlled herself, rising with as much grace as she could muster. The CIA agent couldn't possibly know anything about her suspicions. He couldn't know about the KGB following them last night. He couldn't know about the note. She'd brazen it out.

Trying to gain the advantage, she circled him so that he had to turn with her—just as he had done the last time.

"You don't know anything about Mikhail." She said it confidently, yet she felt as if the words had been squeezed out of her chest.

"And I suppose you do?" Drucker's thin lips drew into a feral smile. "Then, of course, you must know that he contacted the Soviet embassy."

"He what?" she choked out, unable to hide her shock. She stopped dead in her tracks.

"Surprised? But I thought you knew him so well."

It couldn't be true, Natalie thought wildly. In spite of the way her heart was pounding, she managed to assume a calm facade. "I don't believe you."

"You'd better, for your sake. And you'd better start wondering why, Natalie. Why the hell did that Russian son of a bitch contact the embassy when he supposedly has severed all ties with his country?" Drucker moved in on her, but Natalie held her ground. "And why is he trying to get close to you? What does he want? How do you fit into his plans?" He waited a significant beat before he ended with "And what happens to you when he gets what he wants?"

The questions had been coldly issued, all traces of the thin-lipped smile gone. Drucker was staring at her, waiting for her reaction, waiting to pounce. She wondered if he could read all the doubts and worries that had come crashing down on her just when she'd thought she and Mikhail had something special going for them. Drucker's questions made her sick inside.

But then she remembered Faith's call. Her friend believed that something was wrong with this whole investigation.

Drucker could be lying for his own purposes, Natalie told herself. He could be involved in something underhanded, as Faith had suggested; otherwise he would have followed procedure and worked with the FBI. She wished she could verbalize her thoughts, throw her suspicions of him and his motivations back in his face. But Natalie *wasn't* stupid. Letting Drucker know what she was thinking was a very dangerous idea.

She blinked once and licked her lips. "Why should I believe anything you have to say about Mikhail?"

"Nervous? You should be. You believe me already. I can see it in your eyes. They're very readable, Natalie. You ought to do something about that when you're with Korolev, or he'll start to suspect you don't trust him." Drucker paused effectively before adding, "And if the Russian thinks you're a threat . . ." He left the rest of the sentence dangling and Natalie's stomach ready to heave.

"He'd never hurt me," she insisted in a small voice, feeling vulnerable in spite of her determination not to let the CIA agent get to her.

"Is that what he told you?" Drucker was using his social-call tone again. She was supposed to believe he was concerned; someone she could turn to. "Yes, I can see it is. And why is that? Why would Korolev even mention your being hurt unless that possibility existed? Face it, Natalie, he's using you."

Visions of their lovemaking suddenly haunted her. "*No*."

"And you know why as well as I do."

She clenched her jaw as though that would stop the word from forming in her mind. Unfortunately, she heard it echoed off his lips.

"Thwart. That's what he wants from you."

"No." Although she'd come to that same conclusion, she shook her head in denial. "Mikhail didn't even know what Thwart was until . . ."

"Until?" Drucker's dark eyes narrowed. "You told him all about your mother's work, correct? And he was interested, wasn't he?"

"A passing interest. Nothing threatening."

"But you are threatened or you wouldn't be so defensive."

"No, that's not—"

"It *is* true. Korolev is using you to get to your mother. He's making a fool out of you, and you're not doing a thing to stop him."

Drucker was backing her into a corner again, making her suspicions grow and multiply. Natalie was desperate. If she didn't get him out of her home, she would have Mikhail convicted and hanged in her own mind before she learned the truth.

"You've said your piece. Now leave," she said softly but firmly.

Without taking his eyes from hers, Drucker pulled a cigar from an inner breast pocket with a casualness that made Natalie furious. He clipped the tip and let the tobacco fall to the floor. She wanted to scream, but she wouldn't give him the satisfaction. He lit the cigar and puffed so that the acrid smoke reached out to choke her. She wouldn't give him the satisfaction of doing that, either.

"Get out, Drucker," she repeated. "Now."

His smile made gooseflesh run up her spine. "Think about what I've said, Natalie, and if you decide there's any information you'd like to discuss with me, you can either reach me or leave a message for me at this number."

He held out a card. When she didn't take it, he put it down on the coffee table and headed for the door. Then he paused and turned around, shaking his head. For the first time, his eyes held an expression other than threat.

Pity.

For her.

Natalie stood frozen until he exited, leaving a trail of cigar smoke behind him. Then she ran to the door and slammed it shut. Emotions threatened to burst within her like an overloaded dam, to make her whimper and sink into the corner while praying for the nightmare to be over. She fought the overwhelming feeling of helplessness. She wasn't helpless, nor was she a woman who would sit back and allow herself to be deceived and used. Not by Drucker. Not by the man she loved.

She didn't know whether Mikhail had contacted the Soviet embassy, as the CIA agent had claimed, but she had a feeling she could find out if she set her mind to it. The enciphered message held the key to her trust.

All she had to do was figure out how to break the code.

SEVERAL HOURS LATER, Natalie stood at the open French doors that led from her bedroom to the deck outside. A breeze rustled the leaves of the old oak tree whose branches spilled over onto one side of the railing. The clear night sky was sprinkled with stars.

The rustling leaves seemed to whisper Mikhail's name, making her wonder where he was, what he was doing, whether or not he'd tried to call her. She'd purposely turned off the phones, not wanting to be in contact with him until hings had been settled in her own mind, which she hoped vould happen before this night was over. Drucker's visit and iccusations had stayed with her. She'd tried to sort things out but had come to no hard-and-fast conclusions. She could only judge the situation by her own instincts.

If Mikhail were guilty of collusion with the Soviets, it lidn't make sense that the KGB would have followed them he night before. Undoubtedly Drucker would say that the Soviet agents were either guarding Mikhail or helping him out on a show for her benefit.

Natalie believed neither supposition. Mikhail's fear had been as real as her own, but she knew he was keeping secrets from her. She was hoping the note would confirm that he was in desperate trouble. Then, when she could think of him as innocent of betraying her or her country, when she had rid herself of the lingering doubts, she'd force him to let her help. She'd see the man she loved through anything.

Natalie went back inside. On her desk lay *Skating-perfect*, along with the two notes. She slid the original in between the pages of the book, then shoved the duplicate into a spiral notebook into which she'd penciled several variations on a computer program.

Her nerves were strung taut as she waited for the house to grow quiet; the noisy old pipes told her that Catherine was still in the shower. Once she was sure her mother was sleeping, Natalie planned to sneak downstairs and use the computer without fear of discovery. That way, she could be more certain of her facts before telling Catherine anything.

Natalie threw herself across the bed, facedown, remembering how difficult it had been to remain "up" during the early part of the evening while toasting her mother's success and listening to the details of the scientific breakthrough. She'd done a dynamite acting job, though. If she had missed hearing or commenting on a detail or two, Catherine Lundgren hadn't seemed to notice.

Now Natalie was anxious to carry through the plan she'd formulated after Drucker had left. She'd run out to a bookstore and had bought the most comprehensive Russian-English dictionary she could find. Then, before her mother had come home, she'd had a couple of hours to formulate a computer program that would help her to decipher the message.

The terminal in the study was linked to Aircon's powerful Cray mainframe computer because of her mother's work on Thwart. Using it to help her break the code would enable Natalie to accomplish her task in a fraction of the time it would take by strictly human means. She only prayed she had the knowledge and the patience to find the right method, or methods, of deciphering this particular message. The distant, muffled whine of a hair dryer made Natalie wish her mother would hurry up and go to bed so she could get started. Distracted by the noise below, she almost didn't hear the one outside the French doors.

At first she thought the oak tree was making the deck protest, but as she listened more intently, Natalie soon realized the sound was unfamiliar, human somehow. Shoes scraping against the wood for a foothold! Fear pushed her off the bed and toward the doors to close them against an intruder. Too late. A dark figure was stalking the opening.

"Natasha!" came a whisper.

The blood drained out of her in an instant. Mikhail. She couldn't face him; she couldn't avoid it. He was there, in the doorway, his eyes soft and admiring. His arms snaked around her as though he expected her welcoming embrace.

Panicked by his touch, Natalie pushed at his chest and backed away, out of his grasp. Her heart lurched painfully. She wasn't immune to the man, but she couldn't just walk back into his arms until she knew the truth.

"What are you doing sneaking around?" she whispered loudly, her voice competing with the pounding of her heart.

She could see her plans for the night dissolving. "How did you get up here?"

"I used the tree. I did not want to be seen." His brow furrowed when she continued to look at him steadily, saying nothing. "Natasha, I missed you."

She said the first thing that came to her. "Why did you leave without waking me this morning.?"

"Is that why you are so stiff?" he murmured, stepping closer. Not wanting Mikhail to know she was suspicious of him, she stayed put and allowed him to cup her cheek. "I had business to take care of," he said.

KGB business? "What kind of business?" she heard herself ask. She tried not to shiver at his touch.

"I was at the skating club most of the day."

Now his palm was around her neck, his fingertips rubbing the muscles in back. She felt the tenseness leave her in a rush of warmth. "I wondered if you'd gone there," she said softly.

His thumb pressed the tender flesh inside the V made by her collarbone, and she realized he could cut off her air in a second. She wondered if his hand could detect her sudden stab of anxiety.

"Where have you been, Natasha?"

His eyes were filled with such concern. Surely the emotion was real. Surely he'd never hurt her, just as he'd told her. Yet why had he felt it necessary to make that promise? But that was Drucker talking in her head. She shook the agent's image away and concentrated on the one in front of her.

"I have tried to call you many times this day," Mikhail continued, "but no one answered. I feared there was trouble. After last night, I didn't know what to do. I was planning to wait on the deck outside until you returned. And if you did not return . . ." His forehead creased with renewed concern.

"But now that you're here, I'm afraid you'll have to go," she stated firmly.

"I could not stay away."

She heard the implied *although I tried* in his husky tone. The hand behind her neck brought her head inexorably closer, and her body followed, touching his, torturing her. His lips trailed along her forehead, seducing her thoughts, making her want to throw her arms around his neck and tell him everything: her fears, her doubts, the note, Drucker— everything. But she couldn't.

When he slid a hand under the T-shirt and found her unbound breast, she gasped, "My mother is home."

His lips teased her earlobe. "You do not want to be with me?" he said, barely loud enough for her to hear. "We will be quiet."

Yes, she wanted to be with him, more than anything. "No, you've got to go" was what she said.

"How can I leave you, my heart?" he whispered into her hair.

At those gentle words, Natalie closed her eyes and tried to steel her emotions. She searched quickly for an excuse, something not so easily found, with his hands and mouth freely exploring. Her nipple burned where he'd caught it between two fingers. *She* burned, down to the tender flesh that still felt the imprint of his lovemaking from the night before. He was ready to take her now; the proof was pressing against her belly. She felt his need, as terrible as her own, but she couldn't fulfill it. Not until she knew for sure.

"I'd be horribly embarrassed if Mother…suspected. You must leave." The words were probably the most difficult she'd ever had to utter, and before he could suggest going somewhere else, she added, "And I'm very tired. You didn't allow me to get much sleep last night."

He raised his head, and his lips spread into a broad grin that was reflected in his eyes. "I slept even less."

"Because of us? Or the KGB?"

The smile faded. "I have not yet contacted the men who followed us last night."

Why had he been so careful about coming to see her tonight—even climbing a tree in the dark—if he'd *wanted* to contact the KGB men? Or was this some kind of ruse to throw her off guard? Had Mikhail realized that she'd discovered the secret message he'd left in the book?

Natalie thought of asking him about it directly, then changed her mind when she noticed the sudden caution shadowing his eyes and felt his body tense up. On the very real chance that Drucker had been right—that Mikhail had defected merely to get the secret to Thwart and that she would be in danger if he felt threatened by her—she decided to play it safe.

Her way.

"Last night was special," she said truthfully, although her intent was to get his mind back on something more personal than the intrigue surrounding them. "I'll never forget it."

He wrapped his arms around her so tightly that she could hardly breathe. He whispered something in Russian that sounded like a caress. Like love words. Natalie felt a stinging sensation against the back of her eyelids. A lump the size of the Alps seemed to be caught in her throat. She wanted to stay in Mikhail's arms forever, to forget the outside world, Drucker's accusations and her own suspicions.

She wanted to be free of the nightmare.

When Mikhail found her mouth, Natalie didn't hold back this time. She kissed him with all the passion and love she felt—a love free of politics. She put her arms around his neck and held him to her for all she was worth. Even with desire making her heart hammer wildly, a part of her feared that this might be her last opportunity.

As their lips and their bodies parted, she begged. "Hold me for a moment longer, Misha."

He crushed her to him more tightly, forcing her to acknowledge his own uneven heartbeat. His chest heaved against her breasts. Whatever he might be up to, whatever he felt for her, his body couldn't deny her. At least she had that to cling to. It wasn't all she wanted, but it was something.

Mikhail put his hands on her shoulders and pushed her slightly away from him. "I am only human, my Natasha. I cannot take much more of this without doing something about it. If I must go, then it must be now."

She nodded and made an effort to steady her breath as she pulled free completely and turned her back to him. It took her a second to focus and to realize she was staring at the desk. At the book with the message that would either damn Mikhail or prove him innocent.

So great was her need to know the truth that she couldn't conceive of its doing neither.

Hearing softly retreating footfalls, she whipped around. He was halfway to the French doors. "Mikhail, wait." She was going to test him. Her pulse reverberated in her ears. "You forgot something this morning." She approached the desk and with stiff fingers picked up the book. The note was in there; he would know that. How would he react? "Your skating text," she said, holding it out to him.

His shrug seemed innocent of knowledge. "You have finished with it?"

"I've got everything I need from it," she said in a small, scared voice.

Mikhail gave her a quizzical look as he took the book from her outstretched hand, but he appeared to place no importance on its retrieval. He didn't even give it a second glance, and the hand holding it fell to his side. "I will call tomorrow. You will be home?"

"I'll be here."

But what she'd have to say to him was another matter. Still, he'd passed the test. Natalie took a steadying breath. He hadn't seemed overly concerned about the book. That was good. Maybe that boded well.

Mikhail motioned to the French doors. "When I go, you will lock these."

Again, it was an order rather than a request. Again, Natalie didn't protest. She watched him cross the deck and clamber over its side and onto the tree easily, then waited until he was out of sight before closing and locking the doors. Only then did it occur to her that he could have gone down the stairs and out the front door.

All was quiet in the house. Catherine must be asleep. Motivated by anxiety, Natalie picked up her spiral notebook and headed for the study, eager to find out once and for all whether or not she'd been a fool.

Chapter Nine

Mikhail absorbed the shock of the six-foot drop from the oak tree with bent knees. His right leg twinged a little as he landed, reminding him of the way he'd met Natalie. Thinking about his Natasha, he rapidly headed for the front of the house, planning on walking all the way home. The exercise would make him tired enough to sleep, to forget about holding her in his arms.

Damn! He was exhausted now, but he wouldn't forget and probably wouldn't sleep any more than he had the night before. He shouldn't have come here tonight. He shouldn't have involved Natalie. He shouldn't have fallen in love.

So many negatives.

So much truth.

Mikhail shoved his hands into his pockets, gearing himself up for the lonely night ahead. No matter how he tried, he couldn't stay away from Natalie, yet he couldn't bear the thought of her looking at him with hate in her round blue eyes that were as beautiful as the Moscow River in summer. He'd seen her love for him in those eyes, even if she hadn't spoken the words. Knowing that had warmed his heart and tortured his soul.

He'd given up everything he'd ever known or loved for what seemed more and more like a lost cause, and in the end she'd be added to the agonizing list. The burden was too heavy for one man to carry alone. What the hell was he going to do?

"So, comrade, what will you do now?" The echoed thought in Russian came from the rear of the dark blue sedan sitting at the curb. "Hitch a ride to your flat, as you did to get here?"

Mikhail stopped short, feeling incredibly stupid. He'd spent the entire day trying to avoid the KGB agent, while Yuri Simansky had probably known his every movement. The rear door of the auto swung open in command. Mikhail knew there was no point in resisting. He didn't have the energy to run. He crossed to the sedan and slid in, letting his tired body rest against the back of the seat. No sooner had he closed the door than the driver pulled the automobile away from the curb.

"I'm glad to see you are in a more agreeable mood than you were yesterday," Simansky began in a conversational tone. "What was the point of all that drama you went through in order to lose us last night?"

Mikhail answered the question with one of his own. "What was the point of following?"

"I wanted to be sure you understood that my demands were serious, Korolev. I didn't want you to imagine we were bluffing about the woman."

"You didn't have to prove that to me. I know your methods." Mikhail stared at what he could see of the innocuous, bland face disguising a sly, cruel mind. "I believed you, Simansky. All you accomplished was to make her aware of you and to raise her suspicions."

"Then I succeeded, didn't I? Tell me, comrade, what side benefits did you receive last night?" Simansky laughed, the lewd sound echoing through the car, the skin around his pig eyes wrinkling. "Did Natalie Lundgren turn to you for comfort? A man could lose himself in a healthy-looking woman like her. Perhaps you ought to be thanking me."

Mikhail controlled himself. He wouldn't give Simansky the satisfaction of a reaction. He wanted to wrap his fingers around the man's thick neck and squeeze the air out of it until there was no more laughter, but he'd never get the chance. The two agents in the front seat would shoot him dead if he tried.

"So that's how it is. You are serious about the woman. That is good. All the better for me. I know I'll get what I want, because you want to protect her, don't you?"

The agent continued baiting him, trying to force a response he could feed on. Mikhail purposely stared out the window. He vaguely realized they were heading in the general direction of his apartment.

"I want a report on your progress," Simansky demanded. "Now, comrade, before I lose my good temper."

Mikhail could see the Lundgren study in his mind, and as he had done the night before, he felt an overwhelming sense of responsibility to two of the people he loved. "There is no progress. I am not able to give you Thwart. But I can give you the computer board—"

Simansky's growled curse cut Mikhail off. "Don't try my patience. Aleksei Rodzianko is too valuable to be traded off so lightly. And, I imagine, so is your new woman."

"If I could manage to do as you ask—and don't take this to mean that I can—she wouldn't be my woman after she had figured things out," Mikhail said casually, as though that would be the deciding factor. "She'd despise me."

"But she'd be alive, comrade. She'd be alive."

Mikhail grew cold inside. He should have been prepared for the lengths to which the KGB would go. He didn't protest. What good would it do? He knew Simansky could commit murder and get away with it. There were any number of accidents that could be arranged without arousing suspicion, and he wouldn't put it past the bastard to kill Natalie if he was made to look the fool a second time.

Obviously tiring of the game, Simansky lost his friendly tone. "You have until midday on Friday to get me what I want, Korolev. Today's newspapers announced the Lundgren woman's mother has made a breakthrough in the coating formula. I want it. And if I don't get it, I personally guarantee that Rodzianko will be sent to Dolgoryusk."

Mikhail swallowed hard at the mention of the infamous gulag, located in the tundra region of Siberia. Quick deaths at that particular forced labor camp were not unusual.

"Ivan, pull over!" Simansky ordered the driver. The auto came to a sudden stop. "Get out and walk the rest of the way," he told Mikhail. "The fresh air will clear your mind. Perhaps you'll see a way to help your friends. Remember, you have until noon on Friday."

Mikhail had barely stepped to the ground before Simansky slammed the door shut and the auto shot off into the night.

He walked along the street, his legs automatically taking him to the building he now called home. Plans formed and as quickly dissolved in his fevered mind. He could tell Natalie the truth and convince her to run away with him, but Simansky would track them down, no matter how long it took. And their disappearance would not help Aleksei at all.

Mikhail remembered the last time he'd seen his friend. It had been a month ago in a Moscow prison. He'd bribed the guards to let him speak with Aleksei alone. What he'd seen had shocked him. Aleksei had been haggard and filthy, with a purple bruise on his forehead and another on his neck.

"What can I do, Sasha?" Mikhail had asked. "How can I help?"

Aleksei had turned to him, his blue-gray eyes devoid of hope. "Nothing, Misha, nothing. Not here. Not in Russia. My fate is sealed."

"Not in Russia." The words had stayed with Mikhail throughout their frustrating conversation. Aleksei had given

up; there was no fight left in him. Mikhail was already mourning the loss of his friend, for even if Aleksei were granted mercy—transfer to one of the less severe camps or a shortened sentence—he might never be the same man he'd once been. Gulags were known for changing people.

"If only we had a bargaining tool," Mikhail had whispered. "Perhaps we could negotiate."

"Misha, no. Don't say such a thing. You couldn't try that here. They'd throw you in prison. But if you were on the outside..."

Defect. The word had hung between them unspoken, for the very walls had ears. How many times Mikhail had discussed this possibility with Aleksei in the past. But never before had he had such a good reason to go through with it. Aleksei's eyes had come to life once more. Hope, no matter how farfetched, had reached him, if only for that moment. Mikhail hadn't wanted to see that emotion die.

"Why not?" he'd whispered. "I have the opportunity. In two weeks I'll be in Chamonix. I could do it there."

"Then what? You have no bargaining tool."

"I'll get one."

"Where? From who?"

"I don't know, Sasha. If ever your underground political connections could serve you, it is now. Think. What have you heard? What are the rumors?"

Shaking his head, Aleksei had seemed to retreat within himself again. The hopeful expression in his eyes had faded. And then his lips had formed a single word: "Thwart."

This was the first time Mikhail had heard the strange-sounding name. "What is it?"

"A new American military project that the Soviet government wants," Aleksei had whispered directly into his ear. "A couple of my friends were talking about it. I didn't listen closely. I think it's some kind of a jet plane."

A military secret! Mikhail hadn't known how he'd be able to get access to such a thing, but he'd promised to see what he could do if he were successful in evading his KGB guards in Chamonix. He already had several American contacts because of his participation in government-sponsored athletic exchanges. The concept had been vague, but it had given Aleksei something tangible to hold on to.

Nevertheless, the idea of espionage had bothered Mikhail right from the start, so he'd come up with a plan that he considered simple and safe: trading the computer board for Aleksei.

Now it was time he faced facts. He'd been fooling himself all along. Nothing had gone right since he'd eluded his guards at Chamonix. All he'd accomplished was to endanger another person, his innocent Natasha. And he couldn't stall Simansky any longer. He had to take positive steps toward resolving the crisis.

But how?

One name came to mind. There was one person who could help him save Natalie, and maybe Aleksei as well. Mikhail knew he would have to pay a price—undoubtedly his own freedom, but here, not in Russia. He was ready to pay it, whatever the cost to himself.

With a sense of relief, he decided to call Elliott Drucker and tell him the whole truth.

"HEY, SLEEPYHEAD, I wanted you to know I'm heading back for the lab."

Catherine's voice chased away the sleep Natalie had finally found. Groaning, she rolled over and squinted at her mother. "What time is it?"

"A little after eight. I just woke up a half hour ago myself, so I'm in a rush."

Natalie sat up, barely able to open her eyes fully in the well-lit room. She'd forgotten to draw the blinds before falling into bed a few hours earlier. From what she could tell, her mother looked full of vim and vigor. At least one of them was well rested.

"Do you think you'll be home tonight?"

"I know I won't be." Catherine leaned over and kissed her cheek. Then she placed a palm on Natalie's forehead. "Are you feeling all right? Your eyes are bloodshot and you're very pale."

"C.L., don't start coming on like an all-American mom, all right?" Natalie complained, ducking her head. "I'm fine. Go to work."

"If you're sure . . ."

"Positive. I just stayed up reading too late, so I'm a little tired."

"A couple more hours of sleep couldn't hurt," Catherine said, already on her way out the door.

Natalie had gotten to bed just before dawn, after a long and fruitless night at the computer terminal. Although she'd entered her program and spent hours manipulating the message into giving up its secrets, Natalie had finally realized that the task was nearly impossible. The biggest hurdle was her unfamiliarity with Russian. Having to look up combination after combination in the dictionary she'd purchased had been time-consuming and frustrating. She would have to ask someone for help, someone who knew the language well.

Natalie remembered Jerry Lubin's offer. But it was after eight now, and he'd already be in class. She had a few more hours before she could reach him, so she might as well spend them sleeping.

No sooner had she closed her eyes than the telephone rang. Sticking out a hand, she patted the floor in search of the instrument, then pulled the receiver under the covers. "Hello."

"Hi. Is that you, Nat?"

"Faith!" Natalie sat straight up in bed. "It's Wednesday! Good heavens, I've lost track of the days." The background noises on the line sounded like those in a hotel lobby. "Where are you?"

"Actually, I'm still in Washington. I've got a session with several other members of the State Department that'll probably last until noon. I'll leave for our get-together right after it breaks up."

Natalie's head was clearing, telling her that meeting Faith might not be such a good idea until she had something to report. "Maybe we could see each other tomorrow and—"

"Today!" came Faith's urgent reply. "It has to be today."

"Why? What's so important about today? Why not tell me over the phone?"

"I don't think that's the best way to handle this. You remember those friends of mine?" Faith lowered her voice. "Well, they came through as I'd hoped." She paused a second, then said, "Uh, they told me all about this intense new guy who's been showing a lot of interest, if you know what I mean."

Faith's light, teasing tone gave Natalie a queer feeling in the pit of her stomach. *Drucker.* Faith was talking about the feelers she'd put out on him through her contacts. It was obvious that she was reluctant to say anything specific over the telephone and that Natalie would get nothing more from her until they met.

"So," she said, naturally following her friend's lead, "this can't wait, huh?"

"Not really."

"All right. What time and where?"

Faith's sigh of relief was audible. "Our usual place for tea, say at three-thirty?"

"See you then."

Natalie hung up, mentally translating "usual" into Wilmington's Hotel duPont, since it was the only place they'd ever had tea together, and a couple of years ago at that.

Three-thirty. Almost seven hours to wait.

MIKHAIL'S HAND WAS SHAKING as he punched out the numbers he'd been given by the Virginia directory-assistance operator. He could be making the biggest mistake of his life. Each ring at the other end increased his worry, until he almost hung up and left the gas-station phone booth.

A click, followed by a female voice, told him it was too late. "Central Intelligence Agency. How can I help you?"

"I would speak to one of your agents. Elliott Drucker."

"One moment, please."

His eyes roaming the street for anything suspicious, Mikhail ordered himself to relax when he caught nothing out of the ordinary, not even a dark blue sedan. Where the hell was Simansky, anyway? The KGB agents hadn't been around when he'd left his apartment. And where was Drucker? It seemed more like a lifetime than a moment before the connection was live once more.

"Agent Paul Howe speaking."

"Excuse me, but I asked for Elliott Drucker."

"I'm afraid speaking to him won't be possible. But I can help you if you'll begin by giving me your name."

"I need Drucker!" Mikhail almost shouted. "I am sorry. Please."

There was silence at the other end, then a mumbled "Hang on a second."

The man didn't put him on hold; it sounded as though he'd covered the receiver to speak to someone else in the room. Mikhail strained to hear but could only make out low, muffled voices. Then Howe spoke directly to Mikhail. "Agent Drucker is not available at this time."

"When?" Mikhail asked frantically. He couldn't believe he was going to have to do this all over again. "When should I call back?"

"I'm afraid I don't have that information, but perhaps you'll let me—"

Mikhail hung up before the man had finished talking. So Drucker was not available. Now what was he going to do?

THE DARK BLUE SEDAN was following her again. Natalie sensed this before she looked in the rearview mirror and actually saw it. Her skin crawled at the implied threat it represented, and she had to tamp down the now-familiar feeling of panic that made her want to accelerate. She'd have a better chance of getting away from the KGB agents later if they didn't know she was aware of their surveillance. And she *had* to get away from them so Faith wouldn't become more involved in this mess. Her friend had seemed very nervous during their odd conversation that morning.

A glance at her watch told Natalie that it was three o'clock. She had a half hour to park, lose her Soviet guard and make it to the Hotel duPont. Since she'd already entered the downtown Wilmington area, she figured she had plenty of time. She swung the Chevy north on Orange Street, heading for a parking garage.

At least one thing was going right. Before leaving the house, she'd called Jerry Lubin. He'd readily agreed to help her with the message that evening and had sworn to tell no one about it. She was sure she could trust him to keep his word. Since Catherine was staying at the lab that night, they'd have a clear field with the computer.

A glance in the rearview mirror told her the sedan was still with her. She circled the garage at Ninth and Shipley, but it didn't follow her inside. All the better. If there was only one man in the car, perhaps he'd be reluctant to leave it. Or perhaps it would do a disappearing act.

No such luck. When she came out a few moments later, the sedan sat several yards away, its engine running. Her own pulse racing, Natalie gripped her small shoulder bag and kept her eyes on the buildings across the street, not daring to look toward the Hotel duPont, which was a block to her left. Nevertheless, she was aware of the sedan's front passenger door opening. Her stomach did a crazy dip. She crossed the street and headed for the pedestrian-only Market Street Mall, a half-block away. She could try to lose the agent by darting in and out of the shops, but she'd probably be wasting her time. Maybe she could find a rear exit....

The answer lay directly ahead, causing an adrenaline rush at the thought of her successfully eluding a KGB man. The Grand, a four-story opera house designed in the classic revival style of the Second Empire, offered the use of its parlors for business meetings and catered events. Something was going on at this very moment. The glass doors were open and people were milling about. Surely she could become invisible among them.

Aware of the footsteps catching up to her, Natalie stared into the display window of a storefront on her right. The man shadowing her turned the corner and strolled by. She got a quick glimpse of his reflection. The KGB agent didn't look very threatening, even if her heart was pounding furiously. He could blend in almost anywhere in the suit he was wearing. The color was a quiet gray, the antithesis of her own clear-red dress. Dark-haired and clean-shaven, he seemed to have no distinguishing features. She assumed this image was what made him a successful agent.

When he'd gotten as far from her as he was about to go—only two storefronts away—she pretended to lose interest in the window display and moved quickly toward the opera house, ears attuned to the sounds behind her. It wasn't long before she heard the slap of leather against the bricked-in walkway. Swerving around a small group of people who had just exited, she darted into the building. Luckily, she knew it well from the days when a college friend had worked here as part of the stage crew.

Natalie headed straight for the theater section, praying it wasn't locked. The doors were open. She stole a fast look behind and saw the KGB agent trying to get through the crowd. Hoping he hadn't spotted her, she literally ran up the center aisle of the empty, darkened theater, for once unmindful of the splendor surrounding her. She had to get out of the building before he realized where she was.

No sooner had she arrived backstage than she heard the theater doors opening. Damn! Standing on tiptoe so the clack of her heels wouldn't give her away, she slipped behind a set piece and gripped her purse with stiff fingers. She strained to listen but couldn't locate him until his leather soles hit the wooden stage. She took shallow breaths, her chest squeezing painfully. What would he do if he found her?

The theater doors opened again. "Hey, Mike, I thought I saw you come in here. What's up?"

"I'm exploring," a very American-sounding man answered, making Natalie sag with relief and let go of her tight grip on the shoulder bag.

"This place is something."

Leather soles whispered away from her as the man left the stage and headed toward his friend. "Look up there—a frescoed ceiling!"

Tourists! Natalie didn't wait to hear any more. She headed straight for a rear exit she had used many times in the past. The sunlight outside was welcoming. Rather than waste time congratulating herself, she took a roundabout route to the hotel that she hoped would guarantee her safe arrival. Even so, her eyes constantly roamed in every direction. By the time she'd passed the statue on horseback in

Rodney Square, she was positive no one was following her. A few minutes later, she faced the elegant old structure housing the Hotel duPont. She'd come almost full circle from the garage where she'd parked the car.

Today Natalie had no appreciation for the hand-carved paneling, antique furnishings or original artwork on the walls. She immediately sought out Faith Osborne. The blond woman was sitting in the Lobby Lounge, a tea service for one on the glass table in front of her. She was raising a cup to her lips when she spotted Natalie. Her small hand shook as if the fine piece of china had suddenly become too heavy, and she put it back on the saucer.

"Nat, thank heavens!"

Natalie dropped into the gold easy chair next to her. She placed her purse near the fresh flower arrangement on the table and took a deep, relieved breath. "I'm not late, am I?"

"A minute or two. It's just that I thought..." Faith's voice trailed off and she licked her lips. Her golden brown eyes were wide as she admitted, "Oh, hell, I'm afraid!"

It was Natalie's turn to widen her eyes. Faith *never* swore. "Afraid of what? Or should I say of whom? Drucker?"

"Partly."

Faith's narrow shoulders heaved once, and then she regained control of herself. She picked up her cup again, her fingers as white as the porcelain in her hand. Sipping at the tea seemed to calm her.

Before Natalie could demand a full explanation, the waitress arrived with another tea service and asked if she'd like a selection of finger sandwiches, scones with jam or an assortment of miniature pastries. Because she hadn't had anything to eat since dinner the night before, Natalie asked for some of each. The few minutes it took for the waitress to accommodate her and to leave her alone with Faith seemed interminable.

Faith spoke first. "Has anything unusual happened since I talked to you last?"

Definitely. Natalie had fallen in love—a very unusual state for the rational, analytical person she prided herself on being. She cut a scone in half and spread strawberry jam on it, saying only, "KGB agents have been following me off and on for days."

Sputtering, Faith almost doused herself with tea. "KGB? H-how do you know?"

"They're not exactly subtle." Natalie bit into the scone and chewed as she thought about this for a moment. "Though I guess the dark blue sedan was meant to blend into the crowd just like the gray suit."

"What gray suit?"

"The one worn by the agent who was following me a few minutes ago."

Faith's frightened eyes darted around the lobby. "Oh, Lord, Nat!"

"Don't worry, I lost him. I didn't want to involve you any more than I had to."

Silky blond hair curtained Faith's expression when she ducked her head. "It was I who involved *you* in this situation," she said, her voice low and filled with misery. "I never should have asked you to come to France."

"Stop it!" Natalie whispered, reaching out to touch the other woman's arm. It was just like Faith to take the blame for something over which she had no control. "What are good friends for, anyway, if not to provide comfort and support where and when needed? It wasn't your fault that Mikhail had that accident on the mountain and that Peter Baum came looking for help. Besides, if we hadn't been there, I would never have met Mikhail."

Her eyes stricken, Faith said softly, "Nat, please tell me you're not so involved with the Russian that you can't pull back."

Memories of her night with Mikhail flooded through Natalie. The physical sensations had dissipated, but the emotional ones lingered and seemed to grow stronger with each passing hour. She wished she could tell Faith everything and let her reciprocate in the comfort department, but she couldn't. She wouldn't tell anyone about the secret message until she and Jerry had cracked the code. She wouldn't implicate Mikhail without reason.

"I'm sorry, Faith, but I can't reassure you. Mikhail and I have grown very...close."

"Oh, Nat. That's what I was afraid of."

"'Afraid.' That word's becoming big in your vocabulary. Why?"

"Because of Drucker. You haven't agreed to work with him, have you?" When Natalie shook her head, Faith shuddered before adding, "Thank God. That man's dangerous. I told you I thought something wasn't right. Well, it's a good thing I checked on the bast—on him."

"What did you find out?"

"Only that he's considered a renegade agent by his own department because of his unorthodox methods."

"I think we could have figured out that much," Natalie said dryly, although she wasn't so sure that Drucker operated much differently from any other government agent.

"But what we didn't know was that he was suspended right after he handled Korolev's defection." Faith picked up her teacup but was unable to stop it from dancing on its saucer. "As a matter of fact, Drucker was threatened with dismissal if he didn't make an effort to conform to agency policy once he was allowed to come back to work." She took a shaky sip of tea. "And then, to top it off, there's been speculation about his loyalty. Since the suspension, he's made contact with the Soviets without sanction from his superiors."

"He's contacted the Soviets?" Exactly what he'd accused Mikhail of doing, Natalie reflected.

"Nat, I've thought and thought, but I can't figure his angle." Faith was staring into her teacup as though it could provide her with answers.

"Neither can I, Faith," Natalie said slowly while her brain raced ahead.

Drucker had been suspended from the CIA, yet he'd tried to intimidate her into helping him by blackening Mikhail's character. But he'd never explained *how*, exactly. What if he was in on some kind of payoff and wanted to use her to get Thwart for the Soviets? A chill shot through her. There was no black or white anymore, only confusing shades of gray in this dangerous game. It was too much for her to sort out without further data.

The message. So much depended on its contents. But now she was more hopeful than ever that it would clear Mikhail in her own mind.

And if it did . . . then what?

THE PASSENGER DOOR of the sedan opened, and the young agent slid in.

"Well?" Simansky demanded from the rear seat.

"I lost her in the opera house."

"You made sure she was aware that you followed her?"

Gregor nodded without looking around. "She knew."

"Good. Ivan, get us out of here. My stomach is growling with hunger."

And after he ate, he'd telephone his contact and discuss strategy. Satisfied that his carefully laid plans were about to bear fruit, Simansky smiled. It wouldn't be much longer before he would succeed, not only in obtaining the secret to Thwart but also in giving those who thought of defecting and those who would help the traitors a lesson they wouldn't forget.

Mikhail Illyovich Korolev was about to trap himself and Natalie Lundgren in a death spiral from which there would be no recovery.

Chapter Ten

"This is getting us nowhere, and not very quickly at that," Jerry muttered as Natalie made some minor changes to her computer program. After spending hours trying to decipher the message, they were both tense. "We can do this all night and come up with nothing if I have to scan the screen without any kind of reference."

"Can't you pick a common word like *the* or *you*?"

"I've already tried that, but they're too short and nonspecific. I need something longer that we can make part of the program. Then we can let the computer find it. I need a name."

Natalie grimaced and tried to concentrate on what she was doing. Jerry's questioning eyes seemed to be boring into her. Although she was growing more uncomfortable by the minute, she didn't answer him.

"Natalie, don't you think it's time to be honest with me?" he asked.

Her fingers froze on the keyboard, and she tried to work up some honest indignation. "I haven't lied to you."

"But you haven't told me the whole truth, either."

He continued to stare at her until she turned away from the terminal and faced him directly. She swallowed hard. "Thwart," she finally said, not wanting to admit it, even to herself. "Look for Thwart."

"Hell! Your mother's coating formula!" His eyes narrowed, and he drew his lips into a tight line. "Natalie, why didn't you tell me what was involved here?"

"Because I'm hoping it's not. I'm hoping it's a bad guess."

"You're that hung up on Korolev, huh?"

She nodded. "I'm afraid so." It was only fair that she tell Jerry everything that had happened in the past few days. After all, until they had broken the code, she had no idea what she might be involving him in. "I copied this from a message I found in a book Mikhail had on skating techniques. The original wasn't written by him."

Jerry's brow furrowed. "Wait a minute. This sounds innocent enough. It could have been a note from a friend. What made you try to translate it in the first place?"

"Because the KGB followed us the night before I found it."

The string of curses that echoed through the study made Natalie's ears burn. If they'd been directed at her, she couldn't have blamed Jerry.

"Natalie, is there anything else you aren't telling me?"

"A renegade CIA agent has been after me to spy on Mikhail. Today I learned he'd been suspended even before he came to see me the first time. And that's it. That's all I really know. Jerry, I wouldn't have involved you if I could have done this myself. Please believe me. I'm afraid, not only for myself but for Mikhail, too. I think he's in desperate trouble and I want to help him. But I have to be sure."

"Then let's get cracking—although I don't know why I want to give the Russian the upper hand with you," Jerry muttered. "He's done well enough on his own."

Remembering all the times Jerry had asked her out, Natalie thought his cooperation was generous. "Jerry, thanks for being a friend. I appreciate your help...and your discretion."

"Sure." He dropped his gaze to his notebook and penciled in some characters. " 'Thwart' won't have a translation unless they're using some kind of code word for it. If so, you can forget about finding it. Let's assume they're using a phonetic equivalent. That's a tough one, because the *th* sound isn't directly transcribable by using the Cyrillic alphabet. The pronunciation would be different. Something like 'Too-art,' but a single syllable beginning with a soft *t* sound. They might write it out like any one of these."

He flipped the notebook around so Natalie could see the variations he'd printed:

ТЮАРТ ТЮЁРТ ТУАРТ

Natalie nodded. "All right, I'll add a search-and-find to the program, asking the computer to look for all three of these, regardless of spacing."

She made the necessary modifications as quickly as possible, slowing down only when working with the Cyrillic characters. How lucky she was that her mother had access to a computer programmed to work with various foreign languages and alphabets.

Two hours later, she wasn't feeling quite so fortunate. She'd begun with simple letter substitutions and transpositions and had worked up to building more complex matrixes for polyalphabetic ciphers. The computer had literally searched through hundreds of combinations. So far, nothing.

"I'm afraid we're never going to do it," Natalie said wearily. It was well after midnight, and she didn't know how much longer she could last. She got up and stretched her back muscles. "My body is collapsing from sitting in one position and my eyes are starting to defocus from staring at this screen."

"Does that mean we give up?" Jerry asked, leaning back in his chair.

"Do you want to?"

He studied her face, which she tried to school into an expression of acceptance. "It's obvious *you* don't, so *we* won't," he said. "I think it's time we faced the fact that this isn't a simple one-step cipher we've run into. We'd better start trying combinations."

"That makes sense," Natalie agreed, taking her place in front of the terminal. "The Soviets probably used a two-step method involving both letter substitution and a twisted path."

They began again, revising the program to check for a multilayered ciphering system. Natalie only prayed that the message hadn't been coded by more than two levels. She didn't plan to search further. She'd already wasted a whole day. In the morning she'd turn the whole thing over to government experts, but she wasn't sure if she'd do it before or after she faced Mikhail and pleaded with him for the truth.

"That's it!" Jerry yelled, jumping up and leaning toward the terminal as the computer stopped searching. "We found it!"

Natalie blinked and stared at the monitor and at the Cyrillic letters highlighted within the text. Her heart began to pound with the knowledge that she'd wanted to be able to deny. But there they were—some letters vertical, others horizontal, but all connected—spelling out the Russian version of Thwart. The computer had identified the path as being a spiral.

"Can you recognize any other words?" she asked, her tone joyless.

Jerry was already scribbling into his notebook. "Give me a couple of minutes."

He mumbled words in Russian as he worked. Natalie felt the seconds tick by. A sense of foreboding as strong as the one she'd had when facing Mont Blanc grew within her.

Let me be wrong.

The silent words echoed in her head until they were cut off by Jerry's stricken "Good God, Natalie, I don't believe this."

"Read it to me." She felt his hesitation. "Please. I have to know."

"'Computer board desirable. First obtain Thwart as instructed in Moscow.'" He read the translated message deadpan, with no inflection, but each word cut into her heart. "'Remove all obstacles. Failure means exile from motherland.'"

Natalie's vision suddenly blurred, and she couldn't see the screen at all. Mikhail's face was there, looking as it had when he'd made love to her, but it was wet with her tears. "A fool, that's what I've been," she whispered.

"Natalie...I'm sorry."

"So am I. Sorry to have been so stupid, but not sorry to know the truth."

"What are you going to do about it?"

Making an effort to rise above her pain, Natalie became aware of Jerry's concerned expression. "I don't know yet. Something. I have to talk to my mother first. Thwart is her project. You won't say anything...?"

"I promised you I wouldn't." He shifted awkwardly and slipped his hands into his pockets as he backed away toward the door. "Maybe I'd better go now."

"Get some sleep."

"Sure. Will you be okay?"

"Of course I will," Natalie said, rising and drying the tears from her cheeks. Crying was irrational. Her father had told her so. Why hadn't she remembered that? "I'll walk you to the door. Wait. Let me check first." She turned out the light and opened the blinds. No sign of the sedan outside. Nevertheless the sick feeling in her stomach increased. "I think it's safe."

"I can take care of myself." Jerry kissed her damp cheek. "I really am sorry."

She followed him through the living room to the front door to let him out. Then she locked herself in and leaned on the doorframe. A few deep breaths steadied her system, and the nausea that had threatened her subsided. She had to think; she had to overcome the irrational part of herself that had allowed her to fall in love with a man she'd known slightly more than two weeks.

A man who was, in fact, her enemy.

Part of her still wanted to deny it, to declare Mikhail innocent. But she couldn't listen to her instincts anymore. Not in the face of what she'd learned. *"Remove all obstacles."*

Did that include her?

Would Mikhail be willing to kill her to obtain a military secret for his precious Russia?

Dispirited, she reentered the study and printed the copy on the screen, then shut down the system. She took the printout and Jerry's translation with her and headed for her room, the truth haunting her.

She'd been duped. Drucker had been correct when he'd accused her of being naive. She should have seen this coming. She hadn't wanted to give validity to his questions about how she fitted into Mikhail's plans and what would happen to her after he'd gotten what he'd come for.

It was crystal clear to her now.

She'd *allowed* herself to be duped, Natalie thought as her deep-seated insecurities surfaced in a rush. She'd never seriously questioned why a charismatic man like Mikhail Korolev would want to be with someone ordinary like her. And now the purposeful blinders she'd chosen to wear might have put her country's security in jeopardy.

She checked the clock over her desk. It was late—after three—but she picked up the telephone and dialed Faith's number. Faith deserved to know about the message in case there were any repercussions that would affect her. She had gone out on a limb for Natalie by finding out about Drucker, and Natalie hadn't been totally honest in return because she'd been protecting an undeserving man.

The phone rang only once. "Yes?" Faith answered.

"It's me, Natalie. Are you still up at this hour of the morning?"

"Why? Are you disappointed you couldn't wake me?" The smile in her voice sounded false, as though she, too, were worrying about the situation. Natalie was convinced of it when Faith added, "I was having trouble sleeping, so I decided to read for a while."

"After hearing what I have to tell you, you might be awake all night."

"What happened?" Faith asked, her tone changing immediately. "Not something with those KGB men?"

"No. It's Mikhail." Natalie took a deep breath and launched into her story, starting with her discovery of the message and ending with her horror at learning its contents.

"Oh, Nat, how awful for you! And you never even guessed!"

"Yes, I did guess. I merely chose to ignore my suspicions," Natalie admitted. "When I woke up the other morning and came downstairs looking for Mikhail, he was gone. But someone had been in the study. The computer terminal was on and papers were strewn across the desk. I thought my mother had been working in there—until she called from the lab a little while later. Faith, I don't know who else could have been in the study except Mikhail."

"He does seem to be the one with the opportunity, doesn't he? Why didn't you tell me about the note and the incident when you saw me this afternoon? Scratch that. I should know better than to question the motivations of a woman in love. I've done a few questionable things my-self."

"I couldn't believe Mikhail meant me any harm. I thought he cared."

"Maybe he does care." Faith spoke softly, almost as if to herself. "Sometimes people do things for reasons that have nothing to do with those they love. Sometimes the inno-cents get hurt."

"Hurt or killed?"

"Killed?" Faith's voice rose. "Nat, you're scaring me. What are you talking about?"

"I read you the translation. 'Remove all obstacles.' I think that was meant in a very literal sense."

No answer came from the other end of the line, as if Faith had been shocked into silence. Eventually she found her voice. "What are you going to do?"

"I haven't decided. I just can't bring myself to go through legal channels yet, even if I could figure out whom to go to with this story. I certainly can't trust Drucker after what your friends found out about him."

"If you need me, I don't have to leave tomorrow. I could delay my flight back to France at least until the weekend."

"No, Faith, I don't want you to jeopardize your career with the government because of my mistake. I want to keep you out of this if I can."

"Nat, you're the best friend anyone could ever have." Faith's voice held the funny little squeak that was always there when she was trying not to cry. "I'm not without contacts, you know. Not everyone who works for the gov-ernment is an Elliott Drucker."

"Thanks. Just the thought that I can count on a friend is a relief," Natalie said with more confidence than she felt. "I merely wanted someone to know what was going on in case something happened to me."

"D-don't say that!"

"All right, calm down. I'm just tired. My brain isn't functioning properly anymore. I need some sleep. Maybe the solution to this mess will come to me in a dream."

Or in a nightmare.

Whatever the solution, Natalie knew it wouldn't make the memories or the feelings or the guilt go away. She was going to have to live with them for the rest of her life.

"I JUST CAN'T BELIEVE Mikhail Korolev is capable of such treachery," Catherine said later that morning. She sat on the living-room couch, the faint lines around her eyes deepening as she frowned at the paper in her hands.

Natalie paced the room, her exhausted brain and body running solely on nervous energy. "I don't want to believe it either, Mother, but you've read the translation for yourself."

"Couldn't you and Jerry have made a mistake?"

"Two mathematicians, one who speaks Russian fluently, armed with a Cray computer? I hardly think so."

"Well, I guess not," Catherine said, shaking her head, "but it boggles the mind. Mikhail's a skating coach, for heaven's sake, not a minor diplomat. They're the ones you have to watch out for. Maybe this is some kind of mistake." She indicated the translation. "Not the contents, but the fact that Mikhail had it."

Natalie stopped in front of her. "You don't know how much I want to believe that."

Although she was still having similar doubts, Natalie was convinced she was the victim of wishful thinking. The proof of Mikhail's guilt was undeniable...and yet when the KGB men had pursued them in the car chase, his fear had been almost a tangible thing.

All last night her heart had battled with her brain, the escalating inner war keeping her from sleep. She'd tried to formulate a plan that would resolve everything once and for all, something she'd thought translating the note would accomplish. Finally, at seven that morning, she'd called her mother at the lab and insisted that Catherine come home immediately. As it turned out, "immediately" had been four hours later, time enough to put Natalie in a fine state of nerves.

"I'm going to need your help in proving Mikhail guilty or innocent, Mother, but before I ask it of you, I'd better tell you everything that's been going on."

"You mean there's more?"

Nodding, Natalie sat down next to her and began to speak. She left nothing out. Her mother listened quietly until she'd finished.

"My God, Natalie!" Catherine's shocked voice trembled, as did the hand that reached out to touch her cheek. "Why didn't you tell me all this before?"

"Even though I had my suspicions, I couldn't believe Mikhail would do anything to harm anyone. I was sure he had his own private reasons for defecting." Natalie took her mother's hand from her cheek and held it between her own. "I didn't want to worry you or spoil your big breakthrough."

"Your life is more important to me than my work," Catherine stated. "Think about this. You haven't been any more honest with me than Mikhail has been with you, and yet I have no doubt that you love me and that you're a moral person. Maybe that applies to him as well."

Guilt seemed to loom in every direction in which Natalie's mind turned. She hadn't been honest with her mother; she could have endangered her country; she might be condemning Mikhail mistakenly. Renewed agitation made her rise and walk to the windows; she automatically checked the street outside. No dark blue sedan.

She turned back to Catherine. "As I said, I need your help to prove his innocence or guilt."

"What kind of help?"

"Bait—a set of fake plans and a fake coating formula for Thwart. And I need it immediately. I'll find some excuse to get Mikhail here tonight, and when he arrives, the trap will already be set."

"And if he falls into it?"

"I'll do something. He'll leave me no choice."

Natalie didn't know exactly what that would be, but she knew how she'd feel: betrayed, used, stupid, ashamed. Those were only a few words that came readily to mind.

HE WAS GOING TO TELL Natalie everything, Mikhail thought as the taxi turned down her street early Thursday evening. He didn't know what else to do.

As much as he'd like to, he couldn't turn the clock back to the time before his defection, and Elliott Drucker had continued to be unavailable. Mikhail had tried to reach the CIA agent three times the day before and twice that afternoon. Each time the operator had put him through to the same man, Paul Howe. And each time Howe had become more insistent that Mikhail identify himself and state his problem.

Mikhail had wavered during the last call, but he hadn't been able to force the words of truth from his throat. His gut instincts told him that Drucker was the right man to resolve this dilemma. From their initial contact, he'd been aware of Drucker's competence and aggressive nature mixed with enough cunning to put any KGB agent to shame. Mikhail would try to reach him one last time in the morning.

In the meantime, he couldn't allow the woman he loved to be in such imminent danger without knowing it. He had a little more than sixteen hours either to meet Simansky's deadline or to stop the agent from carrying through with his threat. Not being able to speak with Drucker left Mikhail no choice. He had to protect Natalie himself. He'd start by telling her everything before they left for her friend's get-together. Of course, she might not want to go anywhere with him afterward, but that was a chance he had to take.

Still, as the taxi slid over to the curb in front of her house, Mikhail dreaded the upcoming confrontation and wondered if he really needed to tell Natalie the moment he saw her. He'd never considered himself a coward before, but he was fast becoming one where she was concerned.

He paid the driver, left the vehicle and strode quickly toward the house. No sign of Simansky or his men. Their very absence took on a new, ominous meaning for him. He ascended the porch steps two at a time. Natalie must have been watching for him, because the front door opened before he had a chance to ring the bell. The overhead light spilled softly over her. Her full-fleshed curves were accentuated by a belted, polished-cotton dress.

"Mikhail, you're right on time, but I'm not quite ready," she said, holding open the screen door.

"I like this dress," he said. "The clear blue is only a shade darker than your eyes." He entered, unable to stop himself from staring at her. He'd seen her lush body naked and flushed with desire, but never in a garment that played up her femininity as this one did. Familiar stirrings weakened his resolve to do the right thing. He didn't have the heart to alienate her immediately. "Please, do not change it."

"I wasn't thinking of changing. I—I need to put on some makeup and—and do something with my hair."

Her hand swept through her loose brown curls, fussing with them in an uncharacteristic gesture. With the soft light on her, he could see her expression, but he couldn't read it. She seemed distant somehow. He guessed she might be self-conscious or nervous, exactly the way he was feeling. Wanting to reassure her, to feel her in his arms at least one more time before he might read hate in her eyes, he pulled her close against his tightening loins.

"You are beautiful, my Natasha."

Downswept lashes hid her eyes from him, and there was a trace of a quiver in her voice when she said, "We'll be late if I don't finish getting ready."

"Then we shall make a heartfelt apology to our host."

Mikhail met her lips in a kiss that was agonizingly sweet in its intensity. He could feel the sudden flutter of Natalie's heart where her breasts flattened against his chest, but he knew she was holding herself back, fighting acceptance of the passion that could sweep them both senseless so quickly. He thought she might be shy with him, that she might have come to realize she cared for him as much as he cared for her, yet didn't know how to deal with it. Love and the responsibility that went with it were enough to make anyone nervous.

And she didn't even know the odds that were against them.

Natalie pulled away and whirled into the living room, her full skirt swishing around her long legs, her back absorbing this new tenseness in her. She held herself very straight. "Would you like some vodka while I go upstairs for a few minutes?"

"No, no vodka." He needed a clear head, now more than ever. "Nothing." She turned toward the stairs. "Natalya, wait."

She stopped, one hand on the railing, her expression questioning, her breath coming a little too fast. Like him, she must still be feeling the effects of the kiss. She looked so desirable that he had a difficult time remembering what he'd been about to say. But he did remember.

"Yes, Mikhail?" she asked. "Have you changed your mind about that drink?"

Had he? Before he could decide, the moment passed with the sound of an inner door opening behind him.

"Hello, Mikhail. Nice to see you again," Catherine said as she came out of the study. "Natalie, I have a minor crisis at the lab."

"What now?" Natalie asked. Mikhail noticed her fingers digging into the railing. There was an air of expectancy about her that he couldn't define. "Don't tell me you have to work all night again."

"Well, no, not at the lab, anyway." Catherine glanced around the room, her forehead pulled into a frown. "When I get back I'll continue my work here. One of the technicians locked his keys inside the lab and he has to get in again to shut off some test equipment." With a sound of triumph, she crossed to the couch and picked up a purse. "I was the only one David could reach. Now I just need to find *my* keys."

Mikhail followed Natalie's pointed gaze, which had shifted to the study. The door was open, and from where he stood he could see the computer terminal. The screen was lit and papers were strewn around it.

"Aren't you going to shut down before you go?" Natalie asked.

Catherine was rummaging through her purse. "No, dear, I'm right in the middle of revising the supply list for the test model coating," she said. "Don't touch anything. Aha!" She lifted a set of keys from the purse and jingled them. "Success. To the rescue. I'll be back in a half hour or so."

"We'll probably be gone before then," Natalie told her mother, who was already racing out the door. Then, to Mikhail, she said, "I should be ready in ten minutes or so."

It took a few seconds for her words to register. Mikhail was distracted by the fact that the answer to his problems lay in the next room, waiting. It would be so easy... He could steal those papers in there—or take as many notes as he had time for while Natalie was upstairs. He could meet Simansky's deadline if he could close his mind to the moral dilemma such an action posed.

No, he couldn't do it.

But if he allowed this opportunity to slip by, what would happen to the woman he loved?

His pulse racing when he turned toward her, he neatly avoided Natalie's gaze. "Go ahead, then," he said, his voice sounding strange to his own ears. "I'll wait for you down here."

Natalie forced her legs to take her up the stairs. Her heart was pounding by the time she reached the top. She paused there, listening intently. *Let me hear his footsteps,* she prayed. *Let him follow me.*

Silence.

Disappointment made her sick inside, but she told herself that just because Mikhail had stayed below didn't necessarily mean anything. He'd seemed uncomfortable with her, but she hadn't been calm and collected, either. Her mood might have rubbed off on him. Maybe he simply didn't like the idea of her fussing with her hair and makeup.

It was the kiss that had shaken her. It had seemed so real, so full of passion . . . and more. Love? No, she wasn't going to fool herself. She had to wait to see if he took the bait. Her mind revolted against the possibility that he might steal the plans or photograph them with one of those trick cameras hidden in a pen or a lighter. Natalie wondered if she'd been reading too many spy novels.

Getting ready was a more difficult task than she would have imagined. Her hands trembled as she applied eye shadow and mascara and lipstick. She smeared all three and had to deal with the mess. Then her brush tangled in her hair and she had to pull it free, strand by strand. When she had finished, twelve agonizing minutes had passed, enough time for Mikhail to have gotten a good look at the papers lying around the computer.

Had he done it? She wouldn't know anything for sure until she'd returned from the small gathering Jerry had agreed to arrange. Catherine would have an answer for her then.

Natalie had no idea of how she was going to get through the evening.

The clack of her heels on the wooden stairs echoed around her as she descended. She gave herself a mental pep talk in an effort to dispel her growing alienation from the situation. She had to get hold of herself and act naturally, or Mikhail would get wind of her suspicions.

"Ready," she called out, giving him fair warning.

The sight of him sitting on the couch reading a magazine was a welcome one. Surely he couldn't look so normal if he'd just been in the study. She took a deep breath filled with relief and forced herself to keep her eyes on him, away from the study. He set the magazine down on the coffee table and joined her at the bottom step. She tried to smile naturally. His lips turned up, too, but the smile didn't reach his eyes; they reflected some darker emotion.

"Ah, my Natasha," he murmured, his voice filled with a rawness she could have sworn was real. "You must stay close by my side this entire evening."

"Why?" she asked, trying to keep her tone light. *He is innocent,* she told herself as she walked past him toward the front door. *He has to be.* "Will you be jealous if I don't?"

"Of course. We Russians are very possessive of our women."

"I must warn you, the friend we're joining is a man." She waited until they were both outside before adding, "I'm sure he'll expect to be allowed to talk to me."

Mikhail slipped an arm around her shoulders and led her toward the car. "He can speak to both of us, then."

"He'll enjoy that," she murmured. "His name is Jerry Lubin. He's Russian, also." She felt the arm around her stiffen slightly. "Of Russian descent, that is. He was born here in the States."

Surreptitiously she glanced down the street and could barely make out the front grille of Catherine's car, parked under a stand of trees. There had been no emergency at the lab. The story had been part of their setup. Her mother was merely waiting to return to the house as soon as Natalie and Mikhail were out of the way.

Although the air between them seemed to be charged, Mikhail remained silent during the short ride, giving Natalie a chance to relax. Well, not relax exactly. She wouldn't be able to do that until she got home again and her mother could confirm that Mikhail hadn't touched anything.

Jerry had been glad to help her out by asking a few friends to come over for drinks and conversation. She'd hated involving him any more than she had to, but she'd needed a way to get Mikhail out of the house so her mother could check the study. The papers they'd planted were real, not fake. Catherine had produced structural plans and a coating formula for an earlier version of the project. Both had been discarded more than a year before, and they bore almost no similarity to those in use now. But no one except the people working on Thwart would be able to figure that out. Each piece of paper had been set carefully, its edges lined up with and corners tucked under other objects on the desk. Natalie had even placed a hair on top of a middle sheet— another idea from those spy novels. It would still be there if nothing had been touched.

As she and Mikhail got out of the car, she tried to take a positive attitude. Everything would be exactly as she and her mother had left it. Her positive attitude allowed her to move in a little closer to Mikhail as they approached Jerry's town house, which was situated in an area of Wilmington that was being renovated. Just outside the door, Mikhail stopped and turned her to face him. "Natalya, I . . ."

"Yes?" she said when he faltered. His serious tone alarmed her. She could feel the tension in the fingers that gripped her upper arms, and her positive attitude wilted a little. "What is it, Mikhail?"

He seemed to struggle within himself. She could read the war going on in his eyes. Then his fingers loosened and fell away. "Later. It can wait until later."

Disappointed, she turned from him and pressed Jerry's bell, once more wondering how long she would last before her nerves gave out and she screamed for release from this awful tension.

Chapter Eleven

Natalie's nerves held up for little more than an hour before she sneaked off to the kitchen to telephone her mother. She just couldn't wait until she got home. Jerry had invited other university employees and their spouses or dates. Mikhail was busy answering a faculty member's questions about Moscow, so she figured he'd never notice her slip away. Her hand shook as she dialed her home number. Instead of a ring, she heard a busy signal. She cursed to herself as she replaced the receiver.

"All right. Explain," Jerry demanded softly from behind her. He was standing in front of the screened back door, arms crossed over his chest. "What's this all about? Why haven't you turned this case over to the authorities?"

Natalie felt heat rise up her neck to sting her cheeks. She hadn't had time to explain anything but her request when she'd called him earlier. The sound of festive voices filtered into the kitchen from the living room. So that no one but Jerry could hear her in return, she drew closer.

"I had to have absolute proof that Mikhail was after Thwart before I could do anything about it," she whispered. A breeze came through the screen door, lathing her flushed face soothingly. "Before we came over here, I set a trap and left him alone, giving him the opportunity to take the bait."

"What kind of bait? You can't mean Thwart itself?"

Natalie nodded. "I got Mother to help. She left real plans and a coating formula in the study, but they're..."

Jerry's eyes shifted to a spot over her shoulder, his suddenly cautious expression silencing her before she could finish giving him the details. A second later, a possessive arm wrapped itself around her waist. She had to force herself not to stiffen, although she couldn't do anything about the rush of anxiety sweeping through her. Mikhail had been serious about not letting her away from his side.

"I missed you," he murmured.

"I needed air." Natalie indicated her position near the screen door. She took a deep breath, not because she was playacting, but because she really needed one. Mikhail's almost overhearing her conversation was the last straw. She had to get home! She had to know for sure! "I have a headache and I thought fresh air would help. Unfortunately, I was wrong. I think we're going to have to leave, Jerry. It's been fun while it lasted. Thanks for the invitation."

Her friend's hazel eyes held a meaningful expression when he took her hand and said, "Take care of yourself. I wouldn't want anything to happen to your health. Headaches have a way of lingering and debilitating you unless you take positive steps to get rid of them."

Natalie knew his words weren't to be taken literally, and neither were hers. "I have something at home that should take care of it."

She and Mikhail said their goodbyes to the half-dozen people in the living room, then left promptly.

"Since you are not feeling well, perhaps I should drive," Mikhail suggested as they approached the car.

"A headache has never stopped me before." She purposefully circled to the driver's side. "Besides, I remember the last time you drove the car. That hair-raising ride was enough to give anyone a migraine.''

His lips tightened grimly at her not-so-subtle reminder of their flight from the KGB. Again, Natalie remembered his very real fear when he'd sheltered her body with his own. She tried to think positively about what she would find when she returned home, but she grew more uneasy instead.

She waited until they were heading away from Jerry's place and toward Mikhail's before saying, "If you don't mind, I'll drop you off at your apartment."

"Natalya, we must talk." His voice was low and urgent, and she felt his eyes boring into her. She shifted uneasily, but focused her attention on the traffic as she turned onto a main street.

"I'm sure whatever it is can wait until tomorrow."

"No. This is important. We must talk about us. You must understand how much I care for—"

"That sounds serious." She gripped the steering wheel with suddenly sweaty palms. She'd give anything to be able to relax, to act naturally with him. Their personal relationship was the last thing in the world she wanted to talk about when she was aching to learn whether he was innocent or guilty. Then she would know if what he wanted to tell her was the truth or a lie. "Tomorrow," she promised. "We'll discuss whatever you want tomorrow."

"Now, Natalya."

"Please, stop this!" Natalie slapped the steering wheel for emphasis, then took a shaky breath. The timing was all wrong, but she couldn't tell him that. "I'm sorry. It's just my head," she lied. "I can't think straight with a headache."

He withdrew into a frustrated silence that made Natalie jittery. She kept expecting him to begin again. He didn't. He stared out of the passenger window, ignoring her completely. She was relieved when she pulled up in front of his place and he got out without trying to kiss her.

"Tomorrow, then" was all he said.

"Tomorrow."

She repeated the word to herself over and over as she drove home half blindly, seeing nothing between the intersections. Tomorrow she would be able to take positive action one way or the other. Either she'd go to Congressman Harry Simpson with the story and let him handle it—he happened to be an old friend of her father's, and Catherine had agreed he could take care of the problem—or she'd go to Mikhail himself.

It had to be Mikhail!

The short drive home seemed interminable, the walk up to the house all too short. Natalie paused on the porch for a moment, not knowing if she was ready to face the truth. Every nerve in her body was on edge. She could feel a pulse tick in her neck as she entered. Her mother rose from the couch in the living room and shook her graying head. The smile curving her lips took ten years from her face.

"He didn't do it. Everything is exactly as we left it. That must mean he's innocent!"

Strength flowed out of Natalie in a rush. Her knees went weak, and she wedged a shoulder against the wall next to the door for support. "Thank God," she whispered, tears of gratitude stinging the back of her eyes. She squeezed her lids shut and felt the tears seep through her lashes and roll down her cheeks. "Thank God."

"I just knew Mikhail couldn't harm anyone," Catherine said, coming forward to wrap her arms around her daughter. "I knew he loved you."

Shame stole through Natalie as she remembered the way she'd snapped at him in the car. "He tried to tell me how he felt tonight, but I wouldn't let him. Do you think he'll hate me when he knows what we did? I must tell him, if I expect him to be honest with me in return.''

Catherine smoothed a curl away from Natalie's forehead. "He won't hate you. He'll understand.''

"I should go to him and apologize,'' Natalie said, suddenly overcome by exhaustion after the release of tension, a reminder of the emotional stress she'd been under and that she'd hardly slept the night before. "But I can't. I'd probably wreck the car if I tried to drive now.'' Since Mikhail didn't have a phone, she couldn't even call him and say good-night. "I need a few hours of sleep so I can be at my best when I face him. I can't help him if I can't think clearly.'' She swallowed hard before adding, "I'm so afraid, C.L. I haven't seen anything clearly in a long, long time.''

"Sleep sounds like a good idea for both of us,'' Catherine said, locking up behind them.

Arms around each other, they climbed the stairs and hugged at the landing. Natalie had never felt so close to her mother as she did at that moment. Then Catherine broke the embrace and entered the master bedroom. Natalie watched the door close before heading on up to her attic retreat, her feet dragging as if they were carrying hundred-pound lead weights. She fell across the bed, not caring that she was on top of the covers, completely dressed.

Her mind relinquished everything to exhaustion....

In her dream, Mikhail was making love to her again, only this time he was the one doing the questioning. Why hadn't she trusted her instincts? he asked as he ran his hands up the soft flesh of her inner thighs. Warmth exploded through her lower body. She arched toward him, but his hands had already moved on. Why hadn't she believed in him? He'd do anything for her. His palms found her nipples, coaxed them to life, then abandoned them. She'd saved *his* life. He'd protect her with his own. Didn't she know that? His fingers tangled in her hair and tugged her head closer to his. She could see that his gray eyes were filled with disappointment and distrust....

Then something was shaking her shoulders, the sharp movement almost waking her. Mumbling curses, she fought the intrusion, trying to ignore the persistent shaking, trying to find her way back into the dark void so she could make peace with the man she loved. She had to apologize, to tell him she would stand by him and help him through his troubles.

"Natalie, wake up!" Catherine insisted. "Please, you must!"

Her mother's voice finally penetrated the fog of her dreams. Natalie forced her eyes open. The room was dark except for the light coming from the stairwell and the dawn creeping through the open blinds of the skylight.

"What is it, Mother?" Her head still on the pillow, she focused on the face so like her own. The youthful happiness had abandoned it. Still disoriented, Natalie blinked in confusion. "Have I been asleep that long?"

"I don't know how to tell you this...."

Natalie frowned, and a small knot of apprehension settled in her stomach. "What?"

"I woke up about a half hour ago and couldn't fall asleep again. I went downstairs, planning to work for a while." Catherine's voice trembled. "Someone had been in there."

Natalie was instantly awake. "In the study?"

Her mother nodded. "While we were sleeping, someone was going through the blueprints and my notes on the coating formula for the discarded model."

"Are you sure?"

"Positive. I didn't touch anything last night. Whoever it was left the papers in order, but not lined up the way they'd been. The only reason I checked everything a second time was because one of the papers had slipped onto the floor under the chair. The most frightening part is that there was no sign of a forced entry. Whoever was in there was a professional, able to unlock dead bolts or windows without leaving a trace. This whole thing is too much for me.''

Natalie shivered in fear; gooseflesh ran up her spine. Someone walking over her grave—that was what she and Faith would have said when they were kids. She was beginning to wonder if there was any truth to the old superstition, for she no longer had any doubt that she was caught in a veritable death spiral of her own making.

She closed her eyes against the vivid imagery that immediately came to her. ''He must have come back. Those KGB men had no reason to believe the plans were here tonight, Mother.'' She'd trustingly held on to what she'd convinced herself was the truth, until she'd come within a hairbreadth of the very thing that could rob her of life itself. Regretfully she whispered, ''But Mikhail knew.''

FRIDAY DAWNED LIKE ANY OTHER DAY, except that Mikhail remembered Simansky's deadline the moment he opened his eyes. He immediately rose and went to the side window, which gave him a partial view of the street in front of the building. The dark blue sedan sat curbside, patiently awaiting him. There was no sense in stalling, so he got dressed and left the apartment, knowing what he had to do.

He was yards away from the auto when its rear passenger door swung open. Mikhail slid in next to Simansky. He kept his eyes on Gregor's bad haircut.

''I couldn't get them,'' he calmly said in Russian. Every artery and vein in his body felt distended, ready to burst and spill his lifeblood. But there was no other way. ''The security around Thwart is too great.''

''Then why are you here wasting my time, comrade?''

''To make one last offer. I think you might find this one interesting.''

''Amuse me,'' Simansky demanded congenially.

"The computer board—"

"I thought we settled that."

"—and me."

"You, Korolev? Explain yourself."

"Leave the Lundgren woman alone and have Aleksei freed." Bile threatened to rise to Mikhail's throat as he added, "I'll return to Russia. I'll skate or coach or stand trial as the example the KGB always seems to need. Anything you want."

Simansky laughed. "But you've already been tried—and found guilty, I might add."

Mikhail whipped his head around and stared at the man's grotesque grin. "What are you talking about?"

"The Soviet Union has branded you a traitor. Officially, there was no defection. You've been exiled." The mouth between the loose jowls continued to form words that Mikhail could barely hear through the rushing sound in his head. "Even now, your name is being taken off the books, erased from the history of the Soviet people."

Erased. A nonperson. Unofficial. No—*worse*. The next generation of skaters would never know he'd existed.

He should have guessed.

A sense of failure greater than any he'd ever known shuddered through him. He had nothing left to offer. He could call the CIA again and identify himself to Agent Paul Howe. But it would be too late for Natalie. Simansky could get to her in minutes by placing a telephone call of his own. She could disappear, never to be seen again, before he could do anything to save her.

Mikhail thought he was dreaming when Simansky said, "Actually, your offer does interest me. A hero of the Soviet peoples returning to the motherland, cowed, repentant, begging to be taken back into her fold. Yes, I like this picture."

Bastard! What had he expected? Mikhail wondered. That they'd take him back as though nothing had happened? "Then you agree?"

"I feel generous this morning. If you get me the computer board and make a public statement to the effect that you were coerced into coming here and wish to return home, I will spare the woman."

"And Aleksei?"

"Yes, you would be worth Rodzianko, also. The West is welcome to the troublemaker." Laughter rumbled through Simansky's bulk. "It will be quite satisfying to see you humble yourself at a press conference. Not so clever, eh, Korolev?"

No, he wasn't clever at all. But he was learning. "You'll have to give me several more days."

"For what?"

"I don't have the computer board in my possession."

Simansky nodded. "Agreed."

Mikhail wondered why the KGB agent was acceding to his terms so easily. "And I don't turn over the board and give the press conference until Aleksei arrives at an American consulate—safely. Let's say the one in Lyon, Monday morning at nine."

"I am not sure this is possible so quickly."

"I think you're as anxious for this deal as I am," Mikhail stated with certainty. He stared, unblinking. "Make it possible."

Color mottled Simansky's face. "And you make sure you do not cross me this time, Korolev."

"You live up to your part of the bargain. I'll live up to mine."

Mikhail left the vehicle and strode to his apartment without looking back. When he was satisfied that the KGB had departed the area, he pocketed all the change he had and walked to the nearest gas station with a telephone booth.

He'd never bothered to get a telephone of his own because he'd known it would be tapped by the CIA. That was standard procedure in the case of a defector, or so Peter Baum had told him. And even if the CIA had left him alone, Mikhail was sure the KGB would have been delighted to take over. Monitoring people was their specialty.

The first few calls he made were to track down Peter, who was giving a coaching seminar at Lake Placid. He told his friend the whole story this time. Sympathetic but worried, Peter agreed to be in Chamonix late Saturday night, when he'd help Mikhail find the computer board.

Then Mikhail booked a flight to Geneva for that evening and made arrangements to pick up his ticket at the airport. Geneva sat in the Alps bordering France, and from there he could get to Chamonix by bus. He carefully wrote down the flight information on the back of an envelope.

That taken care of, he jogged back to his building, making plans to evade Simansky and his men, who would surely return in hopes of following him to the computer board. Mikhail had no doubts that the KGB would take it from him and renegotiate terms if possible.

He didn't want to think about what would happen after the exchange was actually made. His life might not be worth living, but at least Aleksei would be free and Natalie would be safe. His only regret was that he'd never been able to tell her the truth, about both his defection and his love for her. Now he realized it was better that she didn't know. She might try to stop him.

Back in his apartment, he put the flight information on the dresser so he wouldn't misplace it, then took out his only suitcase. Peter had bought it for him in Paris. It was large enough to hold most of his belongings except for a couple of practice outfits, his portable cassette player and his new ice skates. He picked up one of the skates and ran his fingers across the soft leather of the shoe and along the steel of the blade. Leaving them shouldn't matter—he probably wouldn't be allowed to skate where he was going anyway—but it did.

He wasn't fooling himself. He might be taken to Moscow for a press conference, but they wouldn't let him stay to coach there. Undoubtedly he'd be bundled off to some Siberian gulag and his native Russia would be lost to him once more. This time he'd forfeit everything—country, relatives, friends, the woman he loved and, he was afraid, his work. He wouldn't even have his skating to sustain him.

Suddenly aware of a presence behind him, he whirled around. Her stance and expression uncertain, Natalie stood in the doorway.

"Natasha," he said softly. He'd get to see her one more time, then. He was thankful for the opportunity and filled with regret. Leaving her would be even more difficult afterward. "Please. Come in."

She stepped inside and closed the door, her gaze resting on the skate in his hand. He put it down, and her eyes widened as she spotted the open suitcase on the bed.

"You wanted to tell me something last night." She quickly disguised a vulnerable expression that was filled with disappointment and sorrow, but not before he saw it. "Is this it, then? You're leaving?"

"Only for a few days," he lied, hating the fact that he had to do so for her own protection. It was frightening that inventing lies had become so much easier for him than it had been a month ago. "I have business in Washington with the State Department."

"You're certainly taking a lot of clothes for a few days," she murmured, looking away from him.

"I never pack sensibly. I always fear that I will forget something."

The glint in her eyes was challenging as they met his. "Like your skates?"

"The ice skates stay here, but I hate to be parted from them, even for a few days."

That was true at least. They were a symbol of everything he was leaving behind, and this was the second time he'd had to make the same sacrifice in less than a month.

Natalie began wandering across the room slowly, staying what he saw as a safe distance from him. "So, you were only going to tell me you'd be gone for a few days?" she asked, glancing out the window.

"Yes. I thought you would want to know."

She passed the almost empty closet and headed in the opposite direction, stopping with her back to the dresser. Mikhail could tell she was schooling her face into an impassive expression that didn't suit her at all. He wanted to tell her everything, to make her look at him the way she had when they'd made love together, but he couldn't. He'd put her in too much danger as it was. He had his chance to make things right, and he was determined to take it without doing anything to spoil it.

"You said it was about us," she said, her voice shaky. "That it was important."

"I wanted you to know how much I will miss you. How much your friendship means to me."

"Friendship," she echoed sadly, turning her back to him. She ran her fingers along the design carved into the wood of the top dresser drawer. "I thought I might . . ." Her fingers froze in their aimless search. Her spine seemed to stiffen visibly.

"Might what?" he asked, trying to steel himself so he wouldn't go to her and take her in his arms.

"M-mean something special to you." Natalie cleared her throat before she turned around. Her eyes flashed angrily. "But I guess you were only grateful, right?"

Her tone of voice startled him. "No, you are wrong."

"So you thanked me," she went on. "I didn't expect more. But maybe you had another reason to hang around, to become friends with me and my mother. Did you?"

Mikhail felt his face become ashen. "Natasha—"

"What were you after, Mikhail? Did you think we could do something for you? Were you using us?"

"No! I never used you!"

He hadn't. He'd tried to tell himself it was necessary, but his conscience hadn't allowed it, not even to save *her*. He'd done many things of which he hadn't thought himself capable in the past few weeks, but betrayal of this woman and of the country that had given him shelter hadn't been among them.

"I don't believe you," Natalie whispered hoarsely, as though she were fighting angry tears. "I think you've gotten whatever it is that you wanted from us and now you're leaving for good. I should never have believed in you."

"What are you talking about?" Mikhail asked. Natalie was acting so strangely, almost as if she knew the truth. But that was impossible. He went toward her, intent on removing the accusation from her eyes. He wanted to kiss it away, to hold her one last time.

But Natalie backed off immediately, shaking her head, holding her hand up. "No, don't touch me, Mikhail. I feel foolish enough as it is." The catch in her voice tormented him. "Please, just let me go."

The truth fought to come tumbling from his lips, but he repressed it just as he forced his feet to stay in one spot.

And Natalie left, taking his heart with her.

HER OUTER DEMEANOR DEADLY CALM, Natalie filled the shopping bag with a change of clothes, including a bulky, warm sweater, a light raincoat, a pair of sturdy shoes and a few toiletries. Inside, she seethed as she remembered Mikhail's lies. A few days in Washington—did he think she was stupid? Of course he did. She'd certainly been acting like a woman with more hormones than brains when she was around him. She might even have believed the State Department ploy if she hadn't seen the envelope with his flight plans written on it.

He was going to Geneva, not Washington—to Switzerland, a neutral country that wouldn't want to involve itself in this intrigue. She wondered if there was a bankroll waiting for him in one of those secret Swiss accounts.

How much did one get paid for betraying a woman and her country these days?

She really had been stupid; but no more, never again, Natalie thought, checking her purse for her credit cards and passport. All there. She was set to go. Picking up the shopping bag, she left the house and got in her car. No sign of the blue sedan, but she hadn't seen it for days. Maybe they'd changed cars. Maybe they weren't interested in her anymore. But she wasn't taking any chances. That was why she'd gotten Jerry to agree to help her one more time. She started the engine and headed the Cavalier toward his place.

Her mother would be frantic when she tried to reach Natalie to no avail. Natalie had insisted that Catherine go to the lab as usual while she got in touch with Congressman Simpson. What she hadn't said was that she would visit Mikhail first, give him one more chance to explain what was going on, so that he might offer some small crumb of hope that she hadn't been the biggest fool in the world.

Natalie forced herself to pay better attention to the traffic and check her rearview mirror more often. Allowing her attention to wander could be dangerous.

She couldn't help remembering how disappointed and hurt and brokenhearted she'd felt that morning. Or how confused she'd been by the emotions flitting across Mikhail's face, and the intense tone he'd used when he'd called her Natasha. If she hadn't known better, she would have sworn he really cared.

But she had known better, and Mikhail had left her with no choice. She'd called Harry Simpson. To her amazement, the congressman had been of no help at all. He was in the middle of planning his next campaign, and going on a wild-goose chase after some Russian who had fake plans for Thwart would look like a waste of time and money to his constituents. No, the CIA was her best bet, he'd told her in his most conciliatory tone.

Didn't anyone care what happened to someone else? she wondered as she pulled up in front of Jerry's town house. Were all people so selfishly motivated? Natalie cleared her mind for a few seconds before getting out of the car. She took the shopping bag with her. Any observers—innocent or otherwise—would think she was bringing a package to a friend.

Jerry was waiting for her at the front door. He whipped her inside and demanded, "Do you know what you're doing?"

"For the first time in weeks," she answered truthfully. She spotted a small suitcase next to the couch. She'd asked him to provide her with a lightweight bag so she wouldn't be seen leaving her house carrying one. "Is that for me?"

"Yes, if it's the right size."

"Don't worry, I'm traveling light."

"But I *am* worried, Natalie," he insisted, following her to the couch. She began packing the suitcase with the articles from the shopping bag. "Why not explain it to me? Maybe it'll make *me* feel better if I understand why I'm helping you put yourself in danger."

"I hope I won't be in any danger." Anticipating his objection, she added, "But I'll be careful. I'm merely going to follow Mikhail and see where he goes and with whom. I have a friend who works for the consulate in Lyon. I'll turn over any information I get to her—I promise. Faith has the kind of contacts who can and will do something."

"All to get some stupid military plans back," he muttered.

His words made Natalie's cheeks burn. To cover her discomfort, she headed for the kitchen, suitcase in hand, Jerry right behind her. They left through the back door, crossed several yards and came out on the next street, where he'd purposely parked his car.

Natalie didn't say a word, not even when they were on their way to the airport. Talk about not being truthful. She'd never told Jerry the stolen plans had been old and useless. She was afraid if she told him now, he would immediately blow the whistle on her to Catherine. Her mother would find a way to stop her from leaving the country.

Natalie had no intention of being stopped. This was something she *had* to do. Her plans were vague, not much better developed than she'd described to Jerry. She would beat Mikhail to Geneva by at least an hour. There'd be a rented car waiting for her. She'd follow him and try to obtain some solid evidence against him. And sometime during the next few days she would force a confrontation. Whether or not Mikhail was eventually brought to justice, he would know he hadn't gotten away with his ruse undetected.

"Do me a favor, would you?" she said to Jerry as they walked to her gate. "Don't tell my mother until you're sure my connection out of Kennedy is in the air."

"Sure," Jerry mumbled, but when they got to her gate, he caught her arm. "Natalie, are you positive you want to go through with this?"

She stared into his eyes. "If *I* don't do something, who will?"

Tight-lipped, he nodded curtly and kissed her on the cheek. "Stay safe, then."

"I'll do my best."

It seemed to take next to forever to get to Geneva, what with a change of planes in New York and a short stopover in Paris. After dinner, most of the other passengers slept when the flight attendants turned off the cabin lights. Natalie dozed off and on. At last she arrived in Switzerland. It was Saturday morning. She cleared immigration and customs, then took possession of her rental car, another Ford Fiesta. This one was a drab gray, the perfect color to blend into the shadows.

Next, she bribed an off-duty baggage handler named Rolf to watch for Mikhail as he came out of customs. She told Rolf she was the man's girlfriend and wanted to surprise him, then showed the baggage handler a newspaper clipping with a clear picture of Mikhail that she'd saved since his defection. Rolf was to follow Mikhail closely and find out what kind of transportation he took. She would stay lost in the crowds, far enough away so Mikhail wouldn't see her.

Everything went smoothly, just as she'd planned. The only thing she hadn't counted on was her reaction when she saw Mikhail stride out of customs with Rolf immediately picking up on his trail. Even at a distance, the Russian had the power to disturb her, to wreak havoc with her emotions, to make her short of breath, excited and angry—all at the same time.

But the real kicker came when, after pausing at the bus transportation desk where Mikhail was obviously purchasing a ticket, Rolf bounded back to her. "Chamonix. He will go to Chamonix."

Mutely, Natalie paid the man for his services and forced herself to listen to the details—the gate from where the bus would leave and when. Only after Rolf had left with a tip of his cap did Natalie allow herself to digest what she'd just learned.

Mikhail was on his way to a small town in the French Alps, not far from where she'd saved his life. She'd thought he was taking refuge in Switzerland, but he was going back to France. Why?

Her heart surged, trying to force hope on her. For the first time since her mother had awakened her with the crushing news of Mikhail's betrayal more than twenty-four hours ago, Natalie had some doubts about what she was doing.

Chapter Twelve

Negotiating the hairpin curves and steep grades of the Alps had been harrowing, but no more so than following Mikhail through the small town of Chamonix without being seen. In her rental car a safe distance behind, Natalie watched him enter the Hôtel Mer de Glace. The afternoon sun brightened the whitewashed stucco facade of the five-story hotel that looked like an Alpine villa with its shuttered windows and flower-bedecked balconies overhanging the street.

Mikhail had thrown her with his switch in what she'd considered to be his plans, and she still hadn't figured out what he was up to. Natalie parked and waited. Twenty minutes later, when he hadn't come out, she decided he must have gotten himself a room. She left the car, intending to go in and find out, hoping the desk clerk wasn't above a little bribery. Perhaps he could be more easily persuaded to give her the information she needed if she came up with a sympathetic enough ruse.

Her best bet would probably be to play the jealous wife who was following her husband.

The lobby of the hotel was charmingly rustic. The wide-planked wooden floors gleamed, as did the paneling on the walls. A gentle scent of flowers enveloped Natalie, and she looked around nervously for any sign of Mikhail. Some kind of sitting room opened off the lobby, but it seemed to be empty. She swallowed hard and approached the thin, dark-haired clerk behind the desk.

"Hello, do you speak English?" she asked. If not, she'd have to try her rusty German, because she'd never learned French.

The clerk turned a baleful eye on her. "Of course, ma-dame." His gaze dropped to her hands on the counter. "Excuse me—mademoiselle," he corrected, obviously noting the lack of a wedding ring. "You would like a room?"

She slid a hundred-franc note toward him. "I'd like some information."

He slid the note back. "We are not in the business of selling information."

Terrific. Just her luck to get an unbribable clerk. She stuffed the money into her pocket. "You don't understand," she said, hoping there was the right amount of desperation in her voice to win his sympathy. "That man who checked in a short while ago—he's my lover."

She felt her face and neck redden as the Frenchman studied her intently. Dressed as she was in brown pants and a camel-colored cotton pullover, with her hair smoothed back into a French braid and her face free of makeup, Natalie doubted that she looked like anyone's idea of a mistress. Still, she traded the clerk stare for stare. What she'd said was closer to the truth, anyway, and it wasn't her fault that he'd blown her jealous-wife story.

"I suppose you want to surprise your...lover."

"Yes, sort of. If you could tell me his room number, and maybe whether or not he mentioned meeting someone else."

The clerk's eyes shifted over her shoulder. "Perhaps you could ask the gentleman himself."

She whirled around, feeling her chest squeeze tight at the sight of Mikhail standing there staring at her, his eyes and face empty of expression.

"Natalie. What a surprise." He nodded to the clerk before grabbing her wrist and tugging her toward the elevator. "Come. You can ask *me* these questions upstairs."

"Wait. No!" Natalie tried to dig her heels in the wooden floor, but the leather soles of her loafers slid easily across the waxed surface. "I'm not going up there with you." She tried to pull her wrist free, but she couldn't even loosen Mikhail's determined grip. Her pulse raced with sudden fear. "Excuse me," she shouted over her shoulder to the clerk. "Help me. I don't want to go with him."

But the clerk's back was to her and stayed that way.

"You are wasting your breath," Mikhail murmured. "The French are quite tolerant of affairs of the heart. He will not stop me from taking my lover to my room, especially not when she came looking for me."

Panting from her fruitless exertion, Natalie stopped struggling. She had to recoup her strength.

They were both silent during the elevator ride to the fifth floor. Mikhail's fingers continued to hold her captive. And when she glanced at his profile, his expression seemed to be set in granite. Only a tick in his cheek muscle warned her of his true anger. He wasn't about to let her get away. She'd never seen this side of him before, and she definitely didn't like it. He seemed . . . dangerous.

The elevator stopped and its doors opened with a threatening *whoosh*. When Mikhail stepped out, Natalie followed readily, not wanting her wrist to be further abused. Her pulse was escalating. She tried to think, to formulate a plan, but her mind had gone blank. Good God, what had she gotten herself into? No one knew where she was. No one could help her out of this mess.

Once they were inside his quarters, Mikhail locked the door and pulled her to the middle of the room. "Why have you followed me, Natalya?" he asked grimly, releasing her.

"I thought I was the one who was going to have questions answered." She rubbed her wrist. A sore spot made her wince. When she looked up, she imagined she saw a flicker of regret in his eyes. But no, she was mistaken. His eyes were as remote as they had been the day he'd announced his defection. "What are *you* doing here, Mikhail? You were supposed to be in Washington for a few days. Why did you lie to me?"

"I was afraid you'd try to stop me, and I was concerned for your safety."

Natalie's jaw dropped at the startling answer issued in a monotone. It was a far cry from what she'd expected to hear. "Stop you from what?"

He ignored that. "Why did you follow me?"

Unable to play the game any longer, Natalie snapped, "I wanted to see for myself what you did with your spoils!" She began to pace, glancing out the glass balcony doors at the mountain scenery. The view might as well have been of a slum. She could hardly keep her eyes from the man who had betrayed her so cruelly. "I wanted the satisfaction of confronting you and letting you know that you hadn't gotten away with it!"

His brow furrowed. "I do not understand."

Natalie wrapped her arms around herself so she wouldn't be tempted to hit him. "That's interesting. I am sure you understood exactly what Thwart was developed to do."

"Thwart?"

"Stop it, Mikhail. I'm not one of those people who believe athletes are dumb. Is it your memory that's photographic, or did you use a camera to do your dirty work in our study the other night?"

"Someone got to your mother's plans!"

"You."

"Simansky."

His positive tone made her falter. "Who the hell is Sinansky?"

"The blue sedan. KGB." It was his turn to pace. He rubbed the back of his neck and mumbled to himself while he watched him in silence. Was it possible that he *hadn't* done it, after all? "Now it all makes sense," he said. "No wonder the bastard allowed me to change his mind. He already had what he wanted."

Overwhelmed by the unexpected direction the conversation was taking, Natalie shifted uneasily. "Are you trying to tell me you didn't come back after Mother and I were asleep?"

The exact nature of her accusation finally seemed to register with him. Mikhail glowered at her, and a rush of fresh fear spiraled through Natalie.

"Is that what you think of me?" Mikhail demanded, his tone strident enough to make her back away from him. "That I would use the woman who saved my life?" He advanced on her and stopped her from moving around him by grabbing her upper arms. "That I would betray the woman I love?"

"'Love'?" she choked out, hitting at him ineffectually. "You don't lie to someone you love." And he *had* lied.

"So you mistrusted me all along. That is sad . . . but it is also understandable." He let go of her. "Can you say that you have been any more honest with me?"

"Yes!" But that, too, was a lie and she knew it. Hadn't she set him up? "No, maybe not."

"Then we both have much to explain."

Natalie took a deep breath. "Why did you defect? And don't tell me it was because of the housing shortage in Moscow." She remembered he'd intimated that living with his ex-wife had pushed him beyond endurance.

He turned toward the balcony doors and stared out for several silent moments. Finally he said, "Because I had to.

For myself. And for a friend who is like a brother to me. I had to be free and in the West so I could bargain for Aleksei's life."

Another surprise answer, but one that sounded more like the truth than anything she'd heard so far. Natalie frowned at Mikhail's back and contemplated the enormity of such a selfless undertaking. If it were true...

"And you were going to save your friend by stealing the plans for Thwart?"

"No!" He turned around to face her. "I was foolish enough to believe I could outsmart the inventors of this hellish game. I planned to defect and to regain Aleksei's freedom by trading a computer board I stole from Galina's laboratory. But Simansky wouldn't make a trade for it. Not at first."

"What computer board?" she whispered, thinking of the secret message.

"One used by the Soviet spy network to encipher and decipher information sent to Moscow from around the world."

"If they have something that will encipher straight information and send it in the scrambled form, then why was the message hand-printed as though it had been received in code?"

"What message?" He seemed truly puzzled.

"In the book. The message was folded up and stuck in the book you lent me."

"I know nothing of this message."

"It was in Russian, but there weren't any recognizable words. Jerry and I used my mother's computer terminal to break the code. 'Computer board desirable,'" she quoted from memory. "'First obtain Thwart as instructed in Moscow. Remove all obstacles. Failure means exile from motherland.'"

Mikhail muttered something to himself in Russian; then, as if remembering she couldn't understand, he explained. "The paper on the ground." His eyes narrowed as though he were traveling inward. "I thought the telephone message from you fell from my pocket during the struggle I had with Simansky after he threatened you. I must have put it in the book when I got back to the office."

Fear crawled up her spine. "Threatened me?"

Mikhail's jaw tightened. "Simansky guessed my feelings for you, Natalya. He used them against me so that I would get Thwart for him. I was tempted, I admit it. While I waited for you at your house Thursday night, I wanted to steal the papers. Then Simansky would have left you alone and would have freed Aleksei. It was not the first time I had thought of doing such a thing." He paused and took a deep breath. "I came to Wilmington because I was desperate to free Aleksei. Even then I was tempted to get Thwart. But in the end I could not do it. The moral question was too great for me, so I made Simansky another offer."

His speech had wrought conflicting emotions in Natalie. She wanted to believe in him; she needed to be convinced. "What kind of offer?"

His eyes grew shadowy and he turned away from her again. "The computer board."

Confused, Natalie said, "But I thought you told me he wouldn't trade for it."

"Not before." His voice was as stiff as the broad shoulders blocking the view. "But it must have been far more important than he let on. The Soviets must have gone back to an old code system like the one in the message you found, because they didn't know what I had done with the computer board. Once Simansky had Thwart, he set out to get the board also. That is why I have come to Chamonix." He turned and met her gaze squarely. "To find this bargaining tool which I left on the mountain where you so bravely rescued me—so that you will be safe and Aleksei will be free."

It all made sense. Still, Natalie had an uneasy feeling that he'd left out something. "Why should I believe you?"

He shook his head. "I cannot answer that for you. I should have told you everything as I first planned to do when I knew Simansky meant you harm. I should have forced you to listen in spite of the headache."

The headache...another lie, this one hers. "Is that what you were trying to tell me Thursday night?"

He nodded, but said no more. It was up to her to decide whether or not he was telling the truth. It felt like the truth. His heart was in his eyes. But then, he was a superb actor. She'd seen his theatrics out on the ice. No, those emotions had been real, she thought, and so were these. In the end, it came down to a matter of trusting her instincts again.

In the end, she believed him because she *wanted* to.

"I do believe you," she whispered. "Misha."

He opened his arms and she went into them naturally. He enfolded her in them, kissed the hair at her temples, murmured soft words in Russian. She hoped they were love words.

"All I want to do is hold you one more time," he whispered in English. He slipped a hand under her chin and lifted it so he could look directly into her eyes. "My beautiful Natasha, I love you."

"I love you, Misha, and you can hold me all you want whenever you want," she stated firmly, although the uneasy feeling returned when she studied his open expression. It was filled with raw emotion. Love mixed with something more frightening than anything she'd yet experienced. Frightening because she didn't understand it at all.

Mikhail knew that holding Natalie whenever he wanted wouldn't be possible except in his mind. He'd told her the truth about everything except the trade. He was still part o the bargain. But he couldn't tell her that. She'd never allow him to exchange his freedom for her life. She'd fight back until ...

He didn't want to think about it. He wanted to make love to her. Now. While there was still time.

He took her mouth roughly with an intensity born of fear of loss. She responded in kind, opening for him, seeking, drawing him into another world, one he explored in only two ways—on the ice and in her arms. He tangled his fingers in her hair and loosened it from its plait. He wanted to see the glorious brown spill around her shoulders, stray curls kissing her forehead and cheeks.

"That is good." He admired his handiwork. He picked up a curl and rubbed it across his lips. Only cold wind and snow would kiss his mouth in the near future. "But there is a better way I would see you," he murmured huskily.

Her eyes widened. "I have nothing against making love in the afternoon," she murmured. "But shouldn't we be doing something about retrieving that computer board?"

"In the morning." He opened the doors to the balcony. Crisp mountain air teased his nostrils with the distinctive scent of freedom. He would fill his lungs with it so he wouldn't forget what it smelled like. "Now, come." He led her to the huge bed—actually two smaller beds bolted together side by side. "And let me undress you."

She glanced at the open doors. "I'll freeze."

"Then I'll make you warm under the goose-feather quilts."

She shivered visibly, but he could tell it was from anticipation rather than from the fresh air. He undressed her slowly, taking pleasure from her excitement, which grew with the removal of each garment. He kissed and tasted, savoring every inch of the silky skin he would remember always. When she was naked, he caressed her unbound breasts and sucked the nipples that were already hardened peaks, more enticing to conquer than those outside their room.

"Are you cold?" he murmured.

He trailed his lips down to her stomach, and Natalie made a noise that sounded like a protest. He wanted to hear those sounds from her, those moans of desire a woman makes when she's being well loved. He would treasure each of them on cold, dark nights, when memories would be all he'd have left to keep him warm.

"Misha, please," she whispered, tugging at his hair until he lifted his head. "I want to make love *with* you."

He slid up into her arms for another kiss. Her hands wandered along his back under the sweater he wore, leaving trails of fire that would be imprinted on his skin forever. She found the clasp at his waistband and undid his trousers. He awaited her touch impatiently. When she found him ready for her, he knew he couldn't wait any longer. He helped her remove his clothes, then pressed her back into the bed.

"I want to remember this always," he murmured, feathering kisses down her nose to her chin.

"Mmm." Natalie arched her neck for him. "And I want new memories every time we make love."

Another lie between them, Mikhail thought, nuzzling the soft flesh between her neck and her shoulder. Natalie might hate him when she learned of his devil's bargain, but he couldn't tell her the truth now. He could only make this time together count so that she'd never forget.

Losing himself in the touch of her hands, in the blue of her eyes, in the sound of her voice, Mikhail was tempted to hurry, to push as hard as he did over the ice when setting up for a jump. Instead he drew out their pleasure, gently gliding between her thighs. The world in his head moved in a slow arabesque, a simple but pleasure-filled spiral they created together.

He choreographed their lovemaking as carefully as he did his skating. He kissed and touched and moved within Natalie until she was trembling with need. Plunging deeper, he shuddered when she lifted her legs to encase his hips, taking all of him while binding him to her. Sharp fingernails dug into his back as the woman he loved moved under him, speeding up their pace, making everything blur into one pleasure-filled spin....

When the world righted, he was reluctant to move away. He wanted to take advantage of every second they had left. Natalie looked so beautiful with her hair tossed on the pillow, color flushing her skin, that the loss of her made him ache already.

"Misha?" Her brow furrowed slightly. "Is something wrong? You look so ... sad."

"Only that our lovemaking was so short," he hedged.

A seductive smile curved her lips. "I don't know what you had planned, but I'm staying right here in this bed."

AFTER MAKING LOVE A SECOND TIME, Natalie felt the need to tell Mikhail the truth about the way she and Catherine had set him up. She tried to slide away from him, but he wouldn't let her go.

"We arranged the papers in the study carefully so that we'd know if they'd been disturbed. Then my mother made that excuse about the keys and I went upstairs to get ready. We left you alone on purpose, to see if you'd take the bait."

A shadow of pain crossed his eyes. "With everything that had happened, I understand." But she wondered if he really did. "Have you informed your government that Simansky has them?"

"Not exactly." Not unless she counted Congressman Simpson.

"But everything will have to be changed or—"

Death Spiral

"No. The plans are fakes. I mean, they are real, just not the same Thwart my mother is currently working on, so they won't do the Soviets a bit of good."

Mikhail threw his head back and laughed. "This is a good joke on Simansky. I only wish we could tell him so I could see his face. It would mottle with color...." His words got lost in his renewed laughter.

When Natalie tried to get out of bed a few minutes later, saying she wanted to go down to her car to get her suitcase, Mikhail insisted on doing it for her. He rose and dressed. "You will remain there as you are," he commanded before leaving, but there was a twinkle in his normally serious gray eyes. "I want to see you there when I return."

While she waited, Natalie called Jerry and filled him in on what had happened—everything but the personal part. He promised to call her mother, but to not reveal Natalie's whereabouts. She hung up, wondering where Mikhail was.

A quarter of an hour later he returned, and she saw what had taken him so long. In addition to the suitcase, he'd rounded up a cold supper of bread, cheese, sausage and wine. They picnicked in bed, after which they made love while fighting off the crumbs, finally falling asleep in each other's arms.

Moonlight was filtering through the balcony doorway when Natalie opened her eyes again. Moonlight and cold air. Shivering, she hunched down under the covers, sought the warmth that was Mikhail and curled her body around his back. Lying next to him filled her with an overwhelming sense of contentment that made her wiggle against him. The movement obviously disturbed him, for he turned onto his back. His arm banded around her waist, pulling her closer. He muttered in his sleep, then settled down. She tucked her head in the crook of his shoulder and tried to relax.

Impossible. Her mind was awake and full of questions. There was something going on that she didn't understand.

Whatever Mikhail wasn't telling her was making her nervous. She believed his story and was sure that he cared for her. His words and actions during their lovemaking had revealed that he'd been in search of more than a physical release. Yet she'd sensed a different emotional need, almost as though he'd alternated between complete happiness and the throes of despair.

She ran her hand over his chest and down his stomach and felt a primitive glow of satisfaction when his flesh immediately quickened at her touch. He turned and caught her more closely in his arms, sleepily murmuring the Russian diminutive of her name. His fingers found one of her nipples and coaxed it to life. Suddenly he let go of her and sat up straight, discarding the covers. "What time is it?"

"Late." Disappointed, Natalie scrambled for the protection of the down quilt. "I don't know."

Throwing his legs over the edge of the bed, Mikhail turned on the table lamp and checked the watch that he'd placed next to it. "It's two-thirty." He swore softly. "Peter should be here by now."

"Peter?" Natalie said, sitting up also. It wasn't as cold as she'd first thought, so she merely smoothed the quilt across her breasts and under her arms, leaving her shoulders bare. "You mean Peter Baum?"

"Yes. He planned to be here three, maybe four hours ago."

"Why?"

"To help me find the spot on the mountain ledge where I left the computer board."

"You don't know where you left it?"

"If you recall, I was not at my best after the accident."

"No, you weren't," she said, dazed by this new revelation. Now it made sense, what Mikhail had been keeping from her—fear that he might not be able to recover the computer board. She sighed in relief and leaned forward to nuzzle his shoulder reassuringly. "I'm sure he'll be here if he promised. Where was he coming from?"

"I assume New York." Mikhail kissed the top of her head, but Natalie could tell he was distracted. "Peter was in Lake Placid yesterday morning."

"Perhaps his flight was delayed."

"I must check." He picked up the telephone receiver and gave the desk clerk a number with a New York area code. Natalie wondered what the odds were of his tracking down his friend.

She scrambled out of bed, closed the balcony doors, then headed for the bathroom with her suitcase, regretting that she hadn't packed a robe. Her raincoat would have to act as a substitute. Since she hadn't brought a hair dryer either, she clipped up her hair and wrapped a towel around her head before climbing into a hot shower.

The steady pelting of water on her back and shoulders felt luxurious. She lingered, hoping Mikhail might join her. When it became obvious that she was destined to shower alone, she soaped up, rinsed off, and toweled herself dry in a couple of minutes. Then she slipped into the raincoat and a pair of clean socks and reentered the bedroom.

Mikhail still sat at the edge of the bed, naked, telephone in hand. His face set in a mask of frustration, he hung up. "He's disappeared."

"You can't be serious."

"I am. I made several calls, but nothing. He was staying with a close friend in Lake Placid. I called there. Marlena knew he was supposed to meet me. She said his bags were packed when he left the house—to run an errand, he said." Mikhail took a deep breath. "He never came back."

A chill of apprehension shot through Natalie even as she tried to comfort him. "Maybe he decided to travel light."

"He was not on his scheduled flight. The tickets were never picked up. Natalya, I cannot find the computer board alone. I must ask for your help."

"Of course I'll help—if I can."

"Can you take me back to the place where you found me?"

She closed her eyes and tried to recreate in her mind the route that Faith had taken, but it wouldn't materialize. She'd had her nose stuck in the guidebook and hadn't paid attention to their surroundings. She opened her eyes slowly, dreading his disappointment.

"No," she said regretfully. "I can't. Faith was driving and I paid no attention. I'm sorry." Knowing how much he wanted to free his friend, she hurt for Mikhail, when she probably ought to be worried about herself. "Faith!" she exclaimed suddenly. "I'll call her and ask her to help. She could be here in a couple of hours."

"You think she will come?"

"I know she will."

Natalie squeezed next to Mikhail. Rather than giving her room, he wrapped an arm around her. She placed the call, half distracted by his nearness.

After a couple of rings, a sleepy voice came on the other end. *"Allô,"* it croaked.

"Faith, it's Natalie."

"Nat! What . . . Is something wrong?"

"Yes. I need your help. Can you come to Chamonix, the Hôtel Mer de Glace, as soon as possible?"

"Chamonix? You're here in France?" Faith sounded more awake with each question. "Nat, what's going on?"

"I'll tell you everything as soon as you get here."

"It has to do with the Russian, doesn't it?"

"Yes," Natalie said. "We're in on this together. You have to take us back to that spot where we found him."

"Whatever for?"

"Peter Baum was going to do it, but he should have been here hours ago. Mikhail's afraid something happened to him." Natalie continued rapidly, not wanting to give Faith a chance to protest or ask any more questions. "And I wasn't paying attention to where you were driving that day. You're the only one who can help. But, Faith, before you agree, I have to be honest with you: the KGB is involved in this one."

There was a moment of silence before Faith said, "All right. I'll come. What time is it now?" She groaned. "Three in the morning? Can't you ever have your crises during normal hours? Never mind—that wasn't funny."

"Nothing about this situation is funny, Faith."

"No, I know that, Nat. I'll be there about six."

"Thanks, friend." Natalie replaced the receiver and smiled at Mikhail. "She's coming. She should be here in three hours or so."

His relief was apparent. His body went limp against hers and the frown left his forehead. But, rather than discussing what they would do when Faith arrived, he said, "Three hours gives us plenty of time."

"For what?"

He slid a finger along her collarbone and dipped it inside the sturdy beige material of her raincoat. "To see what is under this disguise."

Although his words were light, his expression was serious. When he touched her, it was with a gentle possessiveness, as if she were something precious that he couldn't bear to lose. And when they were joined, his emotions surfaced more clearly than before. Natalie recognized love, yet once again she could feel his fear as if it were something tangible.

How odd. Faith was coming. She would help Mikhail find the computer board. He knew that.

So what else hadn't he told her?

Chapter Thirteen

"You're sure you want to drive instead of letting me do it?" Faith asked Mikhail several hours later, after having been filled in on the details of their expedition to retrieve the computer board.

"Yes," he said, starting the engine of Natalie's rented Ford Fiesta.

Natalie turned to her friend, who sat in the back seat, road map in hand. "Don't worry. I promise you he does know how."

"I certainly hope so," Faith said with a startled glance at Mikhail's back. "Look here." She scooted forward and held the map out so Mikhail and Natalie could see it. "It was somewhere along this leg of the scenic route rather than the main highway." Faith indicated a strip to the southwest of Chamonix where several main roads paralleled or intersected. She carefully penciled in a rectangle around a small section of the correct road.

"That's got to be at least a five-kilometer strip you marked," Natalie said. "Can't you narrow it down any more?"

"Not really. There are quite a few places for cars to pull over in this area, and they're not marked on this map. But I've been there more than once, so I'll recognize it when I see it."

"The sooner we start," Mikhail said, putting the Ford into gear, "the sooner we will find it."

He nosed the car along the main street of Chamonix. If she weren't so nervous, Natalie thought, she might be able to appreciate the charm of the town. With mountain walls rising on both sides, it couldn't be more than half a mile wide. Even so, the unusually brisk wind swept through the valley and rattled the small car. Suddenly Mikhail swore under his breath.

"Is something wrong?" Faith asked.

"Mikhail?" Natalie put a hand on his arm. Noticing his fascination with the rearview mirror, she glanced out the back window—and at the car behind them. "The brown Fiat?"

"I think so."

Wide-eyed, Faith looked around. "Oh, my God, do you think they're following us?"

"I will find out," Mikhail said determinedly. He gradually increased his speed, eyeing the mirror every few seconds. "It is staying with us."

Natalie watched the car keep pace with them, then turned around. "Look out!"

Mikhail swerved around a woman in the crossing at the main square. The old lady shook her cane after him. Mikhail's fingers clenched and unclenched on the steering wheel, the only sign that he was unnerved. A few blocks later he made a left turn. The brown Fiat did the same.

"KGB—I'm sure of it! They probably have orders to take the computer board from me immediately so they do not have to carry through with their part of the bargain. How the hell did they find us? I was so careful to—"

"There's the main highway ahead," Faith interrupted, her voice shaky. "Make a right when you get to it."

Mikhail turned right, into a parking lot in front of two buildings. "Get out, but act naturally, like tourists," he stated.

"What?" Faith said, her voice rising sharply. "No! Natalie, I don't think this is a good idea."

"Do it, Faith," Natalie said firmly, fighting the strong wind pushing against the car door. This was no time for her friend to argue or panic. "Stay calm. Don't let them know we've seen them."

Faith got out of the car and ducked her head against the wind, but not before Natalie saw how frightened she was. She linked arms with the smaller woman and gave her a reassuring squeeze. Although she didn't know what it was, Natalie was sure Mikhail had a plan.

One of buildings was a transportation terminal, the other a restaurant. Mikhail ushered the women forward to a point between the two buildings, then veered toward the mountain railway station. Natalie's heart sank. She'd been hoping they'd head for the restaurant.

"You're not serious about going up in one of those?" she asked, watching a fire-engine-red tram slide along its thick cable as it came into the station.

"Hurry!" was all that Mikhail said as he grabbed both their arms and made a run for it.

They rushed inside, breathless. While he bought their tickets, Natalie looked out the window in time to see three men get out of the Fiat. "They're coming this way," she said. One of the two dark-haired men was the person who'd followed her on Market Street. The third had receding blond hair. He was older, obviously their leader, but he kept up with the two younger men in spite of his solid-looking bulk.

"It's Simansky!" Mikhail spat, confirming Natalie's suspicion. "Come!"

Faith was white-faced and seemingly frozen to the spot. Natalie had to drag her along through the waiting room to

the boxlike tram where a small horde of people was already
boarding. Her stomach grew uneasy the moment Natalie
stepped off the platform. The car was large, about twenty-
five feet long and eight feet wide. She guessed there were
thirty or more other people standing in it; there were no
seats—little consolation when she knew they'd be going up
through the mountain peaks shortly. She settled herself between Mikhail and Faith and grasped the metal pole in front
of her.

Mikhail muttered in Russian. Natalie followed his line of
sight. The KGB men were in the station, tickets in hand and
running through the waiting room. Too late. The doors in
front of them closed. The tram gave a metallic groan and
started on its journey upward.

Natalie gripped the pole fiercely, her own knuckles turning as white as Faith's. She tried to relax. It was bad enough
her friend was in a near-panic state. She didn't need to add
to the problem.

"What good will taking this ride do us?" Faith asked.
"They'll only be waiting for us when we come back down."

"Not necessarily," Mikhail said. "Perhaps one will wait.
But two will come after us. They won't take the chance that
we might escape into Italy."

"Italy?" Natalie echoed.

He nodded. "There are three stages of ascent to Pointe
Helbronner, which is in Italy. Another skater told me about
his experience the first time I competed in Chamonix. I always wanted to try it myself, but not like this."

The wind whistled around them, the sound penetrating
the tram in spite of its sealed-closed condition. Natalie clung
to her metal post and tried to keep her gaze from the windows. Even so, the view was difficult to ignore, and her eyes
kept wandering where she forbade them to go. Mountain
peaks seemed to be rushing toward them at an accelerated
speed, almost as fast as her pulse.

A child began crying, making Natalie feel silly. She was an adult, for God's sake! She leaned against Mikhail but didn't have long to enjoy the comforting warmth of his body before the tram slid into the station built into the side of the mountain. She didn't say anything until they'd walked the short distance to the next boarding area and stopped behind the people already waiting.

"You don't expect me to get in one of those?" she asked, her heart beginning to thud as a much smaller cable car stopped several yards away. This one had seats—for four people!

Mikhail grimly pushed her forward as the line moved up. "You get in one of those or you wait to face Simansky."

Natalie wasn't sure which danger was preferable, but a few minutes later, when she could see the larger tram coming from Chamonix in the distance, she did as her lover wanted, rushing inside ahead of him. Faith entered and perched on the seat opposite. Mikhail sat down next to Natalie just as the attendant closed the door. The car took off.

"We got on just in time," Mikhail told them. "The tram is now pulling into the station. Simansky will not want to wait in a line. He will follow closely."

They hadn't moved very far when their car stopped as other people got in the next car at the station. When they began moving once more, she leaned into Mikhail, pressing her cheek into his fisherman's-knit sweater. She absently traced the raised white yarn of a cable stitch with one finger. Poor Faith sat alone, staring out the window, her face drained of color. For once, however, Natalie wasn't able to comfort her friend.

When they arrived at their second destination, Natalie didn't hesitate until they were about to begin the third and longest leg of the journey: walking across a chasm-spanning narrow bridge. She set one foot on it and stopped. "No," she said, glancing over her shoulder. "I can't."

"Natalya, Simansky could be on any one of those next cars."

Tension underlaid Mikhail's reasonable tone, reminding Natalie of the previous night when she'd been sure he was still hiding something from her. Was he afraid that Simansky would do something worse than take the board from them when they found it? Did he think the KGB agent might dispose of them as well?

"Come," Mikhail insisted, getting in front of her and offering his hand. "I will lead. Take my hand and look at me."

"I'll hold onto your other hand," Faith volunteered, showing the first sign of courage since their flight had begun. "It's not far."

The short bridge seemed a mile long, but even Faith appeared to have rallied. Natalie couldn't do less. She held out her hands.

"Do not look down."

She wished Mikhail hadn't reminded her. She tried to keep her eyes focused straight ahead, but when the trio had gotten halfway across the chasm, a gust of wind hit the bridge, making it creak and groan in protest. Natalie stopped in her tracks and did exactly what she wasn't supposed to do. She looked down.

Her head became light, and she swayed back and forth. Down was a long, long drop away. Before her dazed eyes, blue sky turned into gray mountain that became a smudge of dark shadows. She wondered if you could hear someone scream when he hit bottom.

"Natalya, look at me."

"Natalie, look up."

She didn't know whether it was the firm voices penetrating the fog of her mind or the warm, encouraging hands making the blood surge through her that pushed her the last few yards to the other side. Natalie told herself it would be easier on the way back, but she didn't really believe that.

She ran with Mikhail and Faith to the next boarding area, her legs pumping furiously. Only a few people waited—obviously not everyone was eager to go all the way up to the top—and here the cars traveled in threes to facilitate loading.

Natalie was about to get in one of them when Faith said, "There they are!" She was pointing in the direction from which they'd come. Natalie's eyes alighted on a bulky man in a gray suit. There was no mistaking Simansky.

Cursing in Russian, Mikhail pushed both women into their car, then slid in next to Natalie. "I hope they have not seen us, as well. I wanted Simansky to wonder if we went ahead or returned." He peered out the window as the tram began to move. "I was correct about one man staying behind. There are only two of them."

The final lap of the trip was the longest and the most frightening. Natalie felt as though they were a minuscule dot on the landscape. They traveled through high mountain passes, between needles of rock and the chasm-scarred glacier bathed in a dazzling sunlight. Her eyes hurt when she looked out. Not that Natalie had any real desire to do so, but for some reason she couldn't stop herself. A feeling of unreality, of being part of another world, pervaded her consciousness. The wind howled fiercely, tossing the car around like a feather in the breeze. Natalie's heart sank and her stomach turned a somersault.

"What now?" she gasped. "Did something happen to the cable?"

"It's all right," Mikhail assured her. "Support towers are not possible over the glacier. The support cable ahead is attached to the mountain peaks on either side, so there is more possibility of movement."

"And of being sick. Don't tell me any more," Natalie begged in a small voice.

If the incessant rocking wasn't bad enough, the car was drafty. Gusts of glacial air attacked Natalie, making her wish she'd brought corduroys and a down vest like Faith's instead of the jeans and the thick blue sweater she'd worn over a lighter blue shirt. She cuddled closer to Mikhail's warmth, praying for the ordeal to be over.

"We will not get off," Mikhail said as they approached Pointe Helbronner. "Let us hope we can evade Simansky and his men and reach your auto without their following us."

"Unless he's second-guessed you," Faith said, a fall of silky blond hair half hiding her face. She was bundled into her corner, her knees drawn up to her chest as if she, too, were trying to stay warm. Her knuckles were white as she twisted her fingers together. Natalie knew it was fear of the chase rather than the cold that was making Faith shake. "They could be waiting down there for us," she said, "like skilled hunters after easy prey."

The car was silent again, except for the moan of the wind and the groan of the cables, the agitated swaying movement causing Natalie's stomach to tumble a few times. She closed her eyes and tried to make her mind a blank.

They finally reached the summit. When the attendant opened their door, Mikhail said a few words in Italian and waved him away. The puzzled-looking young man undoubtedly wasn't used to tourists coming all this way without stopping at the belvedere to take pictures.

On their way down, Natalie glanced briefly at the passing mountain vista of the flank of Mont Blanc, which now seemed close enough to touch. She wondered if staying behind and facing Simansky mightn't have been easier, after all. After a minute or two, her equilibrium steadied, and scrambled thoughts were the only things tumbling around inside her.

What would they do if Simansky had second-guessed them and all three KGB men were waiting in the station at Chamonix, as Faith had suggested might happen? And, as Mikhail had wanted to know, how had Simansky tracked them down in the first place? Mikhail had sworn he'd evaded detection, and Natalie was sure that she had, too.

But Peter Baum had never made it to Chamonix. Had the KGB gotten to the German, either by bribing him or threatening him into revealing Mikhail's whereabouts? There was one other person who had known where they were, Natalie realized. She'd even given Jerry Lubin the name of their hotel.

The thought startled her with its clarity, but Natalie couldn't believe it. Jerry had been too good a friend to her—helping her translate the message, giving the party so she could get Mikhail out of the house, taking her to the airport. He'd have no reason to betray her, she thought, at the same time remembering his fascination with the country of his grandparents, his repeated trips to Russia. He'd been in Moscow during the spring break. . . .

Still, the idea was pretty farfetched. More than likely, Peter had been the informant, either by choice or by coercion.

"The station is just ahead. Keep your eyes open and be quick," Mikhail ordered tersely, bringing Natalie back to the present danger.

When the cable car came to a stop, he was the first one out, looking in every direction. There were many more people milling about than there had been earlier. The thought that someone could hide in the crowd and surprise them kept Natalie glancing over her shoulder. They were only a few yards from the chasm crossing when she spotted

Simansky a short distance behind, alone except for the wicked-looking gun in his hand.

"Simansky!" she whispered, pushing at the others.

Mikhail took her hand. One look at the KGB agent and the gun convinced Natalie that the bridge was the lesser of the two evils. She stared straight ahead at a spot on the other side and ran for all she was worth. A small group of tourists was trying to cross from the other side.

"Get away!" Mikhail yelled at them, waving his free arm wildly. "There's a madman behind us!"

One of the women screamed and the whole group scattered. Natalie glanced back. Only Faith was slowed by their confused hysteria. And Simansky was gaining on them.

Faith's eyes were wild in her ashen face. "Don't leave me to him, please!" she cried, a sudden burst of speed allowing her to catch up in spite of her shorter legs.

"Korolev!" Simansky shouted something in Russian that made Mikhail curse under his breath.

They were a dozen yards from the station, and a car had just been loaded with an older, white-haired couple. The attendant closed the door and the small cable car moved off, about to make its way down to the tram stop.

Mikhail let go of Natalie's hand and, lengthening his stride, caught up to the moving car. "Hurry!" he yelled, reaching for the handle and opening the door. He hopped inside in spite of the couple's boisterous protests and held onto the door with one hand while stretching out the other to Natalie. "Faster!"

Natalie raced forward, grasped Mikhail's hand and leaped up. She flew into the seat and slid hard against the older man, who seemed horrified at the assault. His wife swung her purse wildly and screeched something in German.

"Faith!" Natalie cried, ignoring the couple and scrambling back to the opening. "You've got to help her!"

But Mikhail was already trying. He stretched his arm out farther, hanging dangerously out of the door. Natalie clung to its edge and grabbed onto the back of his belt to give him stability. Faith was running hard, her right arm extended, reaching out, her fingers mere inches from Mikhail's hand. Natalie was so focused on the action before her that she almost forgot about Simansky.

And then the bastard reminded her.

His Russian invective blended with a gunshot that echoed up the mountain walls, sang across the glacier and crawled down Natalie's spine. Faith's body jerked and her hand slipped away from Mikhail's grasp. Her golden eyes wide with surprise, she fell hard.

"Faith!"

Natalie continued screaming her friend's name as the ground dropped out from under them. The cable car was whisking them to safety while Faith lay below, not moving. The fact registered through Natalie's horror that they'd kill themselves if they tried to jump out to help Faith. She felt Mikhail shifting himself inward and prying her fingers loose from the back of his belt.

"The bastard shot her," Natalie babbled. "Oh, God, why did he have to shoot her? She shouldn't have been here. I dragged her into this! If she's dead, it's my fault—"

She stopped only when Mikhail pulled her back from the opening and she landed against the seat. The old man had already moved to the other side, next to his wife. Through dry eyes Natalie watched Mikhail struggle with the door to close it. She should cry. One was supposed to cry when a friend died. She'd never forget Faith's golden eyes wide with surprise. Why wasn't she crying?

And then Mikhail was next to her, putting his arms around her, trying to comfort her.

"Why would Simansky shoot her?" her voice sobbed, independent of her dry eyes.

"He was aiming at me, not at her, and we don't know that she's dead." Natalie shook her head violently in denial of his words and tried to pull away, but Mikhail pinned her to his side. "Faith may be alive, Natalya," he insisted. "If she is, Simansky will leave her alone. He wants me."

Breathing deeply, she ignored the couple huddled together whispering on the other side of the car and concentrated on Mikhail's hand soothing her arm. Maybe Faith wasn't dead. Perhaps she'd merely fainted from the pain.

But the way things were going, how would they ever find out?

STANDING IN THE CROWDED TRAM with his arm around Natalie, Mikhail was relieved that she'd shown no signs of renewed hysterics. If anything, she seemed drained of strength. He only wished he knew if she had the energy left to carry through with his plan to evade the agent who'd stayed behind. Gregor hadn't been at the last connection, so he'd be waiting for them at ground level. Mikhail was sure there would be only one. Simansky would have sent Ivan to Pointe Helbronner, to follow them down the Italian side of the Alps, if necessary.

"Natalya, listen to me."

She stared at him with dry eyes. It would have been better for her if she'd cried, Mikhail thought. She would have released some of the grief she was keeping inside. It would have helped her to think straight.

"I'm listening," she finally said.

"Do you remember the plan?" He'd told her about it, but he didn't know if she'd really heard him.

She nodded. "I remember. I'll be okay."

But she wasn't okay. He could see that. Not knowing what had really happened to Faith had shaken her to the core. He couldn't blame her. Faith was her closest friend, as Aleksei was his. That was why he'd risked everything to free his friend. Natalie would do no less if she thought she could help Faith. In spite of her fear of heights, Natalie was the most courageous woman he knew.

They were coming into the station. "Get ready," he said softly, giving her shoulders a final reassuring squeeze before taking her hand.

A breath shuddered through her, and her eyes lost their vacant stare as she glanced out the window toward the waiting area. "There are so many people. I don't see him."

"He is there," Mikhail said.

He edged them closer to the second set of sliding doors, directly opposite the ones the passengers would leave by. The tram came to a stop and the doors opened. As the people flooded out, he pulled the emergency handle on the other set of doors. Then he and Natalie slipped out in the opposite direction.

Mikhail walked along the outside of the tram to its rear, still holding Natalie's hand. He peered around the end of the car and immediately spotted the KGB agent, whose back was to them. He recognized the bad haircut. Gregor was dutifully watching the exiting crowd.

Mikhail squeezed Natalie's hand. She responded in kind. They moved as one, stealthily, losing themselves in the crowd as quickly as possible without Gregor seeing them. They reached the parking lot and ran to the Ford. Mikhail had the auto started, in gear and out of the lot in less than a minute. He turned right, onto the main highway, as Faith had told him to do earlier.

"Can you read a road map?" he asked Natalie.

"Sure." She reached into the back seat and pulled forth the map Faith had marked. From the corner of his eye Mikhail saw that her hands were shaking a little. "I can get us to the area we want, but then we'll have to find the exact spot by trial and error—take every turnoff until we come to the correct one."

"Can you recognize it?" he asked worriedly.

"I'll never forget it. It's where we met."

Mikhail wished it were a romantic memory for her, but he knew differently. He was afraid Natalie would have few good memories of him when he was gone. Perhaps it would be for the best. He concentrated on the road and on watching the rearview mirror as she followed the map and the road signs and gave him directions.

As they drew closer to their destination, he thought more about what had happened on the cable-car line. It didn't make sense. Simansky had yelled at him in Russian, saying he'd shoot if Mikhail didn't stop and lead him directly to the computer board. Mikhail had taken that as a threat, nothing more. If he were dead, the Soviets would never get their precious computer board back, so why would the KGB agent shoot, if not to warn him?

Maybe Simansky preferred him dead, the computer board lost forever. Then the Soviets could keep Aleksei. But that theory had holes in it, as well. Simansky didn't know the board was out on the mountain. For all the KGB agent knew, Mikhail might have given it to someone who would take it to the Americans if something happened to him.

Before he could sort it all out, Natalie said, "It's along here somewhere to the left. Watch for the turnoffs." After he had pulled the car over three times, she nodded excitedly. "I think this is it," she said, getting out.

Pocketing the car keys, Mikhail did the same, fighting to open his door. The wind was still blowing in strong gusts. Natalie tried to keep her hair away from her face and quickly scanned the area. Mikhail followed her gaze. They had a clear view of Mont Blanc and the gleaming glacier in the distance. Then she walked to a flimsy-looking guardrail separating them from a drop-off and nodded again.

"It looks a little different because of the weather conditions," she said, turning to him. "But I'm sure we're in the right place." Wind again whipped her hair in her face as she pointed to the left. "There! That's the path we took to find you."

"What are we waiting for?" Mikhail asked.

They set out hand in hand, Natalie next to the mountain wall, Mikhail on the outside. The ledge, only five feet wide, would make anyone walk cautiously. Knowing what he did about her fear of heights, he viewed Natalie's agreeing to help rescue him with renewed wonder. He had been a stranger, after all.

They walked in silence, Mikhail thinking about that fateful day. The terrain was foreign to him, as if he'd never seen it before. All he could remember was Natalie and the way she'd kept him going with her inner strength. It was one of the memories he'd cherish most about her.

Mikhail realized he was already thinking about Natalie in the past tense. But how else could he think of her when their time together was almost spent? There was no sense in fooling himself, he thought with a despair that came from knowledge; the computer board would bring them to the final leg of a long and dangerous road together.

He forced himself to concentrate on their journey. To their left, the mountain wall sloped, and scraggly trees and boulders graced the landscape. The path grew narrower, forcing them to walk in single file. Natalie led. Pebbles and small rocks underfoot made walking more difficult.

"There!" she said, stopping suddenly. She pointed to a spot a short distance ahead. "See that rock formation jutting out over the path like a canopy? We found you just beyond that point."

Mikhail was silent. They were almost there. The computer board would be waiting. He moved forward without eagerness, knowing he had to finish what he'd started, knowing he had to save two people who were part of him. He didn't have to like it.

They passed under the overhang, beyond which the path widened again into a large, open area sheltered from the wind. Natalie quickened her steps, stopping only when she came to several small boulders positioned at the base of the slope, rocks still scattered from the slide. "This is it—where we found you."

Mikhail stared at the rock formation. He remembered it as well as other things about the day of his defection. "Peter and I used this back route through the mountains to escape Simansky and his men. They would have caught us if we'd tried to take a main road. We hiked for hours before I had that stupid accident. I tried to go on, to get to the turn-off. A car was to have been waiting to take us to the American consulate in Lyon. This must be where I gave up... where Peter left me when he went for help."

"Someone was supposed to meet you from the consulate in Lyon?" Natalie asked in a strained voice. "You're sure it was Lyon?"

Distractedly, Mikhail nodded as he knelt by the rock formation. "Peter sent a courier with a message to the consulate, asking for assistance."

"Faith works at the consulate in Lyon," Natalie said, but her words didn't register since Mikhail was concentrating on what he was doing. In spite of his pain and the concussion that had threatened him with a steadily descending blackness, he had carefully hidden the computer board in a hollow below the rocks before he'd passed out.

"Mikhail, did you hear what I said?" Natalie asked as he found and removed the loose chunk of rock.

"What?"

"Faith works at the consulate in Lyon."

Mikhail stuck his hand down into a hollow, his fingers feeling for a man-made object. He reached deeper and found the pocket-size computer board, covered with plastic. He pulled it out, intact, exactly as he'd left it!

"Listen to me!" Natalie persisted. "Don't you think that's a pretty weird coincidence—that your friend sends a message to the consulate in Lyon and then Faith takes me to the trysting place?"

Indeed it was odd, but before Mikhail could agree, a thickly accented Russian voice answered in English for him. "Not a coincidence at all, comrade, but part of a very carefully executed plan."

Mikhail spun around to face Yuri Simansky. Blood shot through him, making him rise to his feet. A shaken but very much alive Faith Osborne and a tight-lipped Aleksei Rodzianko were wedged between Simansky and his henchmen, who brought up the rear.

"Sasha!" Mikhail shouted, thrilled to see his friend yet already worrying about why Simansky had dragged Aleksei out here. "Are you all right?"

"Yes, I'm well, Misha," Aleksei said in Russian. Simansky stepped out of the way, so that the two men faced each other directly. "It's your own health you ought to be worried about." His mouth curved grimly, but his eyes held no smile. They seemed as hard and cold as the gun in Aleksei's hand.

Mikhail shook his head, unable to believe his own eyes. "Sasha...what...?"

Simansky laughed, but there was triumph rather than humor in the pig eyes that Mikhail detested. The thick-bodied agent threw an arm around Aleksei's slight shoulders. "The explanation is simple, comrade. Aleksei Rodzianko is one of the KGB's most clever and fervent operatives."

Chapter Fourteen

Stunned by Simansky's statement, Mikhail was silent until Natalie moved closer to his side and asked, "What did he say?"

"That you are not the only one who has been betrayed by a friend. Aleksei is KGB. For how long, Sasha?" Mikhail asked in English.

Aleksei's blue-gray eyes turned to Natalie, carefully appraising her. When he answered, it was in her language, although he spoke directly to Mikhail, his voice flat and hard. "Not long, Misha, though I began to see the error of my ways some time ago. Still, it wasn't until recently that I decided to rectify my life for the greater glory of Mother Russia."

Or to get the KGB off his back, Mikhail thought, guiltily remembering how Aleksei had gotten into trouble the first time by covering for him all those years ago. "But you knew that I would do everything I could to free you from prison."

Aleksei laughed, destroying Mikhail's hope that his friend had entered into this betrayal reluctantly. "You really don't understand, Misha. Prison was my idea. I wanted a way to integrate myself into the West without doing so by working for an embassy or for the United Nations. Soviet diplomats are always suspect, usually for good reason. What better way to gain the Western confidence than to pose as a political prisoner and be 'saved' so I could seek asylum in the United States?''

"So you could get close to sympathetic politicians and other important people without their suspecting you," Mikhail added.

Aleksei nodded. "But I thought, why not accomplish even more while I had your willing help—as in obtaining the plans for Thwart?"

"Or having me do it for you so you could take the credit. Is this what being a hero means to you these days?" Mikhail demanded.

Aleksei's eyes narrowed. "You are one to talk! You have always been in the spotlight, someone to be looked up to because of your skating. Now it is my turn. People will know who I am long after they forget you."

His words made Mikhail realize that Aleksei was jealous of his fame, and probably always had been. To think of what he'd gone through, of what he'd put Natalie through, to carry out Aleksei's plan!

"So the whole thing was a setup. You are an excellent actor, Aleksei. I commend you. When I left that jail—"

"Ah, but the credit goes to Comrade Simansky as well. Perhaps it will amuse you to know we planned the thing together in the Sandunovsky baths. So many important decisions are made while one is cleansing the soul. And I thought there might be some hope for you, Misha. But you would never see the light as far as the Party is concerned. I should have known that you would deviate from the plan, even when it meant risking the life of your friend—your brother, as you called me."

"You are a stranger in Sasha's body, using Sasha's voice. You make a mockery of the man I once knew, Aleksei Feodorovich Rodzianko."

"No, the problem is that you have never really known me. Your childlike idealism made me into something you wanted to see," Aleksei stated, sounding disgusted. "Well, that has served me in the end."

Natalie felt Mikhail stiffen. She had no words of comfort for him, however, for she was just as shattered by Faith's betrayal. She'd thought Faith was dead, or at least desperately hurt, and had immersed herself in grief and guilt. But Faith wasn't even wounded. Natalie stared at the golden eyes that were almost as familiar to her as her own.

"Why?" she demanded of her lifelong friend. "What could have been in this for you?"

Faith's pretty face crumpled and her eyes filled with tears. "I never meant to let it get this far. I was furious when the State Department passed me up for a promotion for the third time, merely because I wasn't as well-connected as the other candidates who got the jobs. So I found connections of my own—Soviet connections."

"All this because of a lost promotion?" Natalie could hardly believe what she'd heard. "Did you ever think about what they will do to us now that our usefulness is over?"

"No!" Faith protested, wiping away the tears that slipped down her cheeks. "You're not supposed to be hurt! No one is. They promised. They said if they had one of the keys to Thwart, the U.S. couldn't use it against them. That's all they wanted! I brought you to France to set the plan in motion."

When Natalie turned her stunned gaze from Faith to Aleksei, he explained. "I knew Mikhail would defect in Chamonix and that he wouldn't go to Geneva. Although that would be the closest place to defect, it would be the most obvious. And there is the international border he would have to cross, of course. I also knew about Faith's connection with you and your mother through Comrade

Simansky's fine work. We were trying to put those pieces of information together to our advantage when Peter Baum sent the message to the consulate. Then everything fell into place.''

''I—I intercepted it before anyone else saw it,'' Faith admitted. ''I was going to bring Baum and Mikhail back to the consulate, and in the meantime the two of you would have a chance to get acquainted. But nothing went like it was supposed to.''

Appalled, Natalie asked, ''Don't you know what these people are?''

Simansky laughed, making Faith cringe away from him. ''I never expected things would turn out like this. I'm sorry, Nat. I really am. When I realized how stupid I was, I tried to get out of it, but they wouldn't let me. They threatened me.... The KGB would never let me back out of the agreement. They'd destroy my career and reputation by revealing my involvement.''

''Your friend speaks the truth,'' Aleksei said. ''I must credit her. She's been almost as clever as I was when I convinced Mikhail to steal Thwart to save me.''

Things were going too fast for Natalie to cope. ''Misha, you didn't take the plans for Thwart, did you?'' she asked in horror, stepping away from him so she could better see his face.

''No, Natalya. I told you I did not do it.''

And as much as she'd believed him, Natalie had sensed that he hadn't told her everything. Had he merely passed on the information to let someone else do it? She had to know. I deserve the whole truth. Tell me.''

''I did not come back to steal the information,'' Mikhail said, trying to put his hands on her shoulders.

She brushed them off and took another step back, retreating from the awful nightmare that had returned full force. Her best friend had betrayed her. Now Mikhail was holding something back. She felt it.

"The truth, Mikhail! The whole truth!" she shouted. "What were you keeping from me last night?"

"Yes, Korolev, why not tell the woman the truth about our little deal?" Simansky said, laughing again.

Natalie covered her ears, not wanting to hear the laughter or any more confusing lies. Without watching where she was going, she backed farther away. Her foot came down on some loose pebbles in the path and her ankle twisted. She slipped, then tried to catch herself, half swiveling in the process. Her stomach lurched as her feet flew out from under her and she saw the drop-off coming at her in slow motion.

Blue sky turned into gray mountains that became a dark smudge of nothingness....

"Natalya!" Mikhail yelled, while Faith screamed, "Nat!"

Natalie was sliding down an incline, clawing at the ground, shooting over the thousand-foot drop. Then a band of steel wrapped around her left wrist, halting her fall, almost jerking her arm from its socket. She dangled there in Mikhail's grip, high above nothingness, her heart in her throat, pain sizzling through her arm and her side where she'd hit the mountain wall. She seemed to be spinning in a dizzying circle...

The ultimate death spiral...

Everything blurred before her eyes.

"Natalya, I can't lift your weight without help." Mikhail was breathing heavily from the exertion. Natalie felt she wasn't breathing at all. "You must help me."

"Don't look down!" Faith added from above.

Natalie forced herself to focus, but she didn't look down. She felt two hands on her arm now. Mikhail turned her slightly so she was facing the solidity of rock.

"Try to find a hold somewhere," he groaned. "A space for a hand or a foot."

She did as he ordered, shuffling her feet along the side of the mountain, scraping the flesh of her fingertips. Finally, her foot found a small niche and she dug her toes into it, the action relieving some of the pressure on her arm.

"Try to find another, higher. I won't let go."

"Hold your other hand up." It was Faith. "I'll help."

Somehow Natalie managed to inch herself higher. And because she had no choice, she reached out to the friend who had betrayed her. Faith grabbed her right arm and sobbed frantically as she tugged with all her strength. At last she and Mikhail succeeded in pulling Natalie up, over the edge, bruising every inch of her body. Natalie crawled the rest of the way to safety before Mikhail helped her to her feet and took her into his arms.

"Natasha," he murmured into her hair while crushing her to him. "I thought you were lost!"

"How touching!" Aleksei spat. "Too bad you wasted so much energy. You will have to die anyway." His chilling blue eyes moved to Natalie once more. "Both of you. I will then defect and tell the media the whole sad story about the brave lovers who were murdered by the KGB in their attempt to free me."

Mikhail tightened his hold on Natalie. "Who would believe you?"

"Everyone," Aleksei assured him. "After the Osborne woman brings me back to Lyon and convinces the State Department it is true."

"You wouldn't do that, would you, Faith?" Natalie demanded, struggling out of Mikhail's arms to face her directly. "Would you help murderers?"

Fresh tears rolled down Faith's tear-stained cheeks. "No. No!" she shouted at Aleksei. "I won't do it if you hurt them. You have to let them go."

As Aleksei's face drew into a cruel-looking scowl, a movement from behind the KGB agent who stood about ten yards away, near the overhang, caught Natalie's eye. "Perhaps there will be three regrettable deaths to report." Before Aleksei finished speaking, the agent crumpled to the ground, and Elliott Drucker stood in his place. Aleksei was unaware of this. "I'm sure I can convince the world of my sorrow at the loss of those who died while trying to save me."

Natalie would never have believed she could be so happy to see the CIA agent. Unfortunately she wasn't the only one who had spotted him. As Drucker rushed forward, Simansky turned and fired a shot at him. The CIA agent ducked, then leaped onto his adversary, sending him sprawling, while Peter Baum came from behind the overhang and grappled with Simansky's other man.

His gun aimed at Mikhail, Aleksei quickly headed toward the computer board, which still lay on the ground. He let his gaze drop for a second as he picked up the board. That gave Mikhail the opportunity to rush him. Natalie drew into the mountain wall, away from the furor. Faith stood a few feet away, her hands jammed into the pockets of her down vest, her face a mask of fear.

Mikhail held onto Aleksei's gun hand and tried to grab the computer board with his free hand. He was larger and obviously in better condition, but Aleksei held his own with amazing tenacity. The two men wrestled until Aleksei elbowed Mikhail in the stomach, winding him. As Mikhail gasped for breath. Aleksei ripped his gun hand from the other man's grasp and put some distance between them, stopping with his back to Natalie.

A quick glance at Drucker told her that he was in the process of securing Simansky's hands behind his back. Peter held a gun on the other KGB agent.

Aleksei began to taunt Mikhail in Russian, and Natalie refocused her attention on them. Mikhail flinched, but stood straight as he answered in kind. Aleksei waved his gun at Mikhail. Although she didn't understand his Russian, no one needed to translate his intent. Mikhail said something that made Aleksei laugh and then go into an angry tirade.

Natalie glanced back at Faith just as the other woman took her right hand from her vest pocket. There was a glint of metal as Faith pointed a small gun at Aleksei, but she was unable to steady her trembling hand. Fresh tears rolled down her cheeks as she mumbled "Mikhail!" and threw the weapon at him. He caught it easily. The small gun seemed ludicrous in Mikhail's large hand, but Natalie knew that didn't make it any less deadly than the one Aleksei held.

The two men continued to argue in Russian. To her dismay, Mikhail lowered the gun, slowly but surely. It was then that she realized he'd never be able to shoot Aleksei, not even to save himself.

Without hesitating, she pushed herself away from her safe mountain wall, planning to shove the Soviet off balance so Mikhail could disarm him. Aleksei must have sensed her intention, because he whipped around, his gun hand first. She ducked its swing and hit him with the weight of her body while he was still in the process of turning.

"Natalya!" Mikhail yelled as Aleksei went flying and she fell to her knees.

Aleksei pitched backward, his body twisting, his feet slipping on the loose pebbles. Natalie watched in mute horror as he flew over the precipice spread-eagled, still clutching the gun in one hand, the computer board in the other. His soul-shattering scream was cut off suddenly when he hit bottom.

The skin along her spine crawled, though it was Aleksei's rather than her grave that was being walked on. Trying to still the sick, shaky feeling inside, Natalie took a ragged breath and rose to her feet. Mikhail moved past her to the edge of the cliff. His shoulders were rounded in defeat.

She put a hand out, wanting to touch him and not daring to. "Mikhail, I didn't mean to…" She let her hand drop. He didn't even glance her way. She'd killed Aleksei, the man for whom he'd sacrificed everything. He'd never forgive her. Certain that whatever they'd had between them was over, Natalie backed away from him. A lump the size of a glacier formed in her throat and settled in her chest, encasing her heart in ice.

Mikhail stared over the precipice into the void below, where Aleksei had meant him to die. Not Aleksei, the brother of his heart, but the monster he had become. How did someone change personal ideals and moral values so easily? he wondered. Or had Aleksei really changed? Mikhail was no longer sure. Aleksei had said that Mikhail had never really known him, and perhaps that was true.

Mikhail swallowed hard and mourned his losses. He'd given up his country, his relatives, his friends—all to save a man who hadn't needed saving; who had, in the end, betrayed the memories of a lifetime. His defeat was final. Aleksei had cheated him of everything.

No, not everything, he reminded himself, turning away from the cliff's edge.

Her face a mask of pain and sorrow, Natalie stood a short distance behind him, her eyes unfocused. She'd wrapped her arms around her body as though she were trying to keep herself warm. There was a haunted look in her eyes, and he knew she was blaming herself for Aleksei's death. He couldn't bear to see her like this.

He was closing the distance between them when Drucker said, "Let's get out of here. Any discussions can wait until we get on solid ground."

With Peter Baum's help, the CIA agent rounded up Simansky and his men, all with their hands tied behind their backs, and hustled them toward the road. Mikhail decided that talking to Natalie could wait until they were alone.

As they silently traversed the familiar path together, he recalled how Natalie had revealed her fears to him, not knowing he understood what she was saying. Maybe he'd fallen in love with her even then. The fates could be strange. Three weeks had brought them full circle, back to where they'd met. He tried to think of that, rather than Aleksei and the pain he felt.

Natalie thought she'd never been happier when she spotted the turnoff in the road a short distance ahead. It would give her some room to breathe. She was still trying to keep a distance from Mikhail as they walked along; she was afraid she might cry if he accidentally touched her. If only he could find it in his heart to forgive her for Aleksei's death...

When they reached the turnoff, Natalie realized there were three cars waiting there; ironically, two were dark sedans. Drucker forced Simansky and his men into the back of one of them while a self-absorbed Faith stood a few yards away. Peter and Mikhail greeted each other.

"You are well, my friend?" Peter asked, briefly throwing his arms around Mikhail, who clasped his back.

"Thanks to you. Many thanks for all your help. I am sorry I could not tell you everything from the beginning. It was not—"

"A man must do what he must do. No apologies are necessary," Peter assured him just as Drucker slammed the sedan door and joined them.

"Would you keep an eye on our Soviet friends for a few minutes?" he asked Peter.

"Of course." The German dipped his head curtly and moved toward the sedan.

"Must be nice to have such good friends who'll do anything for you," Drucker remarked. "Peter Baum and Jerry Lubin."

Startled, Natalie asked, "How do you know about Jerry?"

"Did you think he was going to sit around and wait for you to get yourself killed? He called my department right after the two of you spoke on the phone. I received his message this morning, but by the time Peter and I got to your hotel, you were long gone." Before Natalie could say anything to that, he turned to Mikhail. "Well, Korolev, any other secrets you want to spill?"

Drucker's strident question irritated Natalie, but she had to remind herself that she was glad to see the man. "Aren't you the one who should be doing the explaining?" she asked. "Like, why are you here when you're on suspension for your renegade activities?"

"Is that why you were not available at your office?" Mikhail added.

"So it was you bugging Howe, huh, Korolev? I figured as much. You had Howe going crazy the last few days while I was out in the field tracking down your buddy, Pete," Drucker said, jerking his thumb in Baum's direction. "That's why you couldn't reach me." Turning to Natalie, he asked, "Where did you get the idea I was suspended, anyway?"

"From me," Faith said quietly, her eyes downcast. "I lied about that, Nat, and about Drucker's contacting the Soviet embassy. I was trying to make sure you didn't confide in him."

Natalie stared at her. "It was Mikhail you wanted me to confide in. You wanted me to get involved with him so he could use me."

"No! I knew you'd do anything to help someone in trouble, even a Russian. And your mother is a skating fan with a friend on the Olympic committee. I figured you'd get him a job either at the skating club or at the university. And once Mikhail was there, I knew your mother would want to meet him. That was supposed to be the connection. It wasn't supposed to be anything personal."

Natalie laughed wryly. Nothing personal. She'd only fallen in love. And now she'd have a broken heart.

"How could you have believed that it would be so simple?" Sadly, she looked away from Faith and back to Drucker. "Speaking of the Soviet embassy—you never did tell me how you knew Mikhail had contacted them. I assume that was true."

The CIA agent's expression told her he still thought she was terribly naive for a woman with a Ph.D. "Have you ever heard of wiretapping?"

"You have a tap on the Soviet embassy?"

"Hey, you didn't hear that from me," Drucker said, pulling out a cigar. He hesitated with it in his hand and looked at Natalie questioningly, as though asking for her permission.

She could afford to be generous now. "Have one on me."

"Thanks." He bit off the tip and spit it out. "By the way, Korolev, I admit I misjudged you. I was sure you were a Soviet plant—which didn't prove to be too far off the track.'' He paused to light the cigar. ''But you're in the clear.''

''Why did you suspect him in the first place?'' Natalie asked.

''I'd been working on finding the source of security leaks for months before he defected. There'd been more than the usual 'disinformation' that we put out going to the other side. Agents had to be getting into the States undetected. Like your friend there,'' he said, waving the cigar out toward the precipice. ''And I was just as sure U.S. government employees were being bribed or blackmailed into helping provide the information.''

''Who did steal Thwart?'' Natalie purposely refrained from mentioning that the plans were old and useless. She'd tell Drucker about it later. Let the Soviets think they had the real thing. Even Faith couldn't tell them differently.

It was Faith who answered. ''Simansky stole Thwart.'' She was unable to look Natalie in the eye. ''I told him your mother often brought her work home with her. He or one of his men got into your place more than once. Trying to play the odds, you know. He finally got lucky.''

Thinking about such dangerous men wandering in and out of her home unnoticed made Natalie immediately vow to have an electronic security system installed.

''Nat, I know you won't ever forget what I did, but I hope someday you can find it in your heart to forgive me.'' Faith said. ''I made a mistake . . . and I didn't know how to make it better.''

''Is that why you led them straight to us this morning?''

''I didn't tell anyone about our telephone conversation. Believe me, Simansky was furious with me for going off on my own. That gunshot was a warning to frighten me. I worked. I tripped and managed to knock the breath out of myself. And when he caught up to me . . .'' She shuddered

"I was hoping one of the cable-car employees would try to stop him from taking me back down, but either they didn't realize what was going on, or they were afraid to try." Faith shook her head. "I have no idea how he found out where we were."

"The Soviets may be a little backward in some areas," Drucker said, "but not in wiretaps. They wouldn't have trusted you any further than they could throw you, lady. Now, is 'true confession' time over so we can hit the road?"

"Yes," Faith said, looking away, but not before Natalie saw a new batch of tears sliding down her cheeks.

"Faith, wait."

Despondently, Faith turned back to Natalie. She didn't say anything, merely waited.

"Are you all right?" Natalie asked.

"No."

"Give me some time."

Faith nodded and walked after Drucker. Natalie was reluctant to take her eyes off the woman. She seemed so helpless.

"You'll be hearing from me at your hotel later today," Drucker yelled at Natalie and Mikhail, then conferred briefly with Peter.

The German led Faith to the second sedan; a moment later both cars left the area.

Natalie was alone with Mikhail.

Unable to look at the man she loved, the man whom she had just lost, Natalie asked, "Do you want to drive or shall I?"

"I don't want to go anywhere until we talk."

"You don't have to tell me how you feel," she said in spite of the lump in the middle of her throat. She stared into nothingness. "I understand."

Mikhail took her in his arms. Although her bruised body protested, she tried not to flinch. "No, Natasha, I do not think you understand. I believe Aleksei was responsible for his own death."

She searched his face. "You don't blame me?"

"I love you," he told her, touching her face gently. "So much so that I would have returned to Russia with Simansky to protect you."

She wasn't sure that she understood him correctly. "You were willing to go back . . . ?"

"It was part of my devil's bargain. The computer board and my return, in exchange for Aleksei's freedom and your safety." He tangled his fingers in her curls. "I thought I would never be able to do this again or to look into your beautiful blue eyes that remind me of the Moscow River in summer. I was saying goodbye to you last night."

Tears suddenly burned the backs of her eyelids. "So *that's* what you weren't telling me. I thought . . ." Natalie lowered her head. "I'm so sorry."

"You have nothing to be sorry for. I owe my life to you, as well as a reason to go on living, my Natasha. How will I ever repay you?"

"I don't want to be thanked for killing someone."

He placed a finger over her lips. "I told you: Aleksei was responsible for his own death, but you're responsible for my life. I want to spend the rest of it thanking you."

Natalie looked up at him then—excitement, hope and love filling her. Yet her laugh was nervous. "How? By giving me a lifetime of skating lessons?"

"I can give you much, much more, if only you will promise to be the woman of my heart and soul forever."

Then Mikhail gave her a preview of what he meant as he pulled her closer and covered her lips with a tender kiss. She nestled her head in the crook of his neck, and they gazed out at Mont Blanc, both silent with their thoughts. The mountain had brought them together, this time for good. Only moments ago, Natalie had been afraid she'd lost Mikhail. The experience had given her a new perspective on the importance of things, and she didn't think she'd ever be afraid of heights again—not while she had Mikhail to climb them with her.

ABOUT THE AUTHOR

Patricia Rosemoor began creating romantic fantasies while in grade school, never guessing she would someday share her stories with more than her best friends. A native Chicagoan, she has given up her position as supervisor of the television production facility at a suburban community college in order to devote herself to writing full-time. Her husband, four cats and a dog continue to assist her. Patricia also writes with a partner as Lynn Patrick. *Death Spiral* is her third book for Intrigue.

Books by Patricia Rosemoor

HARLEQUIN INTRIGUE
38–DOUBLE IMAGES
55–DANGEROUS ILLUSIONS

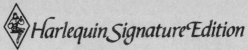

Harlequin Signature Edition

Penny Jordan

Stronger Than Yearning

He was the man of her dreams!

The same dark hair, the same mocking eyes; it was as if the Regency rake of the portrait, the seducer of Jenna's dream, had come to life. Jenna, believing the last of the Deverils dead, was determined to buy the great old Yorkshire Hall—to claim it for her daughter, Lucy, and put to rest some of the painful memories of Lucy's birth. She had no way of knowing that a direct descendant of the black sheep Deveril even existed—or that James Allingham and his own powerful yearnings would disrupt her plan entirely.

Penny Jordan's first Harlequin Signature Edition *Love's Choices* was an outstanding success. Penny Jordan has written more than 40 best-selling titles—more than 4 million copies sold.

Now, be sure to buy her latest bestseller, *Stronger Than Yearning*. Available wherever paperbacks are sold—in October.